The Last
Orphan

BOOKS BY KATE HEWITT

Kate Hewitt

The Last Orphan

bookouture

Published by Bookouture in 2023

An imprint of Storyfire Ltd.
Carmelite House
50 Victoria Embankment
London EC4Y 0DZ

www.bookouture.com

ISBN: 978-1-83790-001-5
eBook ISBN: 978-1-83790-000-8

To my sister Susie, for reading the first Amherst Island story a long, long time ago, and loving it enough to give me the courage to continue. Love you!

CHAPTER ONE

AUGUST 1945

Calgarth Estate, Windermere, the Lake District

"When do you think they will arrive?"

Rosie Lyman carefully propped the teddy bear against the pillow before she turned to the speaker, Jean McGee, another worker at the Calgarth Estate. The staff were a motley crew of well-meaning refugees and volunteers, washed up by the war onto this welcoming shore after peace had been declared, yet the suffering continued. Here, finally, was a chance to help.

Rosie herself had been dismissed from the Canadian Women's Army Corps, known as CWAC, back in March, in an episode so painful she still could not bear to recall its particulars in any detail, and it was her friendship with the charismatic child therapist Marie Paneth back in London that had brought her here, to the shores of Windermere in England's lovely Lake District, waiting for the arrival of three hundred children who desperately needed care and succor.

"How long is it to Crosby-on-Eden?" she asked Jean as she closed the door on one of the many bedrooms that had been prepared for the children's imminent arrival. She had been in Windermere for nearly a month already, helping to get the Calgarth Estate ready for its new visitors, but she still didn't know the area all that well, and had only been off the estate to the nearby village of Troutbeck a few times.

Jean, who had trained as a nursery nurse up in Scotland, admitted her own ignorance with a shrug of her rounded shoulders. She was a friendly-looking woman, in her late forties, her ginger hair pulled back into a neat bun, and Rosie had enjoyed her company from the start.

"An hour, perhaps?" Jean guessed, wrinkling her nose. "I can't be sure."

"Well, then," Rosie said with a smile as she patted her own brown hair, pulled back into a braid, "they should be here quite soon, then, I hope. Although I imagine it will take some time to process them and get them onto the buses."

Several of the staff from the Calgarth Estate, as well as members of the Central British Fund, the Jewish charity which had organized the scheme to bring the children here from Europe, had left to meet the ten Lancaster bombers that had taken off from Prague that morning with three hundred children on board. Members of Parliament and MI5, along with several representatives of the press, were also present for the momentous occasion of Great Britain accepting child survivors of the Nazis' brutal concentration camps. And soon they would be arriving at the estate in Windermere—once the accommodation for workers at a seaplane factory, now a refuge for the most damaged and vulnerable of society.

But no one had any idea what to expect.

Over the course of the last month, Rosie had been advised by several of the staff, many of them pre-war refugees from Germany themselves, to expect the children to be both malnourished and traumatized, potentially terrified or maybe even aggressive, mute or wild. No one quite knew how the children might have had to change or adapt in order to survive the unimaginable experience of life in the camps, what terrors and tragedies they might have seen or endured, and what scars, emotional and physical, they might now have to bear.

The newspapers could hardly show the full horror of such an experience, although what Rosie had already read seemed too terrible to be true, and yet it *was*. All the world was reeling from what had been discovered in the far reaches of Poland, as well as throughout Germany—a system of concentration and extermination camps that dealt in the most grievous of suffering, torture, abuse, and outright murder, of those the Nazis had deemed unfit for society, or even to live.

Some of the Jewish refugee volunteers here had had some experience of their home country under Hitler's reign of terror, while Rosie felt utterly in the dark about it all, gleaning what she knew only from the sparing facts in the newspapers, or on radio programs. Before meeting Marie Paneth at the end of the war in the East End of London, she didn't think she had ever laid an eye on a Jewish person in her whole life. She didn't speak German; she wasn't a therapist or a doctor. A month on, she was still wondering whether she belonged here at all, although Marie had insisted she could make herself useful, and Rosie was determined to do so. She needed to feel useful and busy, craving a distraction from the emptiness at the center of her own life, the deep well of grief she skated away from, in the uneasy quiet of her own mind.

Besides, she acknowledged, what had been the alternative? To find passage on one of the military transports taking demobbed military personnel back to Canada, to go home and pick up the tattered remnants of her life as if she'd never left at all? Her parents didn't even know all she'd experienced, whom she'd lost, the dreams that had been so wonderfully woven and then broken. How could she tell them now, when she could hardly bear to remember the details herself?

No, she wasn't ready to go back home, not yet, and maybe not ever. She'd experienced, suffered, and lost too much serving overseas even to attempt to trip merrily back to Queen's University, to finish her history degree alongside her cousin Violet. She feared she would never again be able to be the cheerful undergraduate she'd been just four years ago, before she'd joined up, at the start simply to appease her cousin.

Although perhaps, Rosie thought, Violet wasn't ready to go back, either; as far as she knew, her cousin and erstwhile best friend was still in England, waiting for Andrew Smith, her GI boyfriend, to be demobbed. Rosie had not spoken to her since May, when they'd fallen out, although not in a dramatic sort of way. Rosie had simply walked away and chosen not to see her again after Violet had, in her usual, indefatigable way, dismissed the pain that had been coursing through her in an unrelenting river.

Maybe it's for the best, Rosie.

Her cousin had meant well, Rosie knew, but it had still been hard to take. Impossible, even, which was why she'd walked away, and not spoken to Violet since.

No, she really wasn't ready to see any of her family or friends yet, to admit her mistakes and her failures, and she wasn't strong enough to pretend they hadn't happened to those who had no idea what had gone on. And so she'd come here, to Windermere in the middle of the Lake District, to help children because she did not know how to help herself.

And yet... broken called to broken. It was what Marie Paneth had told her, back in London, where Rosie had been volunteering with war orphans, under Marie's guidance and care. After the war had ended, she had urged Rosie to come to Windermere and volunteer at the estate. Even though Rosie hadn't told her about the losses she'd suffered mere months ago, never mind the agonizing betrayal, Marie had guessed, or at least imagined, some of it.

So Rosie had agreed to come, because she didn't want to go back and she didn't know how to go forward. This, at least, was a sort of stasis, a limbo land of not having to either dwell on the past or think about the future. Even better, she could think about someone else—the children in need of her help and kindness.

And yet... broken might call to broken, but how could she possibly help to heal these children? The question had been running through Rosie's mind for the last month, for she felt like a fraud on so many counts. But now the children would be here in perhaps an hour, and she, along with everyone else, needed to be ready.

"Cup of tea?" Jean asked with a sympathetic smile, as if sensing the disquieting nature of Rosie's thoughts. Or perhaps she felt the same; she'd worked as a nursery nurse near Glasgow during the war, and although she'd certainly had her fair share of sorrow, losing both her husband and son, she hadn't experienced anything like these children would have. None of them here had.

Perhaps, Rosie thought as they stepped outside into the summer evening, the sun not yet set, even though it was nearly nine o'clock, they all felt like frauds, one way or another, utterly ill-equipped to help children who had suffered so much, yet with a desperate, well-meaning determination to do so.

She and Jean headed down the neat paths that ran along the dormitories to the dining room in the estate's main building, at the center of the property. It was a utilitarian building that served its purpose, squatting in the middle of the neatly laid out paths and dormitories, and, in addition to the dining hall, housed the classrooms and offices for the project.

A few of the ladies from Carlisle's Women's Voluntary Services were bustling around the kitchen, preparing welcoming cups of cocoa for the children when they arrived. The women fluttered around nervously, like Rosie and Jean, not knowing what to expect, and yet so wanting to help, to show kindness where so very little had ever been shown.

"I wonder how many wee ones there will be," Jean mused as she and Rosie took their cups of tea to one end of one of the long trestle tables that had been set up in the dining room. She had been designated to look after the smallest children coming to the Calgarth Estate, under the supervision of Alice Goldberger, a Jewish emigré and childcare expert who had worked in the War Nurseries, set up by Anna Freud, the daughter of the renowned psychiatrist, who had come from Vienna to run homes for war orphans in England. The staff had been told it was more likely that there would be far more older children coming, with the upper age limit set at sixteen, than little ones, who would have struggled in the camps.

Doctors were ready and waiting to do the first medical examinations upon arrival, and a tent had been put up outside for delousing the children as soon as they arrived. Three hundred rooms, in separate boys and girls blocks, had been made up in the former factory workers' accommodation—single-story houses made of concrete and looking much like army barracks. Each room had its own single bed, washstand, and bureau. Every pillow had a bar of Winston's chocolate on it, and several dozen had a teddy bear for the younger children, as well.

Marie Paneth had set up her art studio on the second floor of the main hall, and Oscar Friedmann, the psychiatrist in charge of the whole program, had an office there for talking therapies. Alice Goldberger had set up her own rooms, as well, with toys and games, for the younger children.

There were also classrooms where the older children could learn useful skills; all the children, regardless of age, were meant to learn English, along with arithmetic and British history, in order to give them a useful start in this country. Everything and everyone was ready to receive them, welcome them, *help* them, at least for the next four months, which was all the funding the program had been able to get. All they needed now, Rosie thought as she took a sip of her tea, were the children themselves.

"It's a shame their new clothing hasn't arrived yet," Jean remarked with fretful regret. "All they'll have at the start is underthings—shorts and vests. What with the rationing, it's been so difficult to get enough clothes for everyone. I hope it doesn't make them feel unwelcome, not to be properly dressed at the start. I hate to think they might."

"Could we not have them keep the clothes they are wearing?" Rosie asked, and Jean shook her head.

"No, because of, you know," she replied with an apologetic grimace, "vermin. Everything they have brought with them will have to be burned, I'm afraid."

Rosie nodded in understanding, although it seemed quite sad that the children's personal things would be taken from them and destroyed practically the moment they arrived. Hadn't that sort of thing happened before, at the camps? Of course, she reassured herself, the situation would be completely different here, as different as it could possibly be, and yet even so, she didn't like to think of the children having such an ugly reminder of what they'd endured. But perhaps everything was a reminder already; it was not, she suspected, the sort of experience you would ever forget.

"I'm so excited," Jean confided nervously, "but I'm scared, as well. I'm so worried I'll get something wrong. It's hard to know what to do, how to be, especially with such wee ones." She bit her lip, and Rosie knew she was thinking of the son, Willie, she'd lost during the war. He'd only been six when he'd been killed during a bombing raid, and her husband had died fighting in Normandy. Everyone had lost someone, it seemed; these children the most of all.

"I think we're all worried about that," Rosie told her kindly, "and I suppose we're bound to make mistakes, especially at first.

But we all mean well, and I hope the children will come to realize that, in time." She gave Jean a reassuring smile, although she didn't feel entirely reassured herself, and the older woman smiled back, her eyes still full of worry.

The last month had been peaceful here at Windermere, Rosie acknowledged—setting up the rooms, cleaning and painting and generally making herself useful, but with plenty of time for quiet walks by the lake or in the woods, awash in green during the height of summer, the steep fells stretching upward to the horizon.

It had been lovely to be away from London and all its painful memories—everywhere she turned, she felt as if she could see Thomas, his glinting blue eyes and sweep of blond hair, that ready, charming smile. She pictured them swinging hands in Piccadilly, wandering through Hyde Park, kissing on the doorstep of her old barracks in Mayfair, dancing the night away at Rainbow Corner. Yet Rosie knew she still couldn't escape the crux of those memories, and the questions had continued to torment her up here among the sweeping fells and glittering lakes, even as she refused to let herself dwell on them too long, preferring numbness to misery or grief.

Still, they came in her weaker moments, especially at the beginning, battering her relentlessly. *How* had she let herself be so foolish, so *duped*? She refused to consider the matter or give herself an answer and eventually she was able not to think about any of it all. Merely skimming the surface of her memories was painful enough, like probing a raw nerve, twanging terribly every time she so much as touched it. It was far easier not to think at all, to let her mind empty out as she focused on the physical tasks in front of her—make this bed, paint this wall, sweep this floor. How simple life would be, if she could continue in such a fashion forever.

And yet she couldn't, she knew she couldn't; the memories continued to rise up, with all their accompanying emotions, a tidal wave of feeling crashing over and dragging her under. She pushed them down, again and again, and told herself that helping those who had endured so much more than she had would put her own smaller woes into perspective. Perhaps, one day, she could finally put them to rest.

"I do hope the little ones like their teddy bears," Jean said, clearly still worrying about it all. "I was thinking they might like to go for a walk tomorrow, if the weather's fine. What do you think?"

"I think we will need to give them time to be settled," she told Jean with a smile. "And perhaps let them decide for themselves what they would like to do."

"But they'll need fresh air," Jean persisted. "It's so important for young ones to get outside. Very healthful—"

"I'm sure they will enjoy a walk," Rosie replied, mainly to soothe the other woman's anxieties. She suspected Jean was eager to pour so much into the care of these children because of the loss of her own son. It was easy to understand, and yet these children would be very different from the little boy she'd lost, who could never be replaced. Thinking of her own daughter, whom she had never even been able to hold, Rosie understood that all too well.

"I hope so," Jean murmured as she toyed with her teacup. "I just want to do what's best."

It was so hard to know what to do, to get it right. Everyone at Calgarth was well-intentioned, Rosie thought, if uninformed. Oscar Friedmann had told them that Great Britain had been prepared to offer places for a thousand children, but only seven hundred in total had been found; three hundred would be coming to Calgarth, and the others would travel to Southampton in the coming weeks. Seven hundred children, out of how many millions? It made Rosie want to weep.

"It's getting late," Jean remarked, fretting yet again. "The poor things will be so tired."

"At least they'll be able to have a good sleep," Rosie said as she took a sip of her now lukewarm tea, just as the sound of vehicles could be heard from outside, tires crunching over gravel.

Jean's eyes widened as she gazed at Rosie in a mixture of fear and excitement. "They're here!"

Rosie quickly took their cups back to the kitchen, pausing to straighten her cuffs and pat her hair into place before heading outside with Jean. It was growing dark now, the sun having sunk behind the fells that rose up steeply in every direction, so when Rosie had first arrived, she'd felt hemmed in, even a bit trapped by the way they loomed above her. She'd got used to it now, and enjoyed the sight of the sweeping, heather-covered hills.

Already there was a chill in the air, despite the day's warmth; nights were cold up in the Lake District even in the middle of summer, with the wind sweeping in off the lake and down from the fells.

Bus after bus was pulling into the courtyard by the main hall with its kitchen, dining hall, and classrooms. Rosie and Jean stood outside the front doors with a few other of the staff and volunteers, as well as a couple of doctors who were to assess the children that very evening, in case any of them had a contagious disease such as tuberculosis and needed to be isolated right away.

Rosie folded her hands in front of her, a welcoming smile on her face as the first bus's doors opened, and a man stepped out, mid-thirties perhaps, with rumpled, dark hair, and soulful, brown eyes; his manner was cautious and guarded. As he came toward them, Rosie noticed that although his body was lithe and powerful, he walked with a slight limp.

"Good evening," he said in careful, accented English as he nodded a greeting at them all. "My name is Leon Rosenblat. Thank you for having us here."

Rosie nodded rather dumbly along with Jean and a few

others while Oscar Friedmann stepped forward, speaking in German as he shook Leon's hand. Rosie had learned a few phrases over the years, thanks to the two years during the war that she'd spent as a listener, intercepting Morse code messages from Germany; her training had been at the Isle of Man, where British-resident Germans had been interned, and she had become friendly with a young German woman there. Most of the children coming to Calgarth, she knew, though, would be Polish.

"You are most welcome, of course," Friedmann continued in English. "There is hot food and drink for the children, once they have been medically assessed—a necessity, I am sure you understand."

Leon Rosenblat nodded, looking both solemn and wary, and then he turned back to the bus, calling something to the occupants within.

Rosie glanced at Jean, who looked as apprehensive as she felt, trying to smile and seem welcoming, and probably, like Rosie, afraid that she didn't. Then the first children began to emerge from the bus, slowly, cautiously, their expressions as guarded as Leon Rosenblat's as he ushered them off, speaking gently in Polish to each one.

Rosie's first thought was that these young people were not children, and certainly not in need of teddy bears on their beds. They were practically men—tall, strapping, some even with stubble on their jaws, all of them looking suspiciously around them, shoulders hunched, faces guarded. But though they looked like men, the fear in their eyes reminded her they were really children, and the innocence of their childhood had been stolen from them in the most brutal way possible. She hoped they could rediscover it, at least a little bit, here, no matter what age they were.

Friedmann began to address them in German, his voice carrying on the still, night air. From the few words Rosie was able to understand, she knew he was telling them they would need to be seen by a medical doctor before they could eat and sleep.

She saw several of the boys stiffen, another grab one's arm and take a step back, shaking his head slowly, his eyes wide as his gaze darted around as if looking for an escape. The uncertain, wary looks on their faces were replaced by something that could only be described as true terror.

"Excuse," Leon Rosenblat interrupted Friedmann, bowing his head a little in apology. "They are afraid, because—" He didn't get to finish because one of the boys suddenly bolted, sprinting as hard as he could into the night, the only sound that of his feet hitting the gravel as he disappeared into the darkness.

Friedmann let out a gasp of dismay, stretching one arm out helplessly, and Leon Rosenblat began running after the boy as best as he could with his limp, moving surprisingly quickly, while the others looked on, now huddled together, their anxious expressions making Rosie think that they were wondering if they should run off, as well.

"Oh dear," Jean whispered as she wrung her hands, her face wreathed in unhappiness. "Oh dear, oh *dear*..."

"Everything must seem so very strange to them," Rosie whispered back. "Poor boys. After everything they've endured, they must wonder what on earth is going on now, and whether we can be trusted. How will we convince them that we mean no harm?"

After a taut minute or two, Leon Rosenblat returned with the boy who had run away, his arm around his shoulders. He was murmuring to him in Polish, his face close to his, his formerly wary expression softened into lines of gentle tenderness, while the boy trembled. Rosie's heart ached at the sight.

Another minute passed, everyone waiting, uncertain, and then the boy let out a shuddering breath and nodded jerkily.

Leon, his expression turning grave once more, looked up at

Dr. Friedmann. "I am so sorry," he said in English. "The boys, they are afraid. At the camps, their families were told they would be seeing a doctor, but it was not so."

"It is *I* who am sorry," Dr. Friedmann replied, his voice choking a little as he realized what the boys must have thought. "The last thing I would wish is to cause any of these children fear or harm. They have no need to be afraid here, no need at all, but, of course, I understand it will take time for them to accept that. The medical examinations are merely a necessary precaution, nothing more, in case of contagion."

"Yes, I understand. I will try to reassure them." Leon bowed his head again, and then he turned back to the boys still on the bus, speaking gently in Polish as he tried to urge the rest of the group to leave its safe confines.

Dr. Friedmann turned to address the boys waiting in the courtyard in German, smiling and spreading his hands in apology.

Once more, Rosie was able to catch a few words, and suspected he was trying to reassure them, just as Leon Rosenblat was, explaining again that they would be given food and clothing after they'd seen a doctor.

Jean glanced back at the bus anxiously. "They're all so big. Do you suppose there are *any* wee ones coming at all?" she asked, a waver of disappointment in her voice.

Rosie knew how much Jean wanted a little one to love. "There must be," she said encouragingly. "Otherwise, they surely wouldn't have hired you as a nursery nurse, would they, or Alice Goldberger to run the whole program."

About fifty boys had come off the buses by now, all looking to be at least fifteen or sixteen, if not even older. They were forming a line into the hall, where several doctors waited to assess them. Rosie watched as one boy stumbled up to Oscar Friedmann, looking as if he wanted to speak to him, only to then, shockingly, vomit all over the therapist's suit.

Jean let out a stifled gasp of surprise and Leon Rosenblat hurried up to Dr. Friedmann, his face drawn in lines of anxiety, dark eyes narrowed. "I am sorry, so sorry," he said quickly, fluttering his hands, which were long-fingered and graceful, in apology. His English was accented but excellent. "They were given chocolate and oranges when we stopped in Amsterdam to refuel, and then with the motion of the plane, the bus... they are not used to such rich food—"

"It's fine," Friedmann replied calmly, ignoring the mess all down his front. He touched the boy's arm. "*Komm,*" he told the boy gently. "*Bitte.*"

"Poor things," Jean whispered. "*Poor things...*"

The first bus was now empty of passengers, all of them having been teenaged boys. The second bus was the same, as was the third, all the boys seeming both stunned and wary as they were, en masse, gently shepherded toward the hall, although none had run away like the first boy had. As more and more teenagers emerged from the buses, Rosie began to wonder, like Jean, if there were any younger children coming at all. She knew how disappointed her friend would be if there were no little ones to care for. She saw Leon Rosenblat hurrying by and took a step toward him.

"Please," she asked. "*Bitte.* Do you know if there are any children on the buses?"

Leon's mouth pursed briefly, and something flashed in his dark eyes that looked almost like anger. "They are all children, *Fräulein,*" he told her coolly, and Rosie flushed as she realized her mistake.

"Yes, of course, I'm so sorry," she replied hurriedly, embarrassed by her gaffe. "But I meant... small children. We have prepared some rooms for some very small children—"

"Most of the younger children died in the camps," he cut her off, his tone now flat, his expression hard, making him look all the more severe. "Along with most of the girls, and so here there are only a few of each. They were not strong enough to survive such conditions, you see." His gaze flicked over her briefly. "But if you are looking for small children you can... *cuddle* and *cosset*, then yes, there are some, in the last bus, do not worry. You will have your small children."

"I didn't mean—" Rosie began, helplessly, surprised by his sudden, rather savage outburst, but Leon Rosenblat, his limping gait stiff and dignified, had already walked on.

CHAPTER TWO

The next few hours passed in a blur of activity and barely controlled chaos as three hundred frightened children milled about uncertainly, some clinging to each other, others whispering urgently in tight little knots, many of them seeming more than a little fearful to believe the many assurances that they would come to no harm there.

Rosie ached with sadness to see one boy trembling with terror as a doctor told him to open his mouth and stick out his tongue. Another boy was openly weeping, shaking his head and murmuring prayers that she later learned from the rabbi who had been employed to lead prayers was the Kaddish—a Jewish mourning prayer for grief and death. She saw Leon Rosenblat put his arm around the boy, his face softened into gentle sympathy, and she wondered why the man had seemed to assume the worst of her, before telling herself not to bother about it. This wasn't about her feelings, she reminded herself, but the children's.

True to Leon Rosenblat's word, there were several small children on the last bus—around a dozen, all of them between the ages of four and eight. They came off the bus slowly, peering into the darkness and all of them holding hands, accompanied by a Polish woman in her thirties, who introduced herself as Golda Stein and told Rosie and Jean that she had been with the children all through their time at Theresienstadt.

"They have stayed together all through the camp," Golda explained, after Rosie and Jean had greeted her and the little children as they'd come off the bus. Alice Goldberger, who had met the children at Crosby-on-Eden, had gone to speak with Dr. Friedmann, leaving Jean and Rosie to manage their settling in. "They will not be separated for anything."

Jean eyed the little ones with a hopeful smile; they were dressed in dark coats and battered shoes, huddled together and looking about them with a weary indifference that seemed strange in ones so young.

"They are so dear!" she exclaimed. "They shall all have their very own rooms here…" She faltered uncertainly as Golda shook her head with firm decision.

"I am afraid that to be so alone would frighten them terribly. For tonight, at least, they must be together, all in one room. It is the only way." She spoke with such finality that there was clearly to be no discussion about the matter.

'I… see," Jean said nervously. "Yes, of course."

In the dormitory that had been set aside for the smallest children, Rosie and Jean moved beds around while the children sat on the floor, thumbs in their mouths, eyes wide and unblinking. Not one of them had said a word since they had arrived, and Golda had explained that they did not have much language.

"A few words of Polish, German, some Russian," she said. "That is all. They never had the chance to learn anything."

Jean's eyes were wide as she looked at the children sitting together on the floor. "How on earth did they survive in such a place?" she asked in a whisper.

"Mostly, they hid." Golda turned away quickly, to straighten a bedcover. Rosie saw red, puckered skin all along her forearm, as if she had been burned some time ago and it had never properly healed. Many of the adults who had accompanied the children here, she knew, had been at the camps, as well. They had to be suffering and scarred, too, even if they were able to hide it better. "There was a *Kinderheim*," Golda continued, "a home for the smallest children that the Jewish Council in the camp had made for them, but it was not safe. When the guards came in, the children had to hide."

"Oh..." Jean looked at the children, huddled together so silently, seeming somehow resigned, as if they had already seen too much of life—and death—at their tender age, and she shook her head sadly.

"I will stay with them until they fall sleep," Golda told Rosie and Jean firmly, once the children had settled into their beds, all of them completely silent the whole while.

So, with an uncertain nod, and a longing glance for all the children, sensing she had been dismissed, Jean backed out of the room.

"Perhaps we can help in the dining hall?" Rosie suggested as she gently closed the door on the little children tucked in their beds, Golda singing a soft lullaby in Polish to them, the words haunting and lovely, the mournful tune winding around them. Jean looked at the door longingly, clearly wanting to be in there with the children, and with a sympathetic smile Rosie guided her down the hall, sensing that right now the children needed to settle with someone they trusted—Golda. "The other children must have gone through their medical examinations by now," she added. "Why don't we go and see?"

"They're so *little*," Jean whispered, shaking her head. "Not even as big as my William was."

Rosie patted her shoulder and Jean gave her a small, apologetic smile.

"I know I shouldn't think that way," she said in a low voice.

"Don't worry, I know it. No one can replace Willie, and these children... well, Dr. Friedmann told us not to get too attached, didn't he, and I understand why. They will only be here for a few months, after all, and then they'll go on their way... live their lives."

"Yes." They had all been instructed by the doctor to be kind and warmly welcoming, but to keep a necessary professional distance all the same, for all the children would be going elsewhere by January, at the very latest. It would not be helpful to any of them, or the volunteers, for any meaningful attachments to be formed.

"But how will the little ones be moved on?" Jean asked as they walked along the path toward the dining hall, her tone turning a little plaintive. "The older ones, yes, they will go into hostels or what have you, learn a trade, make lives for themselves here. They are old enough, certainly. But such wee ones..."

"It is not for us to worry about," Rosie reminded her gently. "We will take care of them while they're here, and someone else will decide where they should go." As cold as it may have sounded to Jean, Rosie thought she understood the necessity of it. These children were not theirs, after all.

Jean nodded reluctantly, and they entered the main hall, and then the dining room.

A rabbi who had come from near Newcastle to lead prayers throughout the children's time at Windermere was welcoming the older children into the dining hall for cups of cocoa. The children, having finished with their medical examinations, were all now dressed in nothing but white underwear—pairs of knee-length shorts and vest tops. Just as Jean had said, their clothing had not arrived yet, but what they'd worn on arrival still had to be burned. Dressed only in underwear, their various wounds and scars from their time in the camps were more clearly visible —lacerated backs, the long, puckered ridges the sign they'd been whipped, and, judging by the number and depth of them, often and hard.

Rosie glimpsed patches of burned skin, similar to the one Golda had on her arm—had they been burned on purpose, she wondered, by the guards? Or in their desperation to keep warm, had they sat too close to a fire or stove? Either way, it was utterly lamentable.

Some of the children looked pitifully thin, while others were more robust; for some of them, it had only been three months since their liberation, others six or more, and Rosie saw the truth of it in their eyes, wide and blank and haunted as they sat down at the long trestle tables, their cups of cocoa in front of them, untouched. She watched as many of the children eyed their drinks uncertainly, some sniffing their cups or dipping a finger in the hot liquid and then sucking cautiously, murmuring to each other as they did so.

"I don't think they've ever had cocoa before," Rosie remarked slowly, and Jean nodded in sad understanding.

"Or they don't remember having had it, at any rate," Jean replied. "It has been a long time, I should think, since they've had any decent food at all."

Rosie thought of the poor boy who had been sick all over Oscar Friedmann's front. It would take some time, she supposed, before their stomachs could get used to the plentiful food available here, let alone their minds.

Rosie's gaze was suddenly caught by a girl sitting by herself at the end of one of the tables. There were only about thirty girls among the three hundred children, and most of them were huddled together in groups, chatting in low voices. This girl, however, sat by herself, arms folded, chin tilted proudly, a look of something almost like disdain on her small, heart-shaped face. She had heavy, brown hair that she wore in a thick plait, and hazel eyes under brows that were drawn together in a scowl. She looked to be about eleven or twelve. Rosie watched her for a moment, wondering if she would try to join in with the others, or at least drink her cocoa. She did neither, staying with her arms folded, almost as if she were determined to be above it all. What could be possibly going through her mind?

"Jean," she whispered. "Why do you suppose that girl is there all alone?"'

Jean glanced around the crowded room before her gaze came to rest on the child at the end of the table. "Perhaps she just wants to be alone? This must be quite overwhelming for them all, to be sure."

"Perhaps," Rosie allowed, but her heart still ached for the girl, sitting all by herself, not seeming to derive any comfort from the children seated near her, who had suffered in the camps just as she must have. Why wouldn't she join in, or at least drink her cocoa? Her expression was almost forbidding, as if daring anyone to come close. Yet, surely, she craved some comfort, too?

All evening Rosie had been trying to be as helpful as she could, while feeling fairly useless and ignorant. She could not speak these children's language; she knew she could not begin to imagine what they had endured. She did not know how to comfort or console them, how to explain that she was here to help, not to harm, as much as she longed to do so. She did not know what they needed—silent understanding, space to heal, or someone to draw them closer, with arms to embrace and accept? Her uncertainty had left her feeling helpless, doing nothing because she did not know what to do, yet so much wanting to do *something*. Anything.

Oscar Friedmann had been clear that as much freedom as possible should be given to these children, especially at the beginning of their time in Windermere; after so many years of living under the harshest rules imaginable, they needed the opportunity to explore, to learn, or even simply to *be*. Rules would be kept to a minimum, and the children would have, as much as they could, the complete run of the place, and the freedom to do whatever they wanted or needed.

Yet, Rosie wondered, should she give such space to this girl, right here and now? Something about her—the haughtiness in her face, perhaps, that could hide so much—spoke to Rosie. It reached out to her, and she longed to reach out in return, to offer what little comfort she could.

"I'm going to talk to her," she decided out loud, and Jean clucked her tongue.

"Most likely she doesn't speak a word of English," she said warningly.

"I speak a little German," Rosie replied. A *very* little German, she thought, and absolutely no Polish, but she still felt the desire, and even the need, to try, with this particular girl, although she couldn't really even say why.

She walked over to where the girl was seated all by herself with a purposeful spring in her step, a determined smile on her face.

"*Guten abend,*" she greeted her as cheerfully as she could, although her voice wavered a little in her nervousness. What could she possibly say to this child, that she would want to hear? And yet, Rosie thought determinedly, she could be, at the very least, a friendly face, a kind voice.

The girl looked up at Rosie, her eyes already narrowed in suspicion, her mouth pursed. She did not reply.

Rosie pointed to the cup of cocoa, as yet untasted. "*Ist gut,*" she told the girl, still smiling. "*Trinke?*" Drink. That was more or less all the German she had, and she wasn't even sure the girl understood. Perhaps, like many here, she only spoke Polish.

The girl stared at her for a long moment and then, in a deliberate movement, she pushed the cup of cocoa away from her, hard with the flat of her hand, so it spilled across the table, a pool of dark liquid spreading quickly across the tabletop. Rosie let out a little sound of surprised dismay, and the girl stared at her in defiant challenge, her chin tilted just that little bit higher. Rosie had no idea what to say.

Not, she quickly realized, that she really had the opportunity to say anything. The girl clearly wasn't waiting for her to speak. She pushed away from the table, standing up and walking away from Rosie without so much as a word.

Rosie stood there, struggling not to feel like a failure. This wasn't about her, she reminded herself. She knew that much. And yet the seeming rejection, when she was already smarting from so much, caught her on the raw all the same, even though she tried not to let it.

"She is hurting," someone said next to her, his voice quiet. "That is all."

Rosie turned to see Oscar Friedmann standing next to her, smiling sorrowfully. The girl was nowhere to be seen.

"I know," she told him, with a small smile. He handed her a dishcloth which she accepted with murmured thanks, and then began to mop up the spill. "I don't mean to seem hurt or anything like that," she explained. "It surprised me, that was all." She shook her head as she finished mopping up the mess and righted the cup. "These poor children…"

"What I am coming to realize already," Oscar replied thoughtfully, "is that they do not want to be thought of as 'poor children' at all. They want to fit in, to be accepted. They do not want our pity, not anymore, not after everything. They want our respect."

And it was pity, Rosie realized uncomfortably, that she had been all too willing—even eager—to give to that girl. Had she realized and so rejected it?

"Yes, I can understand that," she told the doctor, and then admitted, "I think I may have made a complete hash of things just now, with that young girl. I'm sorry."

He smiled and patted her shoulder. "We all have the best of

intentions, *Fräulein*," he told her. "We will get there, in the end."

Rosie nodded, grateful for his understanding, even as she wished she'd had more success with the unknown girl, who had now disappeared. Would she get another chance with her? She hoped so.

She went back to Jean with a shamefaced smile. "Well, that was something of a disaster," she said, trying to sound wry.

Jean nodded in sympathy. "It's bound to be hard at first."

"Yes." Rosie shook off any lingering sense of defeat and gave her friend a bracing smile. Most of the children, having had their first taste of the cocoa, had now finished it, and were being guided to their rooms for bed. "Shall we help clear up?" she suggested. "And then I think we'll want our beds, too."

Even though the children had only been at the estate for a few hours, it had felt like a very long day. The apprehension she'd felt waiting for them to arrive, the desperation to get things right... it had tired her out. Well, Oscar Friedmann was right, Rosie supposed. They'd get there in the end. At least they'd try.

It took over an hour to wash all the cups and wipe down the tables, so by the time Rosie headed to the volunteers' quarters, the children had all, thankfully, settled. At least, she thought they had, until she paused mid-step as she walked along the path by the former staff cottages that now housed all the children, disconcerted by an unearthly noise.

It rose from the cottages in a series of anguished moans, sudden shouts, even agonized screams, each terrible sound echoing through the still night. Sounds of torment, agony, and pain—coming from all the rooms themselves, from the *children*. The hair rose on the back of Rosie's neck as she listened to the ghostly sounds, and she looked around for someone to appeal to, to help.

"They're just dreams." Marie Paneth, the art therapist, walked toward her, a small, sad smile playing about her wide mouth. "Nightmares, I should say. Apparently, the children have been having them since they left the camps. These sounds are, unfortunately, quite normal for them."

Another moan rose from a nearby cottage, the sound so full of pain that Rosie had to suppress a shudder. "Can't we do something?" she asked Marie. "Wake them up—"

"Dr. Friedmann told me not to," Marie interjected. "He said it is all part of the healing process, and I must agree with him." She gave Rosie another smile, this one of sympathy. "I know it doesn't seem like it, but it is good for them to dream in this way. It is a way of expressing themselves, of working through the grief and the fear they feel, as with the art I hope they will begin with me tomorrow. You cannot repress these emotions, Rosie, no matter how hard you try."

Marie's voice was gentle, and Rosie tried not to flush, for she had a feeling her friend was talking not just about the children, but about her. There were, she knew, too many things she wasn't ready to think about, much less talk about, and she supposed Marie knew it as well.

"Still, it doesn't feel right," she said quietly as another moan rose into the night sky like some sort of pain-filled offering. "To let them suffer like this, when we could do something. Help them, in some way..." Although how she could help, she had no idea.

"They have already suffered, far more than you or I could ever imagine," Marie replied quietly. "This isn't suffering, even if it sounds like it is. This is *healing*. It just doesn't always look or feel the way you thought it would." Briefly, Marie rested a hand on Rosie's shoulder. "Why don't you help me in the art room tomorrow?"

"I can barely draw stick figures," Rosie warned her. "My mother was an artist, but her gift was sadly not passed onto me."

Her mother, Ellen Copley, had once been on the cusp of world renown, only to leave it all behind for love. She now taught art to little children back at home in Canada, and seemed more than happy to do so.

"Ah, but that is the wonder of what we do here," Marie told Rosie with a smile. "It is not about skill or beauty, not at all. There is no instruction, no assignment, no improvement, even. There is just paper, pencils, paint. The children may do what they like with it all. Express themselves however they choose." She paused. "It will help them, I hope, and it will also help me in my research in how to offer such therapies in the future, to children from all walks of life and experience."

"Well, I'm happy to help, then," Rosie replied, although she still had her doubts as to how effective she could be in such a setting. "What time do we start tomorrow?"

"In the morning, I hope, after breakfast. As you know, Dr. Friedmann wishes the children to do as they please, especially early on in their stay here. There will be time later for them to begin their classes and such things, but I hope tomorrow some of them may wish to draw or paint."

"I'll see you after breakfast, then," Rosie said, and with one last smile for her friend, she walked toward her own quarters—a bedroom much like the ones given to the children, with a single bed, washstand, and bureau.

As she undressed and slipped into her nightgown, the moans and cries continued to echo through the estate. Could Marie be right, Rosie wondered, that these nightmares were part of the healing process? She hoped so, for the children's sake.

She realized she had not dreamed about Thomas—or their daughter, lost before she'd even had the chance to hold her—even once. It was as if her own subconscious was refusing to cooperate and unbend, to allow the memories in, even in its most unguarded moments of sleep, to remember anything at all, because it would hurt too much. Rosie knew a dream of them alive would be painfully sweet; a nightmare of them both dead, a terrible reminder. She wanted neither, and so she hadn't dreamed of anything at all, at least not that she could remember, and no matter what Marie Paneth or Oscar Friedmann claimed, maybe it was better that way. Memories *hurt*, whether they were painful or sweet. Better to try to forget, even if Rosie knew there really was no forgetting at all. There was only pretending to, both to others and to herself.

She paused to stare at herself in the small square mirror above the bureau—auburn hair like her mother's, brown eyes, a pale, ordinary face. What had Thomas seen in her, she'd wondered more than once, sometimes with doubt, sometimes with a thrill of amazement. Now she only felt an emptiness, and looking at her reflection almost felt like looking at a stranger's. She didn't know who she was anymore.

Turning away from the mirror, Rosie slid beneath the bedcovers, staring into the darkness as mournful laments continued all around her, rising up into the night sky.

CHAPTER THREE

Rosie came to the dining hall early the next morning, determined to be as helpful as possible. She'd firmly put aside her own pointless musings about her personal situation to focus on the children in need of care, which was why, she'd reminded herself, she'd come to Windermere in the first place.

She gave the cooks a bright, bracing smile as she helped prepare breakfast—baskets of fresh, white bread, better than any Rosie had seen back in London, and pots of strawberry jam, the likes of which she hadn't seen at all. She was glad the children would be getting such treats, and looked forward to watching them enjoy them.

The children trooped into the hall a little while later, many of them silent, but a few talking, even smiling, which Rosie was happy to see. She looked out for the girl from last night, hoping to at least nod a greeting, but she couldn't see her among the throng.

Jean came in with the smaller children; they walked in a crocodile, the one on the end holding the volunteer's hand, looking around her with wide eyes. Jean seemed to have made a little headway with the smallest ones here, Rosie thought, and was glad for her friend.

After all the children had been seated, the rabbi rose at the head table and said a prayer—"*Baruch ata Adonai Eloheinu Melech ha–olam ha-motz-i lechem min ha'ar-etz.*" Rosie had learned earlier that it meant *Blessed is the Oneness that makes us holy and brings forth bread from the earth.*

Some of the children bowed their heads for the prayer; others looked confused or indifferent. Oscar Friedmann had explained that although the children were all, of course, Jewish, some of them were extremely devout, while others had not practiced their faith at all, either before the war or during it. "Such distinction mattered not at all to the Nazis," he'd said sadly. "But here we must be careful to allow these children to practice, or not practice, their faith as they wish. I imagine that for some of them, the belief that they are the chosen people of a loving and benevolent God would be a difficult one to sustain, but can offer its own comfort, perhaps, even in these difficult times."

Rosie could certainly see how that might be the case. Her own relationship with God was decidedly uneasy at the moment; she'd always been something of a churchgoer, thanks to her parents, but she'd tended to see God as someone far off and somewhat disinterested in her life. How much more might these children feel that way, or even wonder if God was in fact a cruel and vengeful taskmaster, to allow what He had? At least some, it seemed, were partaking in the comfort faith could provide.

At a nod from one of the cooks, Rosie picked up a basket of bread and brought it to the first table, with several other volunteers bringing baskets to the others. She had barely set it down and stepped back when, to her shock, the children lunged for the bread, grabbing it up in handfuls, stuffing slices into their mouths, down their shirts, even in their shorts. A dozen or so of them ran from the room, shoes clattering on the floor, their hands full of bread.

"What on earth..." Rosie began under her breath, only to be silenced by Oscar Friedmann, his voice rising above the din that had erupted as children now fought over the last scraps of bread —some of them shouting, kicking, even biting. The escorts who had accompanied them from Prague were attempting to pull them apart; Rosie saw Leon Rosenblat drag one boy away from another whose lip was split. Every single basket of bread was empty.

"*Kinder, Kinder!*" Friedmann called, his voice nearing a roar in order to be heard. "There is enough bread for everyone to eat, you see? Enough bread." He repeated the sentiment in German, although none of the children looked convinced. They'd stopped fighting, at least, although some were still eating as fast as they could, stuffing whole slices into their mouths, while others simply eyed the doctor suspiciously, clutching their scraps to them protectively. "Enough bread," he repeated. He nodded toward Rosie and the other volunteers who had brought the baskets in from the kitchen. "Please. *Bitte*. Will you bring some more at once?"

With the other volunteers, Rosie took her basket and hurried back into the kitchen, where the cooks were slicing fresh loaves as fast as they could.

"Poor things," one woman was muttering under her breath, like a prayer. "Poor *things*. They think there isn't enough bread to go round. They must have been half-starved all these years, to act in such a way."

More than half, most likely, Rosie thought as she hoisted another basket of bread. How long would it take these children to realize they had enough to eat here, that the food would never run out or be taken away?

The children who had fled the room with their booty were now returning, somewhat sheepishly, with a few of their guardians; once again, Rosie caught the eye of Leon Rosenblat and, this time, she tried to smile at him, but her lips felt as if they weren't quite working as he stared at her with something approaching ferocity, an intensity blazing in his dark eyes that made her feel as if she were pinned in place. Then he looked away, and she felt an unsettling mixture of disappointment and relief.

Expelling a slightly shaky breath, half-wondering if she'd imagined the whole moment, Rosie set the second basket down on the table, smiling at as many children who would meet her gaze—a cheeky-looking boy with freckles, another with a shy, uncertain smile. "There," she said cheerfully. "*Brot.*" She thought for a moment and then added, "*Mehr.*" More.

Unfortunately, she had no more German to say than that, but it seemed to be enough, for this time, with answering smiles and murmurs of thanks, the children took only a slice or two, slathering them thickly, and seemingly incredulously, with jam, darting her uncertain glances all the while, as if they expected her to snatch the slices out of their hands. But no one took more than that, and no one ran from the table to keep their food from being taken.

"They were hiding it in their rooms," Jean told her when breakfast had been finished, and they were clearing the tables while the children trooped outside to play. "In cupboards and drawers, even under their pillows, for later. I suppose they're used to having to do that. Poor things."

Rosie had heard those two words so much they were starting to sound like a litany. "But perhaps they're not *poor things*," she remarked quietly, thinking of what Oscar Friedmann had told her last night. "They survived, after all. They made it all the way here, which is incredible, really. They were strong and brave and lucky enough to come this far. There must be something to admire in all of that, surely? Even though I know we feel sorry for them."

Jean looked uncertain, as if she suspected Rosie had said something wrong, or at least arguable. Perhaps she had. She wasn't sure she entirely believed the sentiment herself, but she was beginning to understand what Oscar Friedmann might have meant. These children wanted to be treated like fellow human beings, not objects of pity, as well-intentioned as the sympathy might be.

Pity, perhaps, only took one so far. At some point, it became unwanted, resented. At some point, perhaps, it felt like a different kind of violence. She wanted to make sure she didn't offer that to these children—and, Rosie realized, to one girl in particular, who she had yet to see again, although she hoped she soon would.

After she'd cleaned up breakfast, Rosie headed to the art studio on the floor above to help Marie set out her supplies. The room was empty, save for the therapist, as Rosie came inside, its long, high windows letting in the morning light, the fells outside gilded in gold, touching the clusters of eyebright—the tiny white flowers that dotted the hills in a gorgeous carpet. Everything looked rich and green and vital, and the sight of such beauty lifted Rosie's flagging spirits.

She glanced out the window at the football pitch, where a dozen or so boys were kicking a ball, while others watched or milled around, chatting and laughing. Girls clustered nearby in tight knots, occasionally glancing over at the boys. Rosie looked for the girl from last night, but she couldn't see her anywhere. Still, she was glad to see so many of the other children seeming happy and relaxed.

"You'd think it was any schoolyard," she remarked with a smile as she turned from the window. "Although it is a bit incongruous to see them all in just their underthings!" She'd almost got used to the white vests and tops all the children were wearing, although she imagined from the outside it might look strange indeed, with not one of the three hundred yet in proper clothing. "Do you know when their clothing will arrive?"

Marie shook her head. "The Red Cross is meant to bring some things soon, but with clothing so scarce... hopefully in the next day or two." She glanced out the window, her lips pursed. "It must be a bit chilly like that! August up here isn't all that warm, is it?"

"I suppose they're used to wearing little," Rosie replied slowly. "But it seems a shame to remind them of it." She turned back to survey the tables and chairs, the crayons and paint pots Marie had set out, along with sheets of butcher's paper, cut into large rectangles. "Do you think many will come to do art today?"

Marie let out a little sigh. "Jean is taking the littlest ones on a walk this morning, around the lake. I spoke to Golda about having them come here, but she did not seem particularly enthused. Alice is hoping to convince her."

"Why is she not keen?" Rosie asked.

Marie shrugged. "There will always be resistance to new or different ideas. And I think she fears I mean to pry and probe, as if I want to make them specimens of some sort, the way some of them were during the war, subjects of experiments and worse, in those hellish camps." Her mouth tightened with disgust. "I assure you, I want to do nothing of the kind." The therapist's voice thrummed with passionate conviction. "This art is for *them*. For their sakes. As with the nightmares they had last night, their trauma must come out. It is the only way. It's like a poison in the blood; it will infect everything if it is not lanced. Only then will they be able to move on with their lives in peace. Alice understands that, and perhaps she will be successful in speaking with Golda, and convincing her that I mean to help, not to harm."

Rosie glanced down at a blank sheet of paper, several glass

pots of paint nearby, along with brushes, all waiting to be used and enjoyed. "But they're so little," she said after a moment, her gaze on the colorful paints. "Couldn't they just... forget, in time? If we give them fresh walks and fun, good food and lots of cuddles... couldn't they forget, as if it never happened at all? Since they're so small? It's not like with the older children, who will always remember..."

"The body does not forget," Marie stated quietly but firmly. "Nor the mind, although sometimes these traumatic events can be buried so deep in our consciousnesses that it seems as if we have forgotten, and we convince ourselves of such, but we have not. Not at all." She lit a cigarette, narrowing her eyes and blowing out smoke as she considered the matter. "I once worked with a child who reacted in fear, in true terror, to something so seemingly small and insignificant—the sound of running water." She paused, and Rosie waited, uncertain as to what she was going to say. "This child would run and hide, or curl into a ball, whenever he heard a tap go on and the water begin to run. It seemed quite unnatural, almost absurd, to be so scared of such a small thing, until I learned that from a very young age, as a punishment, the child would be left in a cold bath—overnight, sometimes, to terrible effect. When he heard the sound of water, he remembered the bath, even though he could not explain it, or even remember that was what had happened to him when he was small."

"That's awful!" Rosie exclaimed quietly. "Who would treat a child in such a terrible way?"

"And yet these children have experienced worse—*much worse*," Marie reminded her. "And their bodies will not forget, nor their minds, no matter how many treats or cuddles we give. The trauma must be brought out into the light, Rosie." Marie's voice was firm. "That is the only way."

"I suppose," Rosie replied reluctantly, for the thought of the three hundred children having to relive their traumatic experiences, through art or otherwise, was terrible, in its own way, if seemingly necessary.

"But not today it seems," Marie finished on a sigh. "Today it seems they are going to play football." She shrugged and then smiled. "Ah, well. I will be here when they are ready, and so will the paints."

"Perhaps when the little ones have finished their walk—"

"Perhaps. I am patient. There is no point, no point at all, in forcing such things. The patient must be ready and willing, otherwise the work is entirely in vain." Her smile gentled as she looked at Rosie with a sudden, shrewd sympathy in her eyes, and Rosie found she had to look away.

Sometimes she wasn't sure when Marie was talking about the children—and when she was talking about her.

"Perhaps I'll go for a walk, if I'm not needed here," she said. "The sun is bright, and I could use the fresh air. Perhaps I'll find Jean and the children."

Marie gave a nod of assent. "As you wish."

Rosie slipped outside, grateful to feel the sunlight on her face. In her month since coming north, she'd discovered the weather was similar to that which she'd experienced on the Isle of Man during the war—often wet and windy and cold, even in the height of summer, as it was now. And yet, Rosie reflected, a lovely day here in the Lake District, with the sunlight making the lake shimmer as if its surface had been scattered with diamonds, the fells rising steeply above, covered in heather and eyebright, was one of the most beautiful things she had ever seen, even more beautiful, in its own way, than the blue-green waters of Lake Ontario, back home, which she had always loved.

She walked past the football pitch where boys were still playing, the girls giving them curious glances. Once again, she looked for the girl from last night, but could not see her among the crowds. Instinctively, Rosie searched for someone standing alone, but there was no one; all the children were huddled in groups. She met a few of their gazes and smiled, and was rewarded with shy, cautious smiles back, the occasional wave, which gladdened her greatly. She so wanted to make friends with these children, to help them, but as her spirits lifted, she wondered if they actually might also be able to help her. *Broken calls to broken.* She'd doubted Marie's words when she'd first heard them, but maybe it worked both ways.

She took the leafy lane through the wood that led away from the estate to the shore of the lake, the sounds of the football game and other noises fading into silence, the only sound the crunch of twigs and the squelch of damp leaves under her feet. As she rounded a corner, she saw Jean and Golda leading the little ones down the road by the hand.

"Jean!" She smiled at her friend in genuine pleasure. She knew how eager she'd been to take the children for a walk, give them fresh air and get to know them. "How are you?" She glanced at the children, who stared at her, as silent and wide-eyed as ever. "How are they?" she added, softly.

"Oh... well," Jean said, giving Golda something of an unhappy glance. The other woman looked, Rosie thought, rather severe.

"Is everything all right?" she asked uncertainly.

"There was a dog," Golda stated in a voice that was both quiet and fierce.

"It was just a little spaniel," Jean explained, rather miserably. "The sweetest thing, really—"

Golda rounded on her quite suddenly. "In the camps, do you know what the dogs did? They tore you apart. Yes, you!" Her voice was shaking. "The guards kept them on chains, and they were always—what do you say? Pulling and growling. And then—like this!" She snapped her fingers. "A guard would give an order, and the dog, it would be on someone. Biting, growling, *chewing*, like with a bone, but with a—a *child!*" Her voice broke, while Jean and Rosie both stared, stricken, and the children's expressions, rather worryingly, did not change at all.

"I'm... I'm sorry," Jean whispered wretchedly, while Golda struggled to compose herself.

"I know it was a small dog," she stated with dignity. "A span —what did you say?"

"A spaniel," Jean whispered.

"A spaniel," Golda repeated, taking her time over the unfamiliar word. "Even so. A dog, any dog... it reminds them."

"I'm sorry." Jean looked near tears. "I'm so sorry. I didn't realize..."

Golda nodded once, sniffing. "I am sorry, as well. It is just... the memories. For all of us."

"Yes," Rosie said softly, finding herself suddenly near tears, as well. The woman's pain was so raw, so real, and as for the children... had they become used to such terrible things, a dog savaging a child? And yet they'd been afraid of the little spaniel, which she supposed could be seen as an encouraging thing, in its own way. They had not become entirely inured to violence. They were not as numb as all that, she thought with a sudden pang, as she still was.

"I am sorry," Golda said again, sniffing, and impulsively Rosie laid a hand on her arm.

"Don't be sorry," she said. "We are sorry, for not understanding."

"I do not usually carry on so," Golda replied, a little stiffly.

"Perhaps you need to, then," Rosie told her. "At least a little bit." She thought of Marie telling her that the body remembered. That the pain would out. For the children, for Golda, for everyone.

"Let's go back to the hall," Jean suggested, her voice wavering a little. "I'm sure there will be bread and jam. I'll warm up some milk. Alice had suggested we might sing some songs..." She looked hopefully at Golda and then the children. "Won't that be nice?"

"Yes, very nice," Golda replied, like a peace offering. She managed a smile, and for a moment, the two women seemed in solidarity. "*Brot, ja?*" she told the children, who had remained completely still and silent the whole time. "*Brot mit Marmalade?*"

A few of the children nodded uncertainly, but none of them said a word. Rosie watched them walk back toward Calgarth Estate, her heart heavy—for Golda as well as the children, for anyone and everyone who had suffered in such a terrible way. *Broken calls to broken.* But why, she wondered, did the world have to be so broken in the first place?

She walked on, letting her mind skate over the surface of such thoughts without really settling. She didn't want to think, didn't want to tie herself into anguished, mental knots about the children—or anyone else. She simply wanted to walk, one foot in front of another, the wood quiet all around, the sun warm on her face, as she enjoyed these simple pleasures.

After perhaps a quarter of an hour, she came to the shore of the lake and found a rock on which to perch, at least somewhat comfortably, her elbows on her knees and her chin in her hands, the water stretching placidly out in front of her, with barely a ripple. A few birds alighted on the water in the distance, their wings a dark and graceful arc against the sky before they skimmed across the surface of the lake.

Rosie squinted to make out their shape, and realized they were geese—Canadian geese, here in England. One of the local volunteers had told her there were such birds in the area, but she hadn't believed them. Yet looking at them now, she knew these were the same kinds of birds she might see skimming across the aquamarine waters of Lake Ontario before taking off into the sky.

A wave of emotion passed through her—not quite homesickness, more like grief. She missed her home, her family, with a quiet desperation she didn't usually let herself acknowledge... but she knew she still wasn't ready to go back. Perhaps she never would be, a thought which brought its own despondency.

For a second, she opened the locked door of her heart and let herself think about Thomas. Her mind settled on an image of him when she'd first met him, at Rainbow Corner, one elbow propped on the bar, blond head tilted back as he'd laughed, his blue eyes sparkling with humor, with happiness, with life.

Rosie had walked up to him on something of a dare, after imbibing a bit too much pink gin and, after asking him to buy her a drink, admitted she was trying to flirt.

Without missing a beat, he'd asked her, "Well, then, how's that going?"

Rosie had burst into surprised laughter, he'd bought her a drink, and then they'd spent the rest of the evening together, dancing, chatting, laughing. Rosie had never felt so alive, as if every sense was on high alert, every nerve positively singing with joy. When he'd asked her if he could see her again, she'd practically floated home. She'd never before realized it was possible to feel that way, that a single person could make you feel so wonderful, so alive and vibrant and *real*.

Oh, Thomas...

Rosie bent over, pressing her forehead to her knees as the pain broke over her in sudden waves she had to brace herself against. She didn't usually let herself remember so much. It had been Marie's insistence that the pain would out that had made her want to remember for just a few seconds, and now she'd relearned why she usually didn't. It hurt far, far too much. Better, much better, to feel numb. Was that how the children felt? Perhaps they would never want to paint or draw. If the trauma was kept deep inside, maybe it never needed to come out. You just kept pressing it down and down and down. Surely that could work if you just kept at it...

"Pardon me... miss?"

The hesitant voice of a girl startled her out of her desperate and melancholy thoughts. Rosie lifted her head and turned to see a young girl, maybe twelve or thirteen, eyeing her uncertainly from the road that circled the lake.

Quickly, she scrambled from the rock to her feet, flushing at how emotional she must have seemed, bent over nearly double. "Yes, may I help?"

"I was wondering... are you from the estate?" The girl sounded shy, and Rosie nodded, smiling her encouragement, forcing the thoughts of Thomas to the back of her mind, the pain thankfully receding like a tide.

"Yes, I am one of the volunteers there."

"It's only... some of the boys have taken our bicycles." The girl ducked her head, seeming embarrassed. "I know they must only be doing it for fun, and it's not that we mind really, but... we need them back. My sister uses hers to get to work, and she's got a shift at the pub down in the village this afternoon."

"Oh yes, I see," Rosie said quickly, although she wasn't sure she did. Had some of the boys from the estate taken local children's bicycles? *Stolen* them? Not, of course, that she would ever use such a word, or even think it, really. The boys simply must not have realized that the bicycles belonged to someone else. "Do you know where the boys went, on the bicycles?" she asked.

"We saw them riding down the lane, toward the village."

"I see," Rosie said again, staring helplessly at the girl while she stared back, clearly expecting her to do something about it all. "Where should they return the bicycles to?" she finally asked.

"From our house. We'd left them leaning against the gate the way we usually do."

"Oh." Oh, dear. Rosie nodded, straightening and throwing

her shoulders back with resolve. "Very well. I shall go see if I can find them. Where should they return the cycles to?"

"Willow Cottage. It's the third house on the right on the road to the village, as you leave the estate."

"Very well. Thank you. And I'm sorry about that. The bicycles, I mean."

The girl ducked her head. "That's all right, miss. We know those boys have had it terribly hard."

"They have, indeed." She smiled at the girl, grateful for her understanding, and then turned to hurry back toward the estate.

A light drizzle was falling as she came onto the field where the boys had been playing football earlier; they had all drifted away now. Rosie's gaze swept the empty field, looking for someone who could help her, but there was no one about at all.

She headed into the main hall, hoping to find Oscar Friedmann or perhaps Marie, who could advise her as to how to get the bicycles back, when she nearly ran into someone else—Leon Rosenblat.

"Oh!" Rosie pressed her hand to her chest, managing a smile as she took a step back from him. Leon stood in front of her, his dark hair rumpled, his brown eyes with their surprisingly long lashes gazing at her with guarded expectancy. He was not a particularly tall man, but his body was muscular, and now taut and alert as he waited for her to speak, unsmiling. "I'm sorry," Rosie said with an attempt at a little laugh. "I didn't see you there."

He gave a little bow of acknowledgement, and Rosie continued stiltedly, "I wonder if you could help. A girl from the village nearby was hoping she could have her bicycle back..." As she spoke, Rosie realized that of all the volunteers, Leon Rosenblat was probably the last one she wanted to explain this particular problem to. He'd already jumped to certain conclusions the last time she'd spoken to him, and, judging by the rather cool expression on his face now, she had a feeling he was about to again. What, she wondered, did he have against her?

"Pardon?" he asked, dark eyebrows drawing together as he frowned. "Bicycle?"

There was nothing for it but to explain the whole thing properly. "Yes, some of the boys, ah, borrowed some local children's bicycles. I think they must have cycled into the village, but the local children would like their bicycles back. One of them needs to cycle to work..."

Leon drew himself up, his body stiffening all the more. "I am sure the boys will return the bicycles when they are finished with them."

"Well, I hope so, but..." She wasn't quite sure how to finish.

"But?" His voice was as cool as his expression.

"It's just that they took them without asking. And, as I said, one of the girls needs her cycle for work. It isn't..." She swallowed any further words, not even sure what they would be. Leon was positively scowling at her now, his eyes narrowed, mouth pursed. She felt as if she'd done something wrong.

"Are you accusing them of stealing?" he asked coldly.

"No!" Rosie exclaimed, flushing. "No, of course not, not at all. It's just... one of the girls spoke to me, and she was asking for her bicycle back. She understands why the boys would have taken them, but her sister needs it for work." Rosie stared at him in mute appeal, hoping he would see her—or really, the girl's—side of the story. Judging by the expression on his face, he didn't.

"Very well," he said in the same cold voice. "I will get the bicycles back for you."

"Not for *me*," Rosie protested, but he was already walking away from her, just as he'd done before, and she had the terrible feeling that she'd made an enemy of the man without meaning to, and she had no idea how to rectify the situation.

CHAPTER FOUR

The next few days settled into a routine, of sorts; Rosie moved between the kitchen, the art room, and helping Jean with the little ones, and through all these activities was able to keep cheerfully busy. The children, in a surprisingly short amount of time, had become used to being at Calgarth; there was no more lunging for bread at mealtimes, or hiding food in spare cupboards or drawers, or trembling in fear that something terrible was about to happen. In fact, they seemed to be growing in confidence and cheer, both which heartened and inspired Rosie. Children could heal, it seemed, with time and care.

The day after the altercation with Leon Rosenblat—and that was, Rosie had thought miserably more than once, the only word for it—several Red Cross trucks drove up the lane, filled with clothes for the children.

It felt like all their birthdays had come at once, to see how the children rushed to the piles of clothes laid out in the hall— trousers, skirts, jumpers, shirts, yet more underthings and good leather shoes. They tried clothes on right there in the hall, wriggling into trousers or skirts, and buttoning up shirts with delight and pride.

Rosie had enjoyed seeing how excited they were about their new outfits, chatting and joking as they struck funny poses and sashayed up and down the hall, their laughter ringing through the space. She'd laughed herself to see a young boy beam proudly as he'd put on a new suit jacket and bow tie, striking a serious pose before he burst into giggles. The uncertainty and fear that had hung about the children like a shroud when they'd first arrived was already melting away, just two days in.

Last night, Rosie had heard the moans and shouts of their nightmares yet again, but it hadn't been as loud or as distressing as the previous night, and she was hopeful that things would continue to improve; the children would shuck their pain and trauma the way they had their old clothes, leaving it behind for this new life in England, bright with possibility.

Of course, Rosie knew, Marie Paneth would not say it was that easy; the second day after the children had arrived, several dozen ventured up to the art room to try their hand at the paints and crayons, picking up brushes and pencils with a cautious, curious air, as if they did not quite know what to do with them. Perhaps they didn't.

Rosie moved among them, murmuring words of encouragement and praise, as Marie had instructed her to do, without offering any instruction or criticism.

"I don't want pretty pictures," she'd explained. "I don't care about how technically accurate or skilled they are. This is about emotion—and the releasing of it. That is all."

Rosie hadn't been sure what sorts of things the children would draw, especially the littlest ones, who could barely hold a crayon, but the pictures they came up with were both shocking and heartbreaking, drawn with an almost emotionless matter-of-factness, their faces set in lines of grim concentration as they'd painted or colored in. There were pictures of stark stick figures behind jagged fences of barbed wire; more stick figures piled up, horribly, like logs; a child standing by himself, looking very small, in an empty landscape of blank paper. Another child had simply covered his page in thick, red paint until the paper had torn beneath the wet weight of it; yet another scribbled in black as hard as he could, until the paper ripped. All of the pictures told a terrible story, in blobs of paints and lines of crayon, a story of trauma and tragedy and loss, silently and stoically endured, simply because there had been no alternative.

"It's all valuable," Marie proclaimed as she hung the paintings up with clothespins to let them dry. The children had tumbled outside into the sunshine like puppies, tearing across the field with joyful abandon, making it hard for Rosie to credit these carefree creatures with the pictures of desolation now drip-drying on a clothesline. "And I do believe it is freeing for them," Marie continued. "Judging from how they ran out of this room, I think it provided a sort of release, just as I'd hoped."

"Yes," Rosie murmured in agreement, her gaze on the children outside now running in silly circles before they fell dizzily to the soft grass, arms outstretched, their laughter carrying on the breeze to the open window. "I can see that."

Her gaze paused on the sight of Leon Rosenblat, standing by the side of the field, arms folded, a faint smile softening his features in a way she'd never seen when they'd been face to face. With her, he was scowling or frowning, but alone in this unguarded moment, he seemed friendlier, kinder. She'd seen that kindness with the children, the way he talked so gently to them, or put an arm around their shoulders. It made her wonder about him—and what he seemed to have against her.

Although Rosie had done her best to avoid him since their last altercation—he'd seen the bicycles returned without a word of it to her—she found her gaze often searching for him in a crowded room, tracking him across the throng of children. Why, she wasn't sure, although she told herself it was simply because she was curious about him, since they seemed to have gotten off on the wrong foot with each other.

"Marie," she asked now, "do you know anything about the volunteers who came with the children? The adults, I mean?"

Marie gave a little shrug. "Only that they were in the camps, as well."

"All of them?"

Marie glanced at her, her curiosity sharpened. "Most of them, certainly, if not precisely all. Why do you ask?"

Rosie turned from the window with an abashed grimace. "I've had a bit of a run-in with one of them. The man who first came off the bus when they arrived—Leon Rosenblat."

"A run-in?" Marie raised her dark eyebrows. "What do you mean?"

"I don't know exactly how it happened," Rosie replied with an unhappy sigh. "I suppose I was a bit clumsy in my speech, and he jumped to conclusions. I asked if there were any children on the buses, and he said they were all children, which of course I know they were. I'd meant the very little ones, but..." She trailed off miserably.

Marie gave a little shrug of acceptance. "Is that all?"

"No, there was another time," Rosie admitted. "A few days ago, some of the boys took some local children's bicycles—"

Marie nodded. "I heard about that."

"I'm sure they didn't mean any harm, but one of the girls from the village asked me to help fetch their cycles back, because her sister needed one for work, and the only person I could find to ask about was Leon Rosenblat. He took offense—"

"Offense?" Marie raised her dark eyebrows. "Why?"

"I suppose I didn't handle it as well as I could have," Rosie confessed. "I think I might have made it sound as if the boys had stolen the bicycles or something, but I didn't mean it like that, honestly." She bit her lip, as the memory of the difficult conversation with Leon Rosenblat roiled through her yet again. "I just wanted to help the girl."

"Hmm." Having finished hanging up the paintings, Marie

wiped her hands on a cloth, her lips pursed in a thoughtful frown. "It sounds as if he took offense rather easily, but I suppose he is feeling—as all the children and volunteers accompanying them surely are—a bit raw. Perhaps he is not entirely comfortable, among ways that are strange to him, and only here on others' sufferance."

Rosie frowned. She had not considered that before. "Do you think he really sees it like that?"

"I don't know," Marie replied with a graceful shrug, "but it must be difficult to lose everything you've ever had, and then be so dependent on others for every single thing—clothing, food, even the roof over your head."

"I never thought about it like that," Rosie replied slowly. It was a variation of what Dr. Friedmann had said, about the children not wanting to be objects of pity. It was surely understandable that the adults wouldn't want to be, either. "Do you know if Leon Rosenblat was in the camps?" she asked Marie.

Marie's frown deepened. "I believe so." She paused in thought. "He wasn't at Theresienstadt, where most of the children were, I don't think. Dachau, if I recall correctly, with some of the older boys."

The older boys, whom he had insisted were children, too, Rosie realized with a lurch. He must have seen them when they were young, vulnerable, in need, in danger. It made his response more understandable—and it made her feel worse for how she'd handled it.

"Do you know anything else about him?" she asked.

Marie gave her a little, teasing smile. "You are so curious about him, then?"

"I want to make amends," Rosie replied quickly, glad she wasn't blushing for once. She certainly wasn't interested in the man in *that* way. She wasn't interested in any man that way, not after Thomas. Not yet, and maybe not ever. "It would be... helpful," she explained carefully, "to know more about him."

Marie shrugged as she spread her hands wide. "I do not know what more I can tell you. I know the other volunteers as well as you, my dear. They are not particularly forthcoming about their past, and of course I understand why. It must be so very painful."

"I don't know any of them at all, really." It occurred to Rosie then how she had, without even realizing she'd been doing it, viewed the volunteers and the children themselves as some sort of *other*. Not maliciously, or even consciously, but she'd seen them as people who were entirely outside of her experience, even her understanding, and worthy only of pity. Had Leon Rosenblat sensed that in her? she wondered uneasily. She knew, as Dr. Friedmann had said, that her intentions had been well meaning, but that didn't mean she'd acted sensitively, or even rightly. She was ashamed of her own instincts, yet thankful, at least, that she'd realized their error. Now she wondered how she could make amends with Leon Rosenblat, because she knew she wanted to. She did not like the possibility that he thought less of her somehow, although part of her wondered why it mattered so much. Still, she knew it did.

"Perhaps," Marie said, "you should try to get to know some of them, then? They all have some English. It would not be so hard as that, to strike up a conversation."

"No," Rosie replied slowly, "I don't suppose it would."

"Then you must do it. Now, *komm*," Marie said, her tone kind. "The next lot of children are coming to paint, and we have not refilled the pots!"

Rosie banished the swirling thoughts from her mind as she hurried to tidy up the table, and refresh the paper, the paint pots, and the tubs of crayons. Within a few minutes, another two dozen children were trooping into the art room, their expressions ranging from guarded to cheerfully curious.

As Marie began to introduce the object of the lesson—that was, simply to draw or paint without any object at all—Rosie's heart leaped, for the last child into the room was no other than the girl with the dark, heavy hair and the disdainful expression in her hazel eyes, whom she'd been keeping an eye out for since that first night.

She sidled into the room as if she didn't want to be noticed, or perhaps she simply didn't want to be there. She didn't look at anyone and she sat at a table by herself, her skinny arms folded, her expression seeming determinedly uninterested as Marie began to speak.

The other children set to their projects, some with eager alacrity, some with more cautious hesitation, dipping brushes into paint or reaching for crayons with grubby hands. As Rosie moved around the room, murmuring words of encouragement or praise, she kept her eyes on the girl, who barely moved, sitting alone at her table, a blank piece of paper in front of her that she didn't so much as glance at, keeping her expression haughty, chin tilted as she stared straight ahead, making sure to meet no one's gaze. Everyone else was, by silent agreement, it seemed, ignoring her.

After seeing that all the other children had begun to draw or paint, Rosie steeled herself to approach the girl. She was just a child, she reminded herself, and a small one at that; although she guessed her to be twelve or so years of age, she was slight, all hair and eyes. Rosie felt intimidated by her all the same, especially after their last difficult encounter, and the froideur she saw in the girl's eyes.

"Hello." She gave a friendly smile as she perched on the chair next to her. *"Maist du?"* she asked, nodding toward the paper. Do you paint? She'd asked Marie how to say it in German.

The girl's lip curled. "I speak English, you know." The words were accented but clear.

"Do you?" Rosie kept her voice cheerful. "How wonderful.

Much easier for me, then, because I'm afraid I don't speak much German! Where did you learn it?"

"My parents," the girl said, and then pressed her lips together as if she did not want to say anything more.

"Well, I am very impressed." Rosie spoke slowly enough to make sure the girl could understand, for although her English seemed good, she did yet know how fluent she was. "I'm afraid I don't speak any other language than English, which is very dull." She nodded toward the paper. "Would you like to draw or paint?"

The girl pressed her lips together, and said nothing.

Rosie decided to try again. "What is your name?"

A second's pause and then offered with reluctance, "Frieda."

"Hello, Frieda. I'm Rosie." She glanced around at the other children, all busy drawing or painting. Even the hesitant ones were now working with concentration and apparent enjoyment. She saw two girls giggle as they splattered a paper with paint, their dark heads bent together, and was glad to see them enjoying such simple pleasures.

Frieda, meanwhile, folded her arms, her expression stonily obdurate.

"Sometimes that's how I feel," Rosie ventured, feeling her way through the words as she nodded toward the piece of paper in front of Frieda. "Like... like I'm blank inside. Empty. Numb. There's nothing for me to put to paper, at least nothing that I want to." Surprised she'd said so much without having really meant to, she stopped, waiting for Frieda to respond.

She said nothing.

"Do you ever feel that way?" Rosie asked hesitantly. Could this be a point of connection?

Frieda turned to her with a sudden, fierce look, before her lips twisted and she reached for the paper. In slow, deliberate movements, her hostile, blazing gaze never wavering from

Rosie's, she crumpled the paper up into a wadded ball and then hurled it to the floor. And then, just as she had before when Rosie had spoken to her about her cup of hot cocoa, she rose from the table, the chair screeching along the wooden floor, and walked out of the room without looking back.

A few of the children looked up as she walked out, some curious, some indifferent, a few of them whispering as they glanced at Rosie. She sat there, trying to smile, determined not to take offense at Frieda's seeming snub. This wasn't about her, she reminded herself. It was about helping this girl, whose name she now knew. *Frieda.*

Marie came over to briefly rest a hand on her shoulder. "What feels like failure," she said quietly, "can actually be success. You are reaching that girl, whether you realize it or not. She would not have responded that way otherwise."

"Still, it's not a very good way to respond," Rosie returned wryly, managing a small smile. "I wish I'd handled it better."

"Isn't it?" Marie replied shrewdly. "Remember, the trauma must come out. Perhaps, for some, that is how."

Rosie nodded, not entirely convinced, and rose from her seat to move around the room, refilling paint pots or crayon tubs, murmuring more words of encouragement and praise, although inside she felt weary and depressed, and she wasn't entirely sure why. It wasn't just Frieda's rebuff; she wasn't as sensitive as all that, surely. Perhaps it was seeing the terrible pictures the children drew, often with such grim, methodical determination. Even though she knew it was part of their healing process, it still had to hurt. Perhaps, she reflected, it was the sorrow she still felt inside herself, when she let herself feel it; seeing the children confront their own grief made her think, reluctantly yet inexorably, of hers. The world felt like a heavy place, a weight on her shoulders she did not have the strength to shrug off.

"Why don't you get a cup of tea?" Marie suggested once the

children had trooped out to play. "You have been working all day."

"So have you," Rosie pointed out, and Marie smiled.

"I might join you when I have finished with these," she said, gesturing to the wet paintings she needed to hang to dry.

Deciding she could use a few moments' sit-down, Rosie headed downstairs, only to be stopped by a smiling Jean. "The post has arrived, and there was a letter for you, all the way from Canada." She took an airmail envelope out of her pocket. "I said I'd give it to you when I saw you. You must be pleased to have news from home."

"Thank you, Jean," Rosie replied as she took the envelope. A wave of trepidation rippled through her as she realized, despite what Jean had said, she wasn't entirely sure she wanted to read the contents of the letter. Had her brother Jamie returned home safely? Hopefully he'd at least been given a date for his demobilization. She knew, thankfully, that he'd come through the war unscathed, at least, working as a mechanic for the Royal Canadian Air Force; she'd seen him back in London, after the war had ended, before she'd traveled up to Windermere.

The last time her mother had written to her, she had not yet received Rosie's letter informing her that she wasn't coming home. By now, her mother would have read that letter, brief as it had been, and Rosie suspected she would have been bitterly disappointed by its contents. Rosie hadn't told her parents about Thomas; they didn't know she'd had a daughter. A daughter who had died before she'd been able to draw a breath. They knew nothing of her life anymore, because she hadn't told them, hadn't been able to bear to, and it felt as if it had gone on too long now for her to say anything about it at all. And so it remained between them, a burden, a barrier, and one they didn't even know was there, although Rosie thought her mother must sense it.

She slipped the letter in her pocket and went to get a cup of tea from the kitchen, where the cooks were stirring an enormous vat of vegetable soup for the children's dinner. She took her tea to the end of a table and then reached for her letter, slowly slitting the envelope and pulling out the single piece of paper.

Dearest Rosie,

I am writing to you from Amherst Island, where I came to visit some old friends, and to visit the island itself, because I have always loved it here so. I know you did, once upon a time; perhaps when you return, you will visit again. The blue-green waters of Lake Ontario are always a balm to the soul, I think!

I will tell you our good news first—that Jamie is set to come home next month, and I will be so happy to see him. He wrote that he is planning to find work as a mechanic in Kingston if he can, but he will travel elsewhere if need be. I hope he finds work here.

I will be honest and confess I was disappointed to receive your news that you intend to stay in England, as I'm sure you knew I would be, but it might surprise you to learn that I do understand it. At the end of the last war, I felt as I imagine you must—although I could be wrong, of course. But after returning from France, I felt adrift, a bit lonely and lost, without any real purpose. It took me some time, but I ended up returning here, to Amherst Island, where I knew I'd always belonged. Your journey might be different, and I know only you can decide what that path is, wherever it takes you. Just know that you do not have to walk it alone, and we will always be here when—or perhaps I should say if—you return.

All my love, Mum.

Rosie blinked back sudden tears as she finished the letter

and then folded it back up again. She'd almost rather her mother had scolded her, or simply said she was disappointed, for her gentle understanding was nearly more than Rosie could bear, and it made her miss her more than ever—her mother, her father, her brother, even her home and the familiar streets of Kingston. And dear old Amherst Island, too, for her mother was right, she'd always loved it there—the way the wind rustled through the meadows, the copse of silvery white birches with sun-dappled leaves that she'd used to play in, the blue-green waters of Lake Ontario sparkling in the sunlight lapping the familiar, rocky shores. She wondered when she would be able to go back, and what she would feel like then.

Rosie looked up as the threat of tears thankfully cleared, and the wave of homesickness that had threatened to engulf her receded. Her mother had said only she could decide which path to travel down—but where did it even go, and what if she couldn't find the way? Her mum had been right, she did feel lost and lonely, utterly adrift, and had for months. She'd told Marie as much back when she'd first met her, and although she'd tried to put on a good front when she'd come to Windermere, she didn't think anything had really changed inside her.

When her mother had been feeling the same, she had found a way back to shore, to her beloved island and Rosie's father. Rosie knew it must have been a long and twisting path, but in many years' hindsight, it seemed a happy ending to a simple story. Her mother had done it, she thought, but could she? Rosie knew she didn't yet have the answer to that question.

CHAPTER FIVE

By the start of September, most of the children seemed to have settled in well to life at Calgarth Estate. They all finally had clothes and shoes, and Dr. Friedmann had arranged for them to receive three shillings a week for pocket money, which many of them liked to spend at the little post office shop in Troutbeck, coming back with paper bags of sweets, or sometimes rather surprising objects—a bottle of shoe polish, a nailbrush, a comb.

"After all their deprivations," Dr. Friedmann explained to the volunteers, "they long to take pride in their appearance. It is a natural thing, a good one. It bodes well for their future."

Soon after their initial medical checks, forty of the children had had to be taken to isolation wards in hospitals for suspected tuberculosis; others had had trips to the doctor or dentist to address the many maladies and ailments that life in the camps had given them. Malnutrition had, unfortunately, taken its toll on their teeth as well as their bodies; Rosie felt for them, staggering back from the dentist in Windermere, clutching their mouths in shocked agony at what had needed to be done.

"I thought I was going to the cinema," one boy, Ari, with

dark hair and a cheeky smile, had moaned to Dr. Friedmann, who had translated into English for Rosie. Ari had rubbed his jaw ruefully as he continued, "I had three teeth taken out instead. I would have rather seen a picture!"

Despite these trials, the children seemed to be in good spirits; they'd begun to have daily lessons in English and arithmetic and British history, and had even formed both a choir and a football team, with some of the boys playing the local lads on more than one occasion. Part of the lake had been cordoned off to make a sort of swimming pool, and dozens of the boys and a few brave girls waded happily into the water, even though Rosie found it to be freezing. It was lovely to see them taking part in such simple and childish pleasures—a sunny day, a swim, kicking a ball across the field.

Many children had also continued to come to the art room to do their drawings and paintings. And, as the weeks had gone on, their artwork had become less bleak and disturbing, and more about what they were experiencing at Windermere. It heartened Rosie to see their pictures of flowers and football, of the lake glinting under the sunshine, of smiling stick figures and happy-looking houses, so different from their first bleak drawings.

"Children are so resilient," Marie murmured as she studied a drawing of the lake surrounded by bright blobs of flowers. "We could learn from them all in that way, I think."

"Do you really think it is that easy?" Rosie asked, unable to keep from feeling at least a little skeptical, even though she was glad. "They draw a few pictures and then they are able to move on, just like that?" She wished it were that easy, of course she did, but she felt instinctively that it could not be. Not for these children, and, she realized dismally, maybe not for herself.

"No," Marie replied slowly as she hung another picture on the line, "not that easy, not at all. It is not one, two—finished!"

She snapped her fingers, smiling wryly. "But it is, perhaps, part of their journey, a necessary step. Perhaps only the first one."

Their journey.

It reminded Rosie of what her mother had written. She had yet to take any of her own faltering steps, as far as she could tell, and she still didn't even know what direction she would go in. The past still felt like a blank canvas, as empty as the piece of paper Frieda had crumpled and thrown away. Rosie refused to think about it.

As for the future... once her time ended at Calgarth, that seemed even emptier. She would need to fill it somehow, to plan her steps, to make a decision. As she looked at the children's cheerful drawings, Rosie felt a stirring of optimism, a flicker of hope that she hadn't felt in a long while. She thought that if these children could move forward, then surely so could she. She just needed to figure out how.

The possibilities continued to dance at the fringes of her mind as she went about the routine she'd fallen into over the weeks: helping in the kitchen in the mornings, getting breakfast on the table and then cleaning up, and then the art room in the afternoons, working with Marie, and finally with Jean and the little ones in the evening, to settle them for bed, before she fell into bed herself, happy to be so tired that she fell asleep almost as soon as her head hit the pillow.

Golda was hoping to join her aunt in Birmingham in the next week or two, and Jean would be in charge of the smallest children's day-to-day care, while Alice Goldberger continued to focus on managing their therapies.

"They are doing so much better," Jean told Rosie one night after they'd tucked them into bed with stories and songs; the littlest children continued to share a single room, beds crammed together side by side. At least, Jean had told Rosie earlier, they were no longer sleeping *under* their beds, which was what they'd done at the beginning, all huddled there together like a nest of mice. Golda had told them they were used to having to hide, a reality that made Rosie ache with sorrow, even as she tried not to think about it too much. "They like to sing and play sometimes," Jean continued, "nonsense songs, I think—at least with no words I can understand, although perhaps I will one day. Alice said she did not recognize the words as either German or Polish."

"And they're learning some English now," Rosie replied with a smile. "They certainly know the word for cocoa!" She loved seeing the children's delighted grins as their small hands reached eagerly for their nightly treat. Yes, perhaps children *were* resilient, after all. These tiny ones, who'd had so little love or kindness in their lives, were now becoming used to comfort, to safety, to affection. It made Rosie deeply, fiercely glad.

As busy as she was, she still tried to keep an eye on Frieda, whom she saw continued to remain on her own, whether it was in the dining hall or out in the yard, and, as far as Rosie could tell, seemingly by her own choice. From a distance, she'd seen other girls approach Frieda occasionally for a game or a chat, but she'd rebuffed them each and every time. After a week or two, the other girls had given up and left Frieda to her own devices, which didn't seem to make the girl feel any better, judging by her determined scowl, the hostility that so often sharpened her delicate features as she stood alone on the side of the yard, slight shoulders hunched, her arms wrapped around her thin body.

Why, Rosie wondered, did Frieda insist on always being so isolated? She supposed Marie or Dr. Friedmann would advise her to simply let her be, that being alone might be part of her healing process, but it still made Rosie both sad and uneasy. It didn't seem right, to let Frieda fester by herself, especially when she seemed so miserable, hiding her pain behind that scowl. Still, Rosie had given the girl the space she seemed to want, all the while hoping for an opportunity to befriend her that had yet to make itself known.

Rosie had also steered clear of Leon Rosenblat, since she seemed to put her foot in her mouth every time she saw him, and it seemed he was just as intent on avoiding her. Whenever their glances inadvertently met, he always looked away first, his mouth tightening in seeming disapproval that Rosie didn't think she was imagining.

And yet, she had reflected more than once, their glances seemed to meet rather often. For some reason, she found herself seeking him out whenever there was a crowd in the dining hall or on the football pitch; his was the one she looked for amidst the throng of now familiar faces, and often when she found him, he was looking back at her. It gave her a funny little jolt, and she wasn't sure what to think about it.

Still, most of the volunteers had become friendly with one another, chatting at mealtimes or in the evening, and there were enough of them that Rosie had managed not to encounter Leon directly again, choosing to spend her time with Jean and Golda, as well as Marie... even if, for some contrary reason, she kept looking for Leon.

In the second week of September, the summer weather, such as it had been, began to turn; the sky turned gray and the wind off the lake became cold and cutting. It began to rain—not the gently misting drizzle of summer that barely got you wet, but a hard, sleeting rain that came in sideways, thanks to the wind, and stung your face.

It was in this grimly unfavorable weather that the children assembled in the dining hall one afternoon, with pencils and sheets of paper. The Polish-speaking volunteers were giving them instructions as Rosie came into the room, wrinkling her nose at the smell of wet wool of damp clothing and boiled cabbage, the day's lunch.

"What are they doing?" she asked Golda, for the children

had set to writing with an almost ferocious concentration, lips bitten, foreheads screwed up into frowns of focus, eyes narrowed as they wrote on their papers in neat, careful letters.

"They are writing the names of their family," Golda explained in her flat, matter-of-fact way. "So the Red Cross can trace them, in case any of them are still alive."

Rosie's heart lurched at the thought. No wonder the children seemed so terribly intent! "Do you think many of them will be?" she asked in a low voice, and Golda gave her a bleak look.

"No, I should think not very many at all. Certainly not mothers or fathers, brothers or sisters. They would have come with their families into the camps, and the children left without them." A distant, haunted look came into her eyes as she glanced away. "Most of them will almost certainly know that those closest to them are dead."

"Did... did you lose anyone in the camps, Golda?" Rosie asked quietly. Somehow it felt like an intrusive question, a presumption even to ask.

Golda turned back to her with a look of mingled resignation and disbelief that Rosie could ask such a thing, without knowing the blatantly obvious answer. "I lost *everyone*," she stated flatly. "Mother, father, sister, brother... Husband." She paused. "Son." She looked away again, pressing her lips together.

"Oh, Golda." Rosie swallowed hard, horrified. She felt as if she'd put her foot in it *again*, simply by asking the question, and she wished she hadn't, even as she longed to show the other woman some sympathy. "I'm so very sorry."

Golda shrugged. "Ask anyone here and it will be the same."

Rosie nodded slowly in acceptance. She'd understood this in theory, of course she had; it was impossible not to when you read the papers or listened to the news, or considered that these children were here at all, with no one else to go to or advocate for them. Yet somehow it felt worse, more terrible and more *real*, having Golda say it to her like this, a simple statement, so terribly powerful in its bleak matter-of-factness.

She glanced at the tables full of children—children who were now ruddy-cheeked and often smiling, on their way to health and happiness, and yet... They'd lost so much. So *many*. How could they keep going, one foot in front of the other, breathe in and out every day, with so much grief to bear?

"But there might be some other relatives alive?" she asked after a moment, longing to find some hope for these young souls, amidst all the sorrow and grief. "Cousins, perhaps? Or an aunt or an uncle? Someone who could take them in?"

Golda shrugged. "Maybe," she replied, sounding unconvinced.

No wonder the children were writing with such determined focus, Rosie thought. They were writing down their hopes for the future, for their family, for love and for life itself. Her gaze moved around the room, from the young men who were earnestly writing lists in neat print, to the children who could barely form their letters and yet were desperately trying to. And then her gaze snagged on one child who was not writing at all, and she realized she was not surprised to see who it was.

Once again, Frieda was refusing to engage with her surroundings or, really, to do anything at all. She sat apart from the other children, the pencil and a piece of blank paper in front of her, her arms folded, her chin lifted, her gaze defiant. *Why?* Why wouldn't she want to write down the names of her family? Even if she knew that her immediate family were dead, heaven help her, there might be others she could trace—aunts, uncles, cousins... Surely she had *someone?* Rosie hated to think that she might not have.

"Golda," she asked, "do you know anything about that girl?"

She nodded toward Frieda, sitting as usual at the end of a table by herself. "The one who isn't writing."

Golda glanced at Frieda, her lips pursed as her forehead furrowed. "Frieda, isn't it? I don't know much. She wasn't at Theresienstadt, I don't think. I believe she joined us at Prague—she was in a different DP."

"DP?" Rosie asked. She'd heard the term before, but she couldn't remember what it stood for.

"Displacement camp. Where they put us after the war ended." Golda's lips twisted. "From one camp to another, but at least they didn't shoot you in those ones."

"I'm sorry," Rosie said helplessly. She felt as if she had no other words, and those ones didn't seem to do much good. "So Frieda didn't come with anyone else?" Rosie surmised. "Whenever I see her, she is always sitting or standing by herself."

"Maybe she likes it that way."

"Maybe..." Not for the first time, Rosie wondered why she cared so much about this one girl. There were three hundred children here at Calgarth, most of them friendly and cheerful and eager to practice their English; why had she focused on getting to know Frieda, when she seemed so prickly and unfriendly? Frieda certainly didn't seem to want to get to know *her*.

She still wasn't writing anything.

"If she doesn't write the names of her family down on that piece of paper," Rosie asked Golda, "what will happen?"

"Nothing, I suppose," Golda replied with a shrug. "The Red Cross can't trace a name they don't have." She glanced again at Frieda. "Perhaps," she said quietly, "she already knows they are all dead. It is very possible, I am afraid."

It was a truly terrible thought, and yet if there was anyone, anyone at all, left for Frieda to find... this could be the only chance she had to find her family, Rosie realized with a lurch.

To find someone who would take care of her, who would *love* her.

Murmuring something to Golda, Rosie started walking toward the girl. When she was about twenty feet away, Frieda saw her coming and her expression froze for a mere second before her eyes flashed with challenge, and she lifted her chin, as if daring Rosie to come any closer.

With some trepidation, Rosie did.

"Hello, Frieda," she said in as friendly voice as she could manage without, she hoped, sounding false or overly jolly. She nodded toward the sheet in front of her with a playful smile. "Another blank paper, I see."

For a second, Frieda looked startled by the gentle teasing, and Rosie almost thought she would smile back, but then she didn't. She scowled instead.

"Your English is very good," Rosie told her. "You said your parents taught you, didn't you?"

The girl's scowl deepened and, after a second's pause, she reluctantly nodded.

Keeping her smile in place, Rosie sat down next to her. "And how did they learn English?"

"My mother learned it when she was young and my father was a professor at university," Frieda replied, her tone a mixture of pride and reluctance. "They spoke it very well, and they wanted us to speak English at home, and so often we did. My mother said it would help us one day."

And now, Rosie thought, it indeed might, even if in such sad circumstances as these.

"A professor at a university," she repeated, sounding impressed. "Which one?"

"The University of Economics, in Katowice." Frieda looked away. "Until it closed, when Germany invaded."

Rosie was silent for a moment, unsure how to move the conversation on, how much to ask, to press. After a moment, she nodded at the paper. "Are you going to write some names down?" she asked gently.

Frieda's expression closed. "No."

"Why not?"

Frieda shrugged, jutting out her chin.

After a few moments, Rosie realized it was all the answer she was going to get.

"The Red Cross is very good at finding people," she told Frieda. "People you might not even think about or remember. You might have aunts and uncles whom they could track down, or cousins, perhaps. Neighbors, even."

Frieda shook her head. "No. No aunts, no uncles."

"None?" Rosie asked, a little surprised, and Frieda shook her head again, more firmly.

"*None.*"

Rosie sensed there was something the girl wasn't telling her, but then, why should she? She was a stranger, and Frieda was clearly a very guarded child.

"Do you not want to try?" she asked, and Frieda glared at her.

"No."

Well, there wasn't much she could do with that, was there, Rosie thought. She kept trying with this girl, but perhaps it would be better for them both if she stopped. And yet...

"What about your parents?" she asked gently. "Perhaps—"

"My parents are dead." Frieda's voice was low and fierce. "I know they are."

"But—"

"Dead!" Frieda pushed her face close to Rosie's. "Dead, dead, *dead!*" she repeated, her voice rising each time until it ended in something close to a shriek, so a few children nearby looked over at them, and then she flung her pencil and paper to the floor before she scrambled up from her seat and ran out of the room.

The ensuing silence felt deafening; the children's chatter died away as Frieda slammed the door to the dining hall behind her. Rosie was conscious of the children's curious stares, a few muted whispers, and as she looked around, she met Leon Rosenblat's gaze, as she so often seemed to. For once, however, he wasn't frowning at her; there was a look of something almost like sympathy in his eyes before he looked away, and so did Rosie.

Slowly, feeling dispirited by the complete lack of success, she bent to pick up the pencil and paper and return them to the table. Then she rose and walked stiffly from the room. No one stopped her.

Outside, the wind was still sending the rain sideways, although it had, at least, downgraded to more of a drizzle. Even though she wasn't wearing her coat, Rosie set out down the lane toward the lake, needing the space and fresh air to clear her head, the rain wetting her cheeks like tears.

She'd come to Windermere in part because she had nowhere else to go—at least nowhere else she'd *wanted* to go. She hadn't truly believed in Marie's idea that 'broken calls to broken,' but she'd still hoped that somehow, in her own brokenness, she could help someone. And, she acknowledged, she'd wanted a distraction from her own sorrows. It all felt rather selfish now; had she even been thinking about anyone else, about *Frieda*, at all?

Even more dispirited, Rosie kept walking, even though the rain was misting her face and wetting her hair; her shoes were soaked right through. She'd catch a chill if she wasn't careful, but at this point she wasn't sure she much cared.

She felt a weary despair lapping at the edges of her mind, her soul, like dusk falling inside of her. She'd managed to march ahead, day after day, for almost six months, since she'd lost both Thomas and her baby daughter, but right now she didn't feel like trying anymore. Not with Frieda, and not with herself.

What was the point of it all? she wondered desolately. The point of anything?

She turned instinctively to the stretch of quiet shoreline where she'd sat before, only to stop in surprise when she saw the rock where she'd perched a few weeks ago was occupied—by Frieda.

Rosie's first impulse was to turn around and walk away before the girl saw her. Frieda would think she'd followed her, was spying on her, even. The last thing she wanted to do was anger or upset her more than she already had.

She'd already started to turn when she heard a shuddering sound, almost like a sob, and Frieda wrapped her arms around her knees and tucked her head low, just as Rosie once had in the same place, her braid falling over one shoulder.

Rosie stilled, her heart aching for the child before her. She'd suspected, of course, that beneath Frieda's haughty manner was a sad and lonely little girl, but she'd never actually seen any real evidence of it until now. Frieda was hurting, of course she was... and Rosie longed to help her. She took an instinctive step toward her, the leaves and twigs crunching underneath her feet.

Frieda lifted her head, then turned around, her expression turning hostile as she caught sight of Rosie. "*You!*"

"Hello, Frieda." Rosie hesitated, poised for flight—in either direction. Which would be better for Frieda? "Do you want me to go?" she asked, and Frieda sniffed and then shrugged.

It wasn't, Rosie thought with a sudden lurch of hope, an outright no. It wasn't a yes, either, but it was enough to make her take another step toward her.

"I like to sit on this rock, as well," she ventured. "It's so pretty here, isn't it, near the water? It reminds me of home." Another shrug. "Was there a lake near where you grew up? Katowice, wasn't it?"

Frieda hesitated and then replied, "There were some small lakes. Sometimes I went ice skating." She rested her chin on her fists, her elbows braced on her knees, as she looked out on the lake. "I wasn't very good. I was only little."

"That must have been fun, though." Frieda would only have been five or six when the Germans invaded Poland, Rosie thought. So very little to have your life completely changed, everything safe and familiar upturned or taken away in an instant. She walked toward the shore of the lake and cautiously settled herself on a stone next to Frieda. "I used to ice skate, as well, back home in Canada," she said, and gave the girl a sideways smile. "I wasn't very good either, and I wasn't even that little!"

She was rewarded by the tiniest twitch of a smile that made Rosie's heart sing. Could it be possible that she was finally reaching this child, if only a tiny bit?

"In Canada," she continued, "it gets very cold—far colder than here in England. And there is snow—so much snow."

"There is snow in Poland, too," Frieda said, and then let out a small, shuddering breath. Rosie wondered what she was remembering; whatever it was, she thought, it hurt. Grief did. She decided to change the subject.

"It really is so pretty here," she said, "even in the rain." It was still drizzling, a mist hovering over the lake in ghostly shreds, obscuring the far shore. Frieda wasn't wearing a coat either, Rosie realized; they really were both going to get completely soaked if they stayed out here for much longer, and yet she didn't want to break the fragile thread of connection they'd finally formed.

She searched for something to say, something pleasant or at least innocuous, and then realized that there simply wasn't anything. She could witter on about Ontario or ice skating or something else, but it didn't feel right or necessary. When she'd been at her saddest, she recalled, still reeling from loss and grief, no words would have helped. Since meeting Frieda, she'd tried to fill those unhappy silences, but maybe that was the wrong thing to do. Maybe she just needed to sit with her in the stillness, and let it be.

The only sound was the constant dripping of the rain; it dripped off branches and leaves onto the ground with the steadiness of a ticking clock. Rosie felt rainwater trickle down the back of her neck and seep into her skirt where she was sitting on the mossy, wet rock, waiting for Frieda to speak. Hoping, although for what she couldn't even say.

Finally, after several long moments during which Rosie tried not to shiver, the rainwater trickling all the way down her neck and back, Frieda spoke.

"My father's dead," she said in a low voice, her arms wrapped around her knees as she stared out at the lake. "He died even before we were taken to the camps."

"I'm so sorry," Rosie said quietly, knowing once again those were the only words she could offer, even if she wished she had other, better ones.

"And my mother, my sister..." Frieda sniffed, running her wrist under her nose as she gazed fixedly at the lake. "I know my mama must be dead. I *know* it."

Rosie hesitated before asking with careful gentleness, "But if there is any way..."

"*No,*" Frieda said firmly, shaking her head resolutely. "There isn't. I know there isn't." And then she pressed her face into her knees as her shoulders shook with sobs.

"Oh, Frieda." Gently, Rosie leaned over to rest a hand on the girl's shoulder, and was thankful she did not resist the gesture. "I'm so sorry. So sorry." They were the only words she knew to say, and yet they felt so paltry. She wished she had more comfort to offer, but she knew there wasn't anything. Marie was right, Rosie realized; grief had to be dealt with, waded through, endured. Perhaps this was the only way.

After a few more seconds, Frieda took a hiccuping breath and then shook off Rosie's hand. She looked up, her face both blotchy with tears and now full of anger. Rosie tensed, waiting for the backlash, for Frieda looked as if she wanted to fly at her, shouting and raging. But then, after a few tense seconds, the girl simply scrambled off the rock and ran back toward the road, leaving Rosie alone by the lake, and feeling almost as if they were right back where they had started.

CHAPTER SIX

"Dr. Friedmann?"

Rosie tapped hesitantly on the door of the director's office, nervous about approaching him. Although he'd been nothing but kind and gentle since she'd come to Windermere, she still felt slightly intimidated by his kindly air of knowledge and expertise.

"*Komm!*" he called, and Rosie pushed open the door.

"Ah, Miss Lyman, isn't it?" Dr. Friedmann rose from behind his desk, in front of a window that overlooked the football pitch. He was smiling faintly, his eyebrows raised in inquiry. "May I help you?"

"I... I wanted to ask you about one of the children here," Rosie ventured.

It had been nearly a week since she'd talked with Frieda at the shore of the lake; the Red Cross had gone away again with the children's lists of names, and all their hopes. Every day, one of the children asked when they would be back, when they would bring news of their families. Every time a truck or delivery van came down the lane, at least a dozen boys would race toward the drive, their faces lit up with hope, only to fall into lines of disappointment when they saw the vehicle in question didn't belong to the Red Cross.

"I know mine are dead, anyway," Ari, the boy who had had the teeth pulled, told Rosie as he kicked a stone with his shoe. "I don't know why I run."

"Because you hope," Rosie had replied gently, "and there is nothing wrong with that."

Golda had told her as much earlier, with a despairing shake of her head. "So many of them still believe. They think the Red Cross is some sort of magic, a—what do you call it?" She'd frowned before finding the word. "A fairy godmother. They think they will bring them back their families like birthday presents, but they won't. No one can."

"You don't know that for certain," Rosie had replied, because, like Ari, she wanted to hope. She wanted to believe at least some of them would find their loved ones, be part of a family again, as impossible as it sometimes seemed.

Golda gave her a bleak look. "I know," she replied, and Rosie had had nothing to say to that. Golda knew far better than she did.

"Oh, yes?" Dr. Friedmann asked now, his tone polite. "What child would that be?"

"Her name is Frieda," Rosie said. Her voice sounded tremulous, and her heart was beating hard. She had no idea if she was overstepping as a volunteer, interfering where she had no right to stick her nose in—and yet she felt she had to do something. She hated the thought of Frieda not finding out what had happened to her family. If there was any chance at all that someone could be found...

"Frieda," Dr. Friedmann replied. "I do not think I know her."

Rosie was not really surprised, as she would not have expected Frieda to avail herself of the doctor's talking therapies, and he did not insist on anyone coming to talk to him if they didn't want to.

"She is about twelve years old," Rosie told him, "and I know that she was not one of the children at Theresienstadt. Golda, who helps to look after the smallest children, said she joined the group in Prague, from another DP camp."

"Hmm." Frowning slightly, Dr. Friedmann riffled among the papers on his desk. "And what is it you wish to speak about, in regard to this child?"

"I am concerned for her," Rosie admitted, flushing a little. "She is so quiet, always off by herself, talking to no one. And when the Red Cross came to collect the names of everyone's family members, she refused to write any down."

Dr. Friedmann looked up from his desk to regard her soberly. "Perhaps there were no names left to write down."

"Perhaps," Rosie allowed, "but from what she said, it sounded as if she came to the camp with her mother and sister. She said she thought her mother had died, but she didn't mention her sister and... well, she couldn't be absolutely sure that they had both died, could she? And what about other, more distant relatives? Most people have aunts and uncles, cousins..." She trailed off uncertainly, a little cowed by the doctor's serious look.

"Do you know why she did not write any names down?" he asked quietly.

"She said there wasn't anyone else," Rosie admitted. "But... it seemed to be such a missed opportunity. I think she was afraid, or perhaps just stubborn. I... care about her." Rosie ducked her head, abashed. "I know I must seem nosy, and I am afraid my good intentions haven't helped anyone so far that I can see, but if any family could be found, any at all..."

Dr. Friedmann let out a heavy sigh. "If she is not willing to write down the names, I do not know what we can do. It is her choice, after all, even if it isn't a particularly wise one."

"But she's only a child," Rosie persisted, "and if her family isn't found, what will happen to her?"

The doctor shrugged and spread his hands on the desk. "Most of these children's families will never be found, Miss Lyman. And if we do not have the names, we cannot search for them. That is the simple truth of the matter."

It was what Golda had said, but Rosie was still reluctant to let the matter go. Perhaps she was the stubborn one, she thought wryly, not Frieda. "I know she is from Katowice," she told Dr. Friedmann. "And her father was a professor of Economics at the university there."

"She told you that?"

"Yes."

He nodded slowly. "Well, then, perhaps we could find something. It is worth a try, although if it is bad news, Frieda might rather not know. Some children prefer it that way, you know. Then they can still hope."

And yet surely knowing was better than not knowing and always wondering, Rosie thought, but didn't say. "I don't mean to interfere," she said instead, compelled to an uncomfortable honesty, "although I realize that is exactly what I'm doing. I'm just worried Frieda will cut off her nose to spite her face. She seems that type of girl." She thought of how she'd spilled the hot cocoa, crumpled the paper, run away. At every opportunity, she'd refused and rejected, and to what purpose? It was almost, Rosie thought, as if she was punishing herself for something.

"Cut her off nose?" Dr. Friedmann looked bemused. "That is not an expression I have heard before, but I think I can guess what it means." He smiled, and then his expression softened, his voice turning quiet. "Every child will respond to their situation, and their trauma, differently, and we do not know what has happened in Frieda's young life that makes her as she is. If she is choosing to do such a thing, then perhaps that is the way she needs to be right now."

"But if it harms her?" She knew the doctor wanted children to have complete freedom at Calgarth, and she understood the reasoning behind it, but she couldn't help but wonder if, in cases like Frieda's, that freedom could be harmful, or, at the very least, unhelpful. Or maybe she was the one being unhelpful, constantly sticking her nose in. Maybe she really should stop. "Am I wrong, do you think?" Rosie asked uncertainly, "In meddling the way I am? Should I just let her be?"

Dr. Friedmann sighed and shook his head. "That I do not know. As I said, every child is different. It is impossible to know how they will respond, or even what they will respond to." He paused, folding his hands on the desk in front of him, smiling at her with genuine kindness, half his face crinkling up, while the other half remained still and frozen—Rosie knew he had suffered from partial paralysis when he'd received injuries at Sachsenhausen concentration camp, before the war. "What I do know," he told her gently, "is that if you feel some affinity, some affection, for this particular child, then that must be a good thing. As human beings, we crave connection, and we must find it where and how we can. I am glad you spoke to me about Frieda. I will look into her background, and see if we can discover some names. And you, meanwhile, can keep trying with her, for I can tell from what you have said that it cannot be easy."

"No," Rosie agreed, smiling, grateful for his understanding, "it's not easy. But then," she added with a smile, "I'm not a particularly easy person, either."

Dr. Friedmann let out a huff of laughter. "Oh, Miss Lyman," he said, "not one of us is *easy*! Not one of us is easy at all."

Feeling heartened by the conversation, Rosie thanked him and bid him goodbye before heading back out into the corridor. She had promised Jean she'd take the little ones for a walk around the lake before they had their afternoon tea.

With her mind full of Frieda, and how to reach her, she didn't see the figure coming toward her down the narrow hallway until she'd almost collided with him, his hands gripping her arms to keep from smacking right into her.

"Oh!" Rosie gasped in shock, blinking up in the dim light to see, of all people, Leon Rosenblat, scowling down at her as usual. His hands still gripped her upper arms and she felt the nearness of his body with a surprised lurch of awareness.

"You are in a hurry, it seems," he remarked dryly, and she let out an uncertain laugh, unsure whether it was meant as a criticism or not.

"I'm sorry, I was miles away," she confessed.

He released her arms and took a step back. "Miles?" he inquired, and she let out another laugh, this one abashed.

"It's just an expression. I was thinking about something else, and I didn't see where I was going. I'm sorry, I should have been looking." She realized she had never stood so close to him before, as she'd been doing her best to avoid him these last few weeks, and he'd been, she suspected, doing the same to her— even if they'd kept glancing at each other. Now she saw that his eyes, although dark, had golden glints in the irises, and his lashes were long and thick and curly. He had a straight nose and full lips that were, unexpectedly, almost lifted in a smile as he looked at her.

"You must have been thinking very important thoughts," he said wryly, and his lips lifted upwards just a little more.

"No, not—not really." She ducked her head, felt herself flush, wondering why such a simple conversation was making her feel so discombobulated. It was on the tip of her tongue to apologize for all that had gone before, although what exactly she would be apologizing for, she wasn't even sure. She felt they'd had a bad start, but she didn't know how to say or explain it, and so she stood there, tongue-tied, as he regarded her somberly; the smile that had quirked his mouth had now disappeared completely.

"Excuse me, then," he said, his tone as cool as ever, and Rosie wondered if she'd been imagining that moment of something almost approaching friendliness. It appeared she had, because Leon Rosenblat moved past her without another word, heading down the hallway at his steady, yet slightly lopsided gait, until he'd rounded the corner and Rosie was alone.

Giving a little shake of her head, she hurried on, toward the dining hall where she had arranged to meet Jean.

Outside, the gray skies of morning had cleared to a pale blue, and the sun felt warm, although the children wore coats, for when the wind came, it was still brisk.

"They're doing so well, aren't they?" Jean murmured as they walked down the lane that led around the lake; the six children walking slightly ahead of them in an uneven crocodile, all of them holding hands, as they always did, silently taking the world in together. Golda had left yesterday for her aunt; she'd hugged the children in turn, and then walked away quickly without looking back.

The children had stared after her, unspeaking as ever, and then Jean had jollied them along to the nursery, where Alice had set up some toys and games. Not one of them asked for the woman who had been with them since Theresienstadt; perhaps they were simply too used to people suddenly disappearing.

In any case, Rosie supposed it was a mercy that they had not caused a fuss about it, even though their lack of reaction made her feel sad. She wanted to see these children cry as well as laugh, frown as well as smile. Little children, she thought, shouldn't have to feel that way. They should feel free and safe enough to cry, to scream, to laugh, to play.

"They are coming along well," Rosie said as they walked

along, for even though she longed for more for these children, she knew Jean was right and they had come along in their development. Their eager hands reaching for their cocoa, the smiles as they painted or drew, were all encouragements.

Even though it was mid-September, many of the leaves had fallen from the trees, thanks to the relentless wind, and the nearly-bare branches rattled in the breeze.

"I shall be sorry to say goodbye to them, when the time comes," Jean remarked. Inadvertently, her glance lingered on the little, dark-haired boy at the end, Isaak, who was only five years old; Rosie knew the older woman had become attached to him in particular. He'd gone to Theresienstadt as a baby, his mother dying when he was still an infant. Golda had said he'd been cared for by the other women of the camp in one of the *Kinderheims*, and when he'd grown into a toddler, they'd taught him to be useful— collecting coal, fetching water, making sure not to get underfoot. Somehow, he had survived. He had soft, round cheeks and wonderfully dark, liquid eyes, now the picture of blooming health. It seemed both impossible and appalling to imagine what he must have endured in his short life.

"What will happen to these children?" she asked Jean. "When their time at Calgarth ends?" She knew there was funding for the children to stay at the estate through Christmas; after that, they would be placed elsewhere. The smallest children, those under four, were going to be taken to Bulldogs Bank, a cottage in West Hoathly, Sussex, next month, to be cared for by German emigré sisters Gertraud and Sophie Dann. But what about the others?

"Alice has said that if their families aren't found, they will be adopted," Jean replied. "Although adoption of foreign-born children isn't technically allowed, but I imagine the Central British Fund will find a way around it. The older ones, the teenagers, will go into homes or hostels. Many of them wish to work or train, most likely in a city."

"Yes..." It seemed an awfully lonely existence, Rosie thought, to end up in the equivalent of a boarding house when you were only fourteen or fifteen years of age. And what about the children who were neither little, like these, nor old enough to live alone? Children like Frieda? "Do you think it will be easy for them to be adopted? For families to be found to take them in, I mean?" she asked Jean.

"I really couldn't say," Jean replied with a shrug. "The Central British Fund have a network of Jewish families who have settled here since before the war. I'm sure many of them would be willing to take in a child who has no one or nothing, especially such wee, dear ones as these." She let out a little sigh and shook her head, and Rosie reached out to touch her arm.

"What about you, Jean? Couldn't you adopt one of them?" She glanced at Isaak, who was tripping along happily in front of them. "You'd provide a good home for one of these children."

"Oh, I shouldn't think so," Jean replied quickly, although her face was full of longing. "A widowed woman on her own? And besides, I'm not Jewish. The Central British Fund feels strongly about that, and I understand it, of course, considering all that has happened. I couldn't teach one of these little ones about their heritage, their history, and that will be very important to them."

"But you'd *love* them," Rosie said quietly, and for a second she found herself thinking of Frieda. "I know you would."

"Oh, Rosie." Jean let out a strangled sound, pressing her hand to her lips. "Don't give me such dreams! I know it's not possible. Besides, I live in a tiny cottage up in Greenock with my mother. I wouldn't be able to offer him much at all." She bit her lip, abashed. "Or any child, I mean."

"It would be more than they had before," Rosie pointed out, before deciding to subside. As much as she or Jean might wish it otherwise, she suspected the other woman was right and she would never be approved for adoption—a middle-aged woman, with a mother to care for, and no real knowledge of Judaism. Still, it seemed hard, when Jean had so much love to give.

As if he sensed their conversation, Isaak turned around, giving them both a sudden, surprising gap-toothed grin before running straight into Jean's arms. She laughed and swung him up before settling him on her hip, her face filled with pure joy.

"Well, well, my wee laddie! Aren't you a bundle?"

Rosie smiled to see them together, looking so happy, before walking ahead to take the hand of Elsa, the little girl that Isaak had been holding. As the autumn leaves crunched underfoot, she was reminded of how fleeting their time at Calgarth really was. In just a few months, they would all have to let these children go, to forge their own futures.

And, Rosie acknowledged, she would have to find her own.

CHAPTER SEVEN

At the end of September, Rosie and several of the other volunteers took a few dozen of the children to the cinema in Bowness-on-Windermere to see a film. It was a merry and boisterous outing, with them all taking the bus, the children dressed neatly, hair brushed, shoes polished, clearly wanting to make a good impression, just as Dr. Friedmann had said, and very excited to embark on this new adventure. Many of them had never been to the cinema before, or ever seen a moving picture. The bus was full of their excited chatter as it trundled down the lane toward Troutbeck and Bowness beyond.

Over the last few weeks, Rosie had tried to befriend Frieda a little more, with some limited success. While the girl wasn't as overtly hostile as she'd once been, and would even thankfully tolerate Rosie sitting next to her during mealtimes or in the art room, she didn't offer too much conversation and she still seemed to prefer being on her own; all the other girls had long ago learned not to bother with her, which saddened Rosie to see. At mealtimes and out in the yard, Frieda still stood alone, shoulders hunched, arms folded, expression determinedly obdurate. It was heartbreaking.

A week earlier, Dr. Friedmann had stopped Rosie as she'd been walking to the art room to tell her what he'd learned of Frieda's family.

"I have written to the university in Katowice," he'd said, "and received an initial response. It turns out that your Frieda is not like the other children here," he'd explained with a small, sorrowful smile. "She is what the Nazis called a *Mischlinge*—half-Jewish. Her father was a Gentile, that is, not Jewish, and her mother a Jew."

"Her father was a... Gentile?" Rosie had exclaimed in surprise. "But Frieda said he had died before the war. She made it sound as if he'd—well, as if he'd been killed by the Nazis."

"Yes, it is so." Dr. Friedmann had nodded soberly. "He first worked in Dresden, where he was pressured by the university to divorce his wife after the race laws were passed in 1936, because she was Jewish. It often happened that way, and many of those married to Jews did divorce, quietly, deciding it was safer for both of them to do so. Frieda's father, however, refused, and not only that, he issued a statement against such a policy at the university." He'd shaken his head in regret. "A truly courageous act, but perhaps a foolhardy one. In any case, it caused him to be sent to a camp—not a concentration camp like during the war, not as bad as that, but one for political prisoners. Still, not a good place." He'd paused then, his face drawn in somber lines, and Rosie had recalled that Dr. Friedmann himself had been in such a camp before the war; half his face was paralyzed as a result. Not a nice place, indeed. "When he was released, he took a position in Katowice," the doctor had resumed. "I suppose he thought he would be safe there, out of Germany, but his health had been compromised. Weakened, you understand, with a bad chest. He died two years later, I'm afraid."

"That's so sad," Rosie had said quietly. How old would have Frieda been then? she wondered. Five, six? Far, far too young to lose her father.

"Indeed. I imagine it must have been very hard for Frieda—both to lose her father, and then to live in Katowice as the daughter of a Jew, without the protection of her Gentile parent. Frieda, her mother, and little sister were all sent to a camp sometime during the war—maybe 1942, 1943. Auschwitz, it was."

"Auschwitz..." Rosie's stomach had cramped at the mere mention of the place. Auschwitz was the concentration camp that everyone had heard of, that had been in all the papers, with the stark photographs—the dreaded gate, the corpses stacked like firewood, the skeletal survivors, every rib able to be counted. Others had been in the papers, too, of course, but that was the one whose name kept coming up, a place of horror and death. Frieda had been *there*, and as a child... with her sister. What had happened to her sister? She had been adamant her mother had died, but perhaps not so certain about her sister. Had they been separated?

Dr. Friedmann had nodded soberly, understanding Rosie's distress at the mention of the notorious camp. "When it was liberated in January 1945, Frieda was put into a DP camp by herself. I think her mother and sister are almost certainly dead, although we cannot know for sure. Her father had a sister in Dresden, a Gentile, of course, but I do not know any more than that. Perhaps she is alive, perhaps not. The Red Cross will try to contact her, if they can." He'd laid a hand on Rosie's arm, as if to console her, but she, Rosie had thought sorrowfully, was not the one who needed consoling. "She is almost certainly all alone in the world, unless this aunt can be found."

"But Frieda didn't even write the name of the aunt down," Rosie had whispered. *Why?*

Dr. Friedmann had shrugged, spreading his hands. "Perhaps she did not know her very well."

"Even so..."

"I cannot give an answer," the doctor had told her. "But in

any case, the Red Cross will do its best to find the aunt—if she can be found. That is all we can hope for."

"And if she isn't found?"

"Then another suitable situation will be." Dr. Friedmann had given her a look of both sympathy and warning. "We have these children in our care for only a short time, Miss Lyman. We can do our best to give them joy, and healing, and kindness, but that is all. At the end of their time here, they will go on—to lead full and interesting lives, I hope, just as you and I will."

"Yes," Rosie had murmured, knowing she had no choice but to agree. She'd felt a little chastised, although she wasn't sure why. Dr. Friedmann had encouraged her interest in Frieda; was he now cautioning her not to care too much out of kindness, or more of a warning? In any case, Frieda herself would see to that, Rosie had thought wryly, with her determined unfriendliness!

And yet she did care. *Why* hadn't Frieda written a single name down? The question bothered Rosie, like a splinter in her finger, a stone in her shoe. Every other child at Calgarth had written down the names of anyone—anyone at all—whom they remembered, who might remember them. Aunts, uncles, cousins, second cousins, distant relations, even old, half-forgotten teachers, or neighbors. They'd made desperate lists, longing to find just one person who knew and remembered them, who could say *yes, I know you. I care what happens to you.* And yet Frieda, and Frieda alone, had refused to write a single name.

Why?

It was a question that felt pressing, urgent, and yet Rosie knew it wasn't necessarily hers to answer. Frieda might know why she'd refused to write any names down, but that didn't mean Rosie did, or should, or should even guess. She didn't want to pry into the girl's affairs, and yet she was desperate to help, if only she knew how.

At the end of their conversation, Dr. Friedmann had

assured Rosie he would continue with his investigations, and
see if he could discover whether Frieda's mother or sister, at
least, were alive, along with the unknown aunt.

"Thank you, Doctor," Rosie had said, and he had smiled
wryly.

"Have you made any progress with Frieda herself?"

"Not really," Rosie had admitted, "but I'll keep trying."

"Good. That is all you can do, and you must continue to do
it for as long as Frieda remains here," the doctor had said, and
Rosie had been heartened by his further encouragement. If only
she could break through Frieda's reticence, her surly silence...

It had yet to happen, but surely that didn't mean it couldn't?

Frieda was one of the children going to the cinema, much to
Rosie's surprise. The girl had not taken part in any social
outings before, preferring to stay on the estate, but for some
unknown reason, she'd agreed to attend the cinema, perhaps
due to someone or other's cajoling, or maybe simply out of bore-
dom, or perhaps because she liked moving pictures. In any case,
Rosie was glad, especially as it gave her the excuse to sit next to
her on the bus ride into town.

The bus was full of noisy chatter, stuffy enough that despite
the decidedly brisk weather, they had all taken off their coats
and put them under their seats.

"Have you been to the cinema before?" Rosie asked as the
bus drove through Troutbeck, and Frieda gave her a rather with-
ering look.

"Yes, back home, before the war, when I was small." She
pressed her lips together and looked away, clearly not wanting
to say anything more.

"I remember one of the first times I went to the pictures,"
Rosie said, refusing to be discouraged by Frieda's responses, or
lack thereof. "When I was seven, in California, back in the

United States. I'm sure I must have gone before, but I can't remember. But I remember that day. It was in a special theater, all decorated like it was in China."

Frieda did not bother to reply, and Rosie fell silent, lost for a moment in the memory of the happy months she'd spent in California as a child with her brother Jamie, her mother, and her Aunt Gracie, all for her brother's health. She remembered the theater shaped like a pagoda, the footprints of famous people preserved in the concrete sidewalk outside, the excitement she and Jamie had felt about it all. They'd had banana splits at some fancy hotel afterwards, Rosie recalled.

It felt as if it had all happened to someone else a million years ago, like a fuzzy image on a screen or a photograph blurred by time, and yet it still gave her a pang of homesickness, a lurch of longing for the life she'd once known, the people she still loved.

She hadn't seen her parents in nearly two years, and even before then, it had only been for a day or two at a time, months apart. She hadn't seen them properly since February 1942, she realised, when she'd started her basic training, and she'd only seen her brother a handful of times when they'd both been stationed in England. When would she next see them all?

She glanced back at Frieda, who would never see her family again, unless this aunt or some other distant relation could be found. What would happen to her if they couldn't? Dr. Friedmann had not been particularly forthcoming on the matter. Would Frieda be adopted the way the little ones were likely to be, or would she be considered too old for that? She was too young, surely, to go to a hostel like the older teens, to learn a trade, and yet something would have to be done.

Frieda had turned toward the window. Her arms were folded, her expression closed. Rosie struggled to think of something to say, wishing this were easier. Then Frieda shifted in her seat, and Rosie saw a flash of livid red on the inside of her elbow.

"Frieda, you've hurt yourself!" she exclaimed, and the girl turned to shoot her a dark look.

"I haven't."

"Your elbow—" Rosie persisted, genuinely concerned, and Frieda scowled.

"I haven't," she repeated, fiercely this time, and turned back to the window, hunching her shoulders.

Rosie fell silent. She'd seen the patch of reddened skin again as Frieda had moved, and it looked sore and swollen, maybe even infected. It didn't look like an old wound, like one of the many scars various children had from their time in the camps, but something new and painful. What was it, and why was Frieda pretending it wasn't there?

Rosie knew she wouldn't press the point, and yet she wondered. Had one of the girls hurt her somehow? Was she being teased or bullied and *that* was why she kept to herself? Rosie had seen fights occasionally break out among the boys when things got heated on the football pitch or elsewhere; it was usually one of the Polish volunteers who waded in and gently but firmly pushed them apart. She'd seen Leon Rosenblat do it, his face drawn in serious lines as he spoke to each boy in turn, his arm around their shoulders, until they nodded, smiled and then made up.

But were such things happening among the girls, as well? She hadn't seen any evidence of it, but that didn't necessarily mean anything. Or, Rosie wondered sadly, was it really just that Frieda didn't want to talk to her about it, or anything? No matter what encouragement Dr. Friedmann had given her, maybe she really should stop trying with this girl.

She didn't try to engage Frieda in any conversation for the rest of the bus trip, which seemed to suit her. She spent the remainder of the journey staring determinedly out the window and acting as if Rosie didn't exist at all. Rosie looked out the other window, doing her best to enjoy the rolling fells, now gray-green under the misting drizzle as the other children continued to chat and laugh; a few boys got in a tussle in the backseat, and Leon Rosenblat rose to sort them out with a quick word.

His gaze met Rosie's as he returned to his seat, with that now familiar jolt, but before she could think to venture a smile, he looked away again, quickly. She wondered whether he would ever be friendly with her. For a moment, outside Dr. Friedmann's office, she'd hoped so, but now he seemed as cool as ever. Perhaps she should try to make an effort with him, just as she was with Frieda, even if she doubted the success of such an endeavor.

Getting all the children off the bus in front of the Royalty Theatre in Bowness was a noisy and confusing affair, as many of the children hadn't been to a cinema before and were very excited simply to enter such a grand venue, never mind actually see a film. Then there was the matter of tickets and, of course, the sweets and bags of popcorn that they were all eager to try; Rosie had learned that popcorn had only been recently introduced to British theaters by the Americans during the war. Judging by their shouts of enthusiasm, the children loved it, although they seemed to enjoy throwing the kernels at each other as much as eating them. Fortunately, the other members of the audience didn't seem to mind; one woman stopped Rosie to tell her it was heartening to see the children enjoying themselves after what had happened to them during the war. Rosie had encountered this kindly attitude before among the locals, and was grateful for it, especially when the popcorn was flying through the air, with one piece hitting a man right in the middle of his forehead.

By the time Rosie found her seat at the end of the row, she felt a little frazzled by all the commotion, and grateful for an hour of two of peaceful quiet as the film started. Her gaze moved over the rows of children, looking instinctively, as always, for Frieda, and making sure she was all right, even if she was seated by herself.

As Rosie counted heads and listed names, however, she realized she could not find Frieda among their number. She frowned, leaning forward in her seat, squinting into the darkness. The newsreel had started with a segment on the recent victories in Japan as well as the rebuilding of Germany, and the children fell silent. Some of them looked stricken to see the pictures of Germany reduced to rubble, footage of a line of German women handing each other pails of broken-up concrete, smiling with a desperate fervor for the camera.

Rosie was distracted for a moment by the sight; she'd seen plenty of bombed-out buildings in London, and from the newsreel, it seemed Germany had fared even worse. All this ruin and suffering, she thought, and for what? She thought of her mother's friend Ruby telling her how pointless the first war had felt, yet this too felt pointless, and worse, evil. Could there be a worse combination? It gave her a swamping sense of futility, that so much horror had happened, and even in her own small way, with one little girl, she could neither combat nor ameliorate it.

Fortunately, the film started then, with a burst of music that made everyone cheer, and a few more kernels of popcorn sailed through the air as the children straightened in their seats, gazing intently at the screen. Rosie resumed looking for Frieda; the light from the film sent moving shadows along the children's rapt faces, but she couldn't see the girl's. Where was she? She'd come into the theater, Rosie was sure of it, although she'd refused any popcorn or sweets, which had been offered for free by the kindly proprietor.

As quietly and unobtrusively as she could, Rosie rose and began hunting among the seats, looking for Frieda.

Leon Rosenblat, sitting on the end of an aisle, caught her eye and frowned in inquiry.

"Sorry," Rosie mouthed, and kept looking. She was conscious of Leon's curious and possibly annoyed gaze on her as she moved through the aisles, blocking the children's view, whispering sorry again and again. She felt her cheeks flush as she realized she was making a scene, but she kept looking anyway, determined to find Frieda... except, after a few tense minutes, it became clear she wasn't in the theater at all.

Whispering another apology, Rosie hurried out into the foyer, which was empty, save for a girl cleaning up the popcorn that had spilled when the children had all been herded into the theater.

"Have you seen a girl?" Rosie asked her. "She came with our group, she's about twelve, rather slight, with dark hair kept back in a plait."

Wordlessly, bent over her broom, the girl shook her head.

Rosie checked the ladies' and the coatroom, just in case. They were both empty. As she stood in the foyer, she felt a wave of helplessness wash over her, and worse, of fear.

It was obvious Frieda was gone.

CHAPTER EIGHT

What on earth should she do? Rosie stood in the foyer in a welter of indecision. She knew what Dr. Friedmann would say; give Frieda the freedom she craved. He was insistent that the children be subject to as few rules as possible, and if she would rather wander around Bowness than see a film, well, what of it? It was a small town, a safe place, and Frieda would come back when she chose.

Rosie couldn't agree with that attitude, however, at least not when it came to Frieda. A big, strapping lad of fifteen or sixteen, yes, he would most likely be all right walking around here by himself, but Frieda was young, small and slight and most decidedly vulnerable. Rosie hated to think of her wandering about on her own, who knew where or why, but she was also afraid she'd pushed in enough. Maybe it would be better for Frieda to let her be.

"Is something wrong?"

Rosie turned to see Leon Rosenblat coming through the theater doors, his face drawn, as ever, into a frown, although she thought the look in his eyes was one of concern rather than condemnation.

"I don't know," she admitted. "Frieda, the young girl I was sitting next to on the bus, isn't in the theater."

Leon's frown deepened. "Where is she, then?"

"I don't know. I think she must have left here completely." Rosie shrugged helplessly. "I don't know where she's gone."

Leon continued to frown as he glanced around the foyer, almost as if he were expecting Frieda to pop up from behind the popcorn machine.

The girl who had been sweeping up the spilled kernels dumped them in the bin before retreating to the ticket booth.

"Do you think I should go and look for her?" Rosie asked.

Leon turned to face her. Rosie felt slightly jolted by the intensity of his expression, the golden glints in his eyes that she remembered from before blazing all the more brightly. She felt a ripple of feeling go through her, and she wasn't quite sure what it was.

"Was she distressed about something?" he asked. "Angry, perhaps?"

"No more than she usually is, I should think." Leon pursed his lips and Rosie continued in a hurry, "And just in case you're thinking I'm being presumptuous, saying she is often angry or something like that, the truth is, she *is*. Which is why I'm worried about her."

Leon's thoughtful frown turned to an expression of confusion. "Why would I—"

"Oh, never mind," Rosie interjected hurriedly. She feared she might have given a bit too much away with her last remark. "Do you think we should look for her?" Belatedly, she realized the assumption she'd made, in saying *we*, and yet she also knew she didn't want to handle this by herself. "I can, I mean," she amended quickly, even though she'd really rather not have. "I just didn't want to... interfere. You know how Dr. Friedmann wants them to have as much freedom as possible."

"Yes, that is true." Leon shook his head slowly, still frowning. "I think perhaps you are best placed to decide if Frieda should be found or not. You seem to know the girl better than anyone. I'm afraid I cannot even place her in my mind."

"That's because she always keeps to herself." To her embarrassment, Rosie realized she was, quite suddenly, near tears. "She doesn't chat or laugh with anyone at Calgarth. But the truth is, I don't know her at all. I've tried, but I haven't been very successful. I wish I had been."

Leon looked at her seriously, his eyes dark and so very intent. There was a softness to his expression that made Rosie feel as if he cared, at least about where Frieda was. "Do you think she should be left alone," he asked, "or would it better if she were found?"

Rosie hesitated and then said as firmly as she could manage, "I think she should be found."

"Then we will look for her," Leon replied simply, "and we will find her."

The quiet certainty of his statement both heartened and humbled her. It was, she realized, exactly what she'd hoped to hear.

"What about the other children?" she asked.

Leon smiled faintly. "There is at least another hour left of the film, and they are all completely—what is the word?"

He paused, and Rosie suggested, "Spellbound?"

"Something like that, I think, yes." He let out a small, rusty-sounding chuckle, and she realized it was the first time she'd heard him laugh. It sounded as if he did not laugh very often, like a creaky door or a rusted spring that received little use. "Besides, there are the other volunteers to watch over them." He nodded toward the doors to the street. "Should we go?"

Gratified by his willingness, Rosie headed outside, followed by Leon. They stood in the street under a dark, drizzling sky. The air smelled of rain and coal smoke, and Lake Road was empty of pedestrians. Rosie had no idea where Frieda could have gone; Bowness-on-Windermere was not a particularly large town, but it was certainly big enough for a child to get lost in, should she so desire... or even if she didn't.

Leon looked up and down the road, scratching his head. "I suppose," he said, "she could be anywhere."

"Yes." Rosie tried not to sound as despondent as she felt. "Most likely, she just wanted to be alone."

"So where would you go, if you wanted to be alone?" Leon asked, turning to look at her. The seriousness of his expression gave the question a feeling of intimacy that Rosie knew it did not possess.

"I suppose I would go to the lake," she answered slowly. "And I think that's where Frieda would go, too."

He squinted into the distance. "How close are we to the lake here?"

Rosie shrugged. "Half a mile, perhaps? We drove past it, on the way."

"Perhaps you should go to the lake," Leon decided, "and I will look through the town, just in case she is there."

It seemed a wise idea, although Rosie had been hoping to stay together, even if she wasn't sure why. This was the first time Leon Rosenblat had been anything even close to friendly to her, and she was very grateful for his kindness.

"Very well," she said. "Shall we meet back at the Royalty before the film is finished—in an hour?"

"Yes, in an hour."

As Rosie set off down Lake Road, the rain misting her face and hair, she wondered if she'd find Frieda at all. The lake was a good ten-minute walk away, across the main road. Would Frieda really venture that far? And even if she did find her, what would she say? Every time she tried to reach Frieda, she felt as if she got a little nearer, but still fell lamentably short. Would this time be the one where she finally got close to Frieda? Rosie knew she kept hoping so, but now she wondered if there wouldn't be any big breakthroughs, just a careful inching forward, step by laborious step. Maybe that was all anyone could hope for; maybe it could be enough.

Windermere swept out in a long, slate-colored stretch of water under a sky like a blank canvas, the color of pewter. The wind coming off it was chilly, and Rosie tried not to shiver. It was far more exposed here than the wooded stretch of shoreline by the Calgarth Estate. She couldn't see Frieda anywhere along the lakeside, and she realized she might have been ridiculously hopeful to think she'd find her at the lake the way she had last time. Had she been thinking they would sit by the water again and have a nice, cozy chat?

Annoyed with herself, with her absurd hopefulness, Rosie began to turn away from the water, only to stop at a blur of movement in the corner of her eye.

She turned, squinting out at the water, and with a jolt of pure alarm, actual fear, she realized Frieda wasn't by the lake... she was *in* the lake. Waist deep, walking purposefully deeper, step by agonizing step, her chin lifted at that determined angle as she stared straight ahead.

"Frieda!" Rosie started running, shedding her coat and shoes as she went, her heart thudding with anxiety, while Frieda waded in deeper, her arms wrapped around her body, as if she were steeling herself. "Frieda," Rosie called again, and this time the girl turned back to give her a surprised, frightened look. The water had to be freezing—and deep. Why on earth was Frieda wading in, fully clothed, as if she was *going* somewhere?

Rosie was all too afraid she knew why.

Thanks to her years on Amherst Island, she was a strong swimmer, and she plunged into the water without a thought, shocked by its coldness but determined to reach Frieda, who had waded in deeper now, nearly all the way up to her neck. Could she even swim? Although many of the boys had swum and played in the water back at Calgarth, the girls and younger children had been less sure of the deep and cold waters of the lake; some had been scared even to go in up to their ankles. Rosie didn't think she'd ever seen Frieda in the water before, and certainly not like this, fully dressed, wading out, ever deeper...

"Frieda, stop!" she called as she kept going, the water soaking her right through, making her shiver. "Stop, *please*. Why are you doing this? You'll catch your death of cold—"

"Leave me alone!" Frieda cried, her voice high and thin, the voice of a frightened child. She turned back to look at Rosie, her face pale, lips bloodless. She had to be utterly freezing.

"Frieda, what are you doing?" Rosie demanded desperately. "Let me help you!" She waded in a bit farther, knowing that she didn't have the strength to drag Frieda back to shore by herself, not unless she wanted to go with her. "Can you swim?" she asked and, looking miserable, Frieda shook her head.

"I... I didn't mean to go in so far," she confessed in a small voice. "I just wanted to—" She never finished that sentence for she lost her footing and with a sudden scream she began flailing in the water, arms windmilling helplessly. "Rosie, *help!*" she cried, and as she plunged through the water, taking several long, sure strokes, Rosie realized it was the first time Frieda had used her name.

She reached her in just a few seconds, one hand hauling at the back of her jumper, the other wrapped around her ribs as she kicked desperately back to shore, until she could find her footing. It was only a dozen feet or so, but in the cold water, with the weight of the girl in her arms, it felt like forever. With immense effort, Rosie managed to drag Frieda onto the rocky shore, where they both collapsed, choking and sputtering as the rain continued to drizzle down.

For a few minutes, neither of them could speak, and then Frieda managed to roll onto her hands and knees, still gasping, before, to Rosie's amazement, she struggled up to her feet and starting walking down the shore, back to the road.

"Frieda, wait!" Rosie called, an exasperated, exhausted plea. The girl was amazingly, immensely stubborn. "Don't just run off, please! You're soaking wet, for a start."

Frieda turned back to her, arms folded, shivering visibly. "So?" she demanded, and her voice trembled.

"You can wear my coat, at least. It's still dry." Rosie heaved herself up from the shore. Her heart was thundering in her chest, and her body felt strangely leaden, every movement laborious, her head fuzzy from fatigue. "You ought to take your jumper off, as well," she told Frieda. "Did you leave your coat at the theater?"

Wordlessly, Frieda nodded. She was shivering uncontrollably now, her arms folded and her head tucked low, her hair in dark, wet strands like seaweed, sticking to her cheeks.

"Here." Rosie helped Frieda off with the soaking jumper, and then put her coat around her shoulders, wrapping it around her shivering form as best as she could. "We should head back to the theater. The film will be over soon. People will be wondering where you are."

Frieda looked as if she wanted to resist even that, and then she burst out suddenly, "Why did you come to look for me?"

"Because I was worried," Rosie replied honestly, "and... I care about you."

"Care...!" Frieda made a scoffing sound as she looked away.

"I *do*," Rosie repeated. The effort of swimming in the freezing water, or perhaps the emotion of seeing and saving Frieda from it, compelled her to a deeper and more reckless honesty than ever before. "I don't know why I do, but I do. Perhaps because you remind me of myself, a little bit."

Frieda looked surprised, and a bit skeptical. "Of *you*?"

"Yes, of me, but... oh, I'll have to explain it to you another time," Rosie said with a shake of her head. Frieda's lips were turning blue, and she was shaking like a veritable leaf, the coat sliding off her trembling shoulders. "We'll both catch the flu if we stay out here in our soaking clothes for much longer. Let's head back and try to dry off a bit." Although Rosie wasn't sure how they would get dry; neither of them had any spare clothes with them.

They started back to the town in silence, but it wasn't, Rosie thought, or at least hoped, a hostile one. Perhaps this had been the breakthrough she'd been longing for, and yet... why had Frieda waded into the lake like that? It was an alarming question to consider, and one whose answer Rosie feared she knew.

As they came down Lake Road, a kindly looking woman wielding a broom and wearing a pinafore poked her head out of a teashop. "Goodness, what happened to the pair of you? Did you fall in?"

Rosie glanced at Frieda, who shot her an uncertain, fearful look. "Yes, we fell in," she replied. "You wouldn't happen to have a blanket we could borrow?"

"Come in, come in." The woman waved them toward the empty shop. "I can't have you walking down the street like that, you'll catch your deaths!" She glanced kindly at Frieda. "Are you one of the Windermere children?"

Frieda stiffened, saying nothing, and Rosie replied, "We're from the Calgarth Estate, yes."

"Ah, I thought so," the woman said. "I'm Mary Barwise and I run this place. Come in and set yourself down. I'm sure you could do with a cuppa."

Rosie hesitated, for the film would be ending soon, but then she decided this was exactly what they both needed. They had another quarter of an hour or so before the children would be getting back on the bus, and they could both certainly use a bit of warming up.

As Mary Barwise bustled about, getting their tea, Frieda

shot Rosie another uncertain look. "Why did you go into the water after me?"

Rosie gave her a bemused glance. "Why do you think I did, Frieda? The same reason why I went to look for you. Because I wanted to help you."

Frieda shook her head. "You should have left me," she whispered.

Rosie rested her hand on Frieda's cold one. "Please don't say that," she said quietly. "Whatever is troubling you, Frieda, whatever sorrows you've faced..." She swallowed hard. "You don't need to do something like that."

Frieda pulled her hand from Rosie's as she huddled into her coat. "I was just seeing how deep the lake was," she said in a low voice, looking away.

Mary Barwise came back, not only with tea but a plate of warm buttered scones, and spare sets of clothing for both Rosie and Frieda.

"The skirt and blouse might be a bit big for the girl," she told Rosie, "but they're clean and serviceable."

"I can't take your clothes—" Rosie protested, for she knew how precious such things were in these days of rationing and clothing coupons.

"You can return them when you're back in Bowness," Mary replied firmly. "They belonged to my daughter, and she's down in London now, so I won't be needing them anytime soon. You can change back in the kitchen, it's private."

A few minutes later, Rosie and Frieda had both changed into dry clothes, the skirt and blouse hanging off Frieda, and Mary had kindly hung up their wet things by the stove. They drank their tea and ate their scones gratefully; Rosie was both touched and humbled by a stranger's kindness.

"We should get back to the others," she told Mary when they'd finished. "I can't tell you how thankful I am for your generosity. I think we might have both come down with something dreadful if we hadn't changed out of our wet things."

"It's the least anybody can do," Mary replied, "especially, considering..." Her face full of sympathy, she nodded toward Frieda, who quickly looked away. "Here are your wet things." Still damp, the clothes were wrapped in newspaper. "God bless you both."

By the time they returned to the Royalty Theatre, the other children were milling around outside, waiting for the bus. Leon caught sight of them almost immediately, and started forward, a smile splitting his face. He looked, Rosie thought, so much kinder when he smiled, and so much more approachable. Her heart gave a strange little flutter.

"Ah, she is found!" His smile dropped away as he took in their wet hair and clothes. "What on earth happened? Did you... did you fall into the lake, Frieda?"

Frieda glanced at Rosie, and in that second's silence, Rosie saw a flash of understanding cross Leon's face and he frowned, a tension bracketing his mouth and scoring a deep line between his eyes as he gazed unhappily at Frieda.

"Yes, she fell into the lake," Rosie replied, having no idea if it was the right thing to say or not. It was one thing to say it to another stranger; another to someone like Leon. She didn't like to lie, and she wasn't at all sure she should have.

"Rosie rescued me," Frieda added, and Rosie turned to her in surprise, her heart flooding with gratitude at the simple, seemingly heartfelt statement.

Leon glanced between them, looking even more tense and unhappy, the affability he'd had moments ago completely vanished. "Thank goodness for that," he finally replied quietly.

CHAPTER NINE

Rosie and Frieda didn't speak as they climbed onto the bus with the other children, who were excitedly jabbering about the film they'd just seen. Now that it was all over, Rosie realized how shaken she felt by the entire episode, trembling inwardly as she remembered seeing Frieda in the lake, yet also feeling strangely leaden inside. Despite the dry clothes, Frieda was still shivering beside her.

"I hope you don't catch a chill," Rosie remarked in concern, and Frieda did not reply for a moment.

"I wasn't... I wasn't going to do anything bad," she finally said, her voice so low Rosie strained to hear it. "That's not why I went in the lake."

Rosie rested her hand on the girl's arm. "Why did you go into the lake, Frieda?" she asked gently.

She shrugged, looking away. "I... I don't know. I just wanted not to *feel*, for a little while. Not to feel anything. The water was so cold... it made me feel—I don't know the word." She screwed up her forehead in thought. "Empty, maybe. I liked it." She turned back to look at Rosie, her expression both anxious and fierce, dark eyebrows drawn together as she nibbled her lip. "Does that sound strange?"

"No," Rosie replied quietly. "It doesn't sound strange at all."

"Really?" Frieda looked at her almost hungrily, as if she longed to believe what Rosie had said, as if it made a difference... and maybe, amazingly, it did.

Rosie nodded, smiling, although she felt terribly sad, both for Frieda and for herself. "No," she told her, "it really doesn't."

"You won't... tell anyone about what happened, will you?" Frieda asked, and Rosie hesitated. Frieda plucked at her sleeve. "*Bitte*," she said, desperation edging her voice in a way Rosie had never heard before, not even when she'd been in the lake, asking her to help her. "Please."

"Why don't you want anyone to know, Frieda?" Rosie asked, putting her hand over hers once more.

"Because they might think I... I need help. Some of the children have been sent away—"

"That was for tuberculosis," Rosie replied gently. "A contagious disease that must be treated in a sanitorium."

"Still." Frieda's eyes were full of worry as she nibbled her lip again, leaving a reddened mark on the tender skin. "I do not want to be sent away."

Would she be sent away if Dr. Friedmann believed she'd tried to harm herself? Rosie didn't know the answer to that question, but she hoped the doctor would be understanding.

"Do you like it here so much, then?" she asked with what she hoped was an encouraging smile.

"It is better than anywhere I have been before," Frieda replied honestly, and Rosie nodded slowly.

"Why don't you try to get to know the other girls?" she asked.

Frieda's expression closed up, and she looked away, toward the window, her lower lip jutting out stubbornly.

Rosie felt as if any advantage she'd had, any hope of confidences being shared, was slipping away, and yet she felt she had to persist. "Wouldn't you be happier here, Frieda, if you could make some friends? I'm sure they would want to get to know you, if you let them."

Frieda gave a little, determined shake of her head, her gaze still averted.

Reluctantly, Rosie decided to leave it, at least for now. They were almost back at the estate, anyway. "I have a responsibility to Dr. Friedmann, to tell him anything of concern," she said instead, keeping her voice gentle but firm. "It would be difficult for me to keep this from him, but I don't think he would ever—"

She stopped abruptly as Frieda whirled back toward her, all the old hostility visible in her expression, her eyes flashing, her face screwed up in anger. Rosie's heart sank. "So you *will* tell," she practically spat, "and make me go away! And I thought you said you cared about me!"

"Frieda, I do care about you," Rosie protested in a low voice. "But I also have a responsibility. Please understand—" Rosie fell silent again as Frieda twisted away from her.

The bus had pulled up to the main hall of Calgarth Estate, and before anyone else had moved, Frieda was scrambling up, flinging Rosie's coat back at her before she ran down the aisle and pushed her way out of the bus.

With a sigh, Rosie slumped against the seat, her damp coat clutched to her. She had no idea what the right thing to do was. She did have a responsibility to tell the doctor, she *knew* that, but the last thing she wanted to do was betray Frieda's trust.

"Is everything all right?"

Rosie glanced up to see Leon standing by her seat, a look of kindly concern on his face, making his eyes droop in a way Rosie rather liked. It made him look approachable, and in that moment she was very glad for it.

"I... I don't know," she admitted. "I suppose I need to speak with Frieda a bit more." Somehow, she must find a way forward that she and Frieda could both accept.

Leon nodded and moved on with some of the boys, and with another sigh, Rosie heaved herself up from her seat. Her head was aching now, and her body still felt leaden and heavy. She longed for a hot bath, but supposed she would have to make do with a cup of tea instead.

Even that was denied her, however, as she came off the bus and into the hall; Jean was in something of a tizzy because Isaak had been sick after eating too many plums. He was in bed with a poorly tummy, but far worse, he was inconsolable.

"I've never seen him cry so," Jean told Rosie as she wrung her hands. "It's as if his heart has broken and I don't know why. It's just a stomach ache, after all."

"I don't suppose any of us will know why," Rosie replied, "considering how little we know about what these children have experienced. The important thing is, I think, that he is comforted." Seeing how anxious Jean was, she added, "Why don't you sit with him, Jean? I'll manage the others."

Jean agreed with grateful alacrity and hurried off; Rosie took the coat that Frieda had flung at her in the bus, and hung it over a chair. Five pairs of eyes regarded her solemnly as they sat on a bench, all lined up, Rosie thought, like peas in a pod. She tried to smile at them all, but she really did feel so tired, and her mind was full of Frieda.

Where had she gone, and did Rosie really need to speak to Dr. Friedmann about the incident at the lake? She still wasn't sure, and the uncertainty of it all was making her feel as if she was in a ferment. Should she rush off to find Frieda—or Dr. Friedmann? In any case, she couldn't do either, right now, because she had five children waiting on her.

"Well, then," she told the children bracingly. "Now that you've had your snack, shall we go to the art room?"

Not one of them replied, but they scrambled off the bench

and one little girl, Iska, slipped her hand into Rosie's. Smiling down at her, Rosie led the way.

The art room was empty in the late afternoon, rain streaking down the long windowpanes, the sky already darkening to the color of wet concrete, the yard empty below, devoid of any life save for a few crows pecking on the ground. In the distance, the lake looked flat and gray and forbidding, reminding Rosie of when Frieda had been floundering in its dark depths. A wave of tiredness crashed over her as she turned from the view to fetch pencils and paper, giving each child a sheet.

One of the children, Daniel, silently pointed to the paint pots on a side table; Rosie had been hoping to avoid the whole palaver of getting the paints out, but with both a sigh and a smile, unable to resist his silent yet plaintive query, she agreed.

"I suppose we can," she told the little boy, and she went to retrieve paints and smocks for the children. Soon, they were happily painting or drawing away, their sheets splattered with streaks and blobs of color, as Rosie sat with them, her cheek resting on her hand. Her head ached and she still felt strangely heavy inside, like her limbs were weighing her down. She kept thinking about Frieda.

Then she felt a tug on her sleeve, and Daniel was pushing a pencil into her hand.

"Draw," he said, and Rosie stared at him in surprise. She didn't think she had ever heard him speak before, and certainly not in English.

"You want to draw something?" she asked, and he shook his head, pointing first to her, and then to the paper. Rosie let out a little laugh as she took his meaning. "You want *me* to draw? Goodness. I wouldn't know how..."

"Draw!" he said again, this time a command.

A few of the other children had stopped their own artwork to watch Rosie, clearly wondering what she would do.

With another little laugh, Rosie sketched a few lines on the paper—a tree, a flower. She glanced at the boy, who, she thought wryly, looked rather unimpressed by her initial attempt.

"I'm afraid I'm not much of an artist," she told him, like an apology, and he simply shook his head, now looking stubborn. "Oh, all right, then," she said at last, laughing a little. If these children could put pencil to paper with such enthusiasm, she supposed she could, as well.

Quickly, she began sketching in the drawing as best as she could—sun, sky, a few birds winging their way over the lake. An island in the distance, no more than a smudge, a hint of trees. It was all in rudimentary stick figures, a child's picture that was barely legible, and yet Rosie found herself feeling it—the sun on her face, the wind in her hair, the lake stretched out in front of her in a dazzling sheet of blue touched with gold.

"Windermere," one of the children crowed triumphantly, and Rosie looked up from her drawing, blinking the children back into focus. Another word she hadn't realized they'd known, and yet...

"Yes, Windermere," she told them after a second's pause, smiling as the emotions the picture had brought from within her faded away. "Do you see it? The lake, and the trees?"

They nodded eagerly, and then Daniel leaned over and began, painstakingly, to draw a few more flowers onto the shore-line, carefully rounding the petals, sketching in the leaves.

Gently, Rosie touched his head, his hair soft beneath her fingers as a few of the other children watched on. "That's lovely... lovely," she murmured. "Such beautiful flowers."

He grinned up at her and she smiled back, cherishing the moment and all it meant. This tiny child, who had suffered so much, was drawing a flower. He could look up at her and smile, and it was so simple, and yet so very profound at the same time. It felt important, even sacred—this scribbled pencil drawing a thing of beauty and wonder. Yes, the pain had to come out, but

Rosie hadn't quite realized until that moment that something beautiful could replace it.

And the funny thing was, she thought as she gathered the papers up a little while later, before taking the children back to the dining hall for their supper, she hadn't been drawing Windermere at all. She'd been drawing Lake Ontario.

By the time the children had been fed, bathed and tucked up in bed, with Isaak thankfully on the mend and seeming more cheerful with Jean happily sitting next to him, it was getting quite late and Rosie still hadn't seen Frieda... or Dr. Friedmann. The dining hall had been its usual noisy commotion at meal-time, and though she'd looked for Frieda amidst the melee, she hadn't been able to see her, and her absence made Rosie feel anxious. What if Frieda had run off again? What if she'd done something worse?

She had to talk to the doctor, Rosie decided. She couldn't leave it another moment, even though her head was aching and she felt so tired, all she wanted to do was curl up in a ball and go to sleep.

Somehow, when the little children were in bed, she made herself head back to the main hall, and the doctor's office upstairs, but when she knocked on the door, there was no answer.

"He's gone to London for a few days, I believe, to speak with the Central British Fund."

Rosie turned, recognizing the voice, knowing who would be standing there. Leon, and he looked concerned, his eyes dark and thoughtful.

"I... see," she said, after a moment. It felt strangely hard to think, as if her brain was fuzzy. And she was still so tired...

"Did you need to see him about something important? I have come to turn the lights off in the hall."

"I... I wanted to talk to him about Frieda."

Leon took a step closer to her as he nodded, the corners of his mouth pulled down into a frown of concern. "Yes, I wondered if you might. She seemed distressed earlier?"

"Have you seen her?" Rosie asked anxiously. "Is she upset still—"

Leon shook his head. "I have not seen her since the trip to the theater. But she seemed distressed when she was getting off the bus. That is what I meant."

"Yes, she was, but..." Rosie shook her head wearily. "I don't know what has happened since then. I need to find her, make sure she's all right." Her stomach was swirling with nerves. She should have found Frieda hours ago, rather than be distracted by the little children and their needs, important as those were.

She started to walk past Leon, but then he caught at her sleeve.

"All the children will be in their rooms now," he told her, his tone surprisingly gentle. "It is late. You can see if Frieda is there, but I am sure she must be. There is always a check before their lights are turned off, to make sure they are in their beds. If she wasn't there, someone would have noticed."

"Still," Rosie persisted, and then found herself swaying slightly on her feet. She threw a hand out to the wall to balance herself.

Leon looked at her in concern. "I will check, if you like. I think perhaps you need to sit down and have a cup of tea. It has been a trying day, perhaps. The cold water..." For a second, it almost seemed as if he was resisting a shudder, but then he straightened with a small, sad smile. "It is very hard to endure."

"Yes, but—"

"Come."

Without waiting for her reply, he steered her down the hall-way, one hand on her elbow, toward the dining hall, and then sat her down at a table, and fetched her a cup of tea, and all the while, Rosie simply let herself be led like a child, grateful that, for a few moments, someone else was in charge.

She sat and sipped her tea, thankful to have it, and hoping her head would clear so she could think properly. She'd check on Frieda herself, she thought, and then make sure to talk to her in the morning...

When Leon returned a few minutes later, he was smiling faintly, his eyes crinkling at the corners. "I have been assured Frieda is asleep in bed," he told her. "So I am glad to say that whatever concerns you have shall keep for another day."

"Thank you," Rosie replied, her tone heartfelt. "Although, the truth is," she confessed, "I still don't know what to do."

"About Frieda?" Leon sat opposite her, his hands folded on the table, his expression alert and thoughtful. When he wasn't scowling, Rosie thought, he really did look kind, even gentle, his dark eyes drooping slightly at the corners, those full lips upturned into a faint, inquisitive smile. She had a sudden urge to confide in him, which seemed odd, since for weeks now she'd been so sure he hadn't liked her—and she hadn't particularly liked him either, although, she realized with a pang of awareness, she'd wanted to like him. And she'd wanted him to like her. The realization was unsettling, and she did her best to push it away.

"Yes, about Frieda," she confirmed, and then as Leon waited, his head cocked slightly to one side, she confessed in a rush, "She didn't fall into the lake. She... she went in on purpose."

Leon did not look shocked by this surprising admission; rather, he seemed sorrowfully unsurprised as he nodded slowly in acceptance. "Not for a swim, then," he clarified quietly, and Rosie shook her head.

"No, not for a swim." They were both silent for a moment, absorbing this terrible fact, and then Rosie continued hesitantly, "She told me she wasn't trying to... to *harm* herself, in that way.

She just wanted to be... empty, she said. Not to feel... anything, I suppose, except a sort of numbness. And I... I understood that."

The look Leon gave her was both surprised and assessing, his eyes narrowing slightly. "Did you?"

"Yes," Rosie replied, lifting her chin a little, bracing herself for his incredulity, or perhaps even his scorn. "I did."

But neither the incredulity nor the scorn came, only a small, sad smile. "Well," Leon replied after a moment, his voice soft and sorrowful, "I suppose I can understand that feeling as well."

The admission shouldn't have surprised her, considering what he must have endured at the camps, far more than she'd ever had to, certainly, but somehow it did.

She looked down at the table. "I'm sure you can," she murmured. "I didn't mean to imply that I... that somehow I was..."

"You didn't," Leon assured her, although Rosie wasn't entirely sure what she'd been trying to say. In any case, she couldn't get into all that now, not with Leon. They had to focus on Frieda.

"The important thing is," she resumed, "that Frieda wasn't... well, you know." It didn't feel right to name it, somehow. "And she asked me not to tell anyone about what happened, because she was afraid she might be sent away."

Leon gazed at her thoughtfully. "And yet you've told me."

Rosie drew back, stung by the seeming accusation, wondering if she'd been imagining his kindness and understanding. "And you think I shouldn't have?" she asked, unable to hide the hurt from her voice.

"No, no, I didn't mean that." The smile Leon gave her was surprisingly rueful. "I feel as if we have been at—what do you call it?" He frowned in thought. "At... opposite ends?"

"At odds, you mean," Rosie said, smiling a little herself, and he smiled and nodded in return.

"Ah, yes. Yes. At odds. Since that first night."

Rosie flushed and ducked her head. She hadn't expected him to state it outright; she wasn't even sure he'd noticed. "Perhaps we have," she agreed. "I know I spoke clumsily then—"

"No, no, it was I who spoke out of turn." Leon gave her an abashed smile. "I was nervous and afraid, and it all seemed very strange, to be here, with the children. I did not know what to expect and it made me... sharp, I think."

"That's understandable," Rosie replied quietly. She could only imagine how unsettling it must have been, to arrive in the dark, to not know anyone and yet be at their complete mercy. She was glad, that they might now be finally putting those awkward interactions behind them, perhaps even forming a friendship of their own... but there was still Frieda to consider. "What should I do?" she asked Leon. "Should I tell Dr. Friedmann about what happened back at the lake?"

"I think you could, and it would not go badly for Frieda," he replied slowly, his forehead furrowed in thought. "She would not be sent away, I am certain of that."

"How can you be so sure?"

"Because this is the safest place for her," Leon replied simply. "It would take a very great threat of danger for Dr. Friedmann to send any child away from here before he had to. He knows how unsettling it would be for them, to be moved on in such a way."

"And yet they will be moved on, as you say, in a few months' time, won't they?"

"Yes, but they know that. They will be ready for it, and they will receive support. It is part of their journey and they understand that."

"Yes, I suppose so." Rosie still felt heavy inside at the thought of that day, coming ever closer. "Thank you," she told Leon. "For listening." She realized she definitely felt better about the whole thing, and she was glad she'd confided in him.

"I think I will tell Dr. Friedmann, then, when he returns. It feels wrong not to, somehow."

"Yes, I can see that."

"I suppose I should get to bed," Rosie told him with a small sigh. "It's been quite a day, and I'm afraid my head is aching abominably." When she wasn't thinking about Frieda, she realized how tired and ill she actually felt, every movement difficult, as if she was swimming through thick soup.

"A swim in the lake at this time of year is not advisable, I suppose," he said, and although his voice was light, there was a darkness in it, just as there had been before, when he'd met her and Frieda coming back from the lake. Did he not know how to swim? Rosie wondered. She couldn't remember seeing him in the lake with the boys, only standing by the shore. Perhaps he was afraid of the water.

"No, I don't suppose it is," she replied, "although the boys were swimming and splashing about only last week. They must have a stronger constitution than I do." She started to rise, only to stop as the room suddenly started spinning around her, and she had to grip the edge of the table to keep from staggering or even falling to the floor.

"Rosie?" Leon asked, and she realized she was surprised he knew her name. He had not used it before. "Are you all right?"

She pressed one hand to her head; the room was still spinning and she felt dizzy and nauseous and so very faint. "It's just my head," she told him. "It aches so..." It was thundering now, and her vision was blurring, and her body felt both heavy and cold. She didn't think she could take a single step.

"Rosie!" Leon called again, sounding alarmed. He stood up, reaching for her, and his kindly, anxious face was the last thing she saw before she crumpled to the floor.

CHAPTER TEN

Rosie blinked her eyes open slowly, waking to sunlight filtering through the curtains of her small bedroom. She was lying in bed, and her body felt sluggish, her mouth dry, her mind blank. She couldn't remember a single thing. Where was she? What had happened to her?

Then it came back to her, in flashes of memory like streaks of lightning: Windermere. Frieda. The lake, *Leon*. She must have collapsed in the dining hall, she realized fuzzily. She remembered that she'd stood up and the room had spun, everything swirling, while Leon had reached out to her...

She tried to push herself up in bed, but her head felt too heavy, her limbs not seeming to respond to her commands, and she fell back upon the pillow.

"Oh, thank goodness, you're awake."

Jean came into her bedroom with a tea tray, smiling as Rosie blinked blearily up at her. "How long have I been ill?" she asked, her voice no more than a rasp.

"Oh heavens, it's been three whole days," Jean replied cheerfully. "You had such a fever... we were a bit worried, for a while, I must confess. Dr. Friedmann had one of the local doctors take a look at you, just in case. He said it could turn into pneumonia, but fortunately your fever broke last night. I was hoping you'd come to this morning so we could get some food into you."

"Three days..." Rosie could hardly believe it. Three whole days! She couldn't remember anything, not even in blurry or fragmented snatches. Then she remembered Frieda again, and she tried to lurch up from her bed again, to no avail.

"Frieda!" she gasped out.

"Oh yes, Frieda," Jean replied, unperturbed, as she set the tea tray down on the bedside table and began pouring out a cup. "She's been here every day, asking about you. Sometimes two or three times a day, in fact. Poor wee lass has been ever so anxious."

"She... has?" Rosie couldn't quite imagine it. Frieda, so concerned, about *her*? She was gratified, and she was also glad Frieda seemed to be all right. It didn't matter, then, that she hadn't been able to talk to Dr. Friedmann yet, or to Frieda herself...

Rosie found her eyelids fluttering closed. Already the effort of simply trying to lift her head from the pillow had exhausted her. She couldn't remember when she'd last felt so weak and ill.

"Oh yes, she has, most certainly." Jean leaned over her. "Are you feeling strong enough for me to sit you up for a wee while? You haven't had a bite to eat since this all began, and I'm sure you could do with some toast and Marmite."

Rosie actually hated the taste of Marmite, but she wasn't about to argue with kindly Jean, and she supposed she should try to eat something. She let the older woman prop her up against her pillows, where she sagged like a limp rag doll, a cup of tea placed between her shaky hands, the effort of it all almost overwhelming her.

"Tell me more about Frieda," she begged Jean, and her friend clucked and put a plate of toast on her lap.

"First, eat. Three days with nothing in you and now you're almost a bag of bones! Not a scrap of fat on you."

Obediently, Rosie nibbled at the toast, trying not to make a face at the salty taste of the Marmite. She knew Jean was right and she did need to keep up her strength.

"Frieda was awfully concerned for you," Jean told her as she settled herself on a stool opposite Rosie's bed. "She was near in tears the first time, she was, and said it was all her fault you'd come over so poorly. I told her that was a nonsense, and gave her two pieces of bread and butter, as well."

Jean gave a brisk, little nod, and Rosie found herself smiling faintly. Of course, Jean would think some bread and butter would help matters. In fact, it probably had.

"She came back again later, looking a little less peaky, but was awfully concerned that you still had the fever. Begged me to tell her as soon as it broke... said she had to know right away. I didn't even know you knew the girl, although I recall you said hello to her on that first night. Didn't she shove her cup at you, and spill her cocoa all over?"

Rosie closed her eyes, still smiling. It gratified her to no end to know Frieda had been so concerned for her, even though she didn't like to think of the girl being upset on her behalf. "Yes," she told Jean. "She did." And a host of other things besides, none of which seemed to matter quite so much anymore, now that she knew Frieda was safe—and concerned about her.

"Well, we don't know what these children have been through," Jean conceded with a sigh. "Or what manners they might have been taught in those forsaken places! But, in any case, she seemed ever so anxious on your behalf. I'll have to go and tell her your fever's broken."

"Can you have her visit?" Rosie asked. "I do want to see her."

"Not for a while yet, I should think," Jean replied briskly. She seemed to have taken it upon herself to act as Rosie's nurse and guardian. "You're far too weak still. You're looking tired out already, and you've only had half of your toast."

Obediently, Rosie took another bite. "Please, Jean," she said as she swallowed down the salty mouthful. "I don't want her to worry about me."

Jean frowned. "Rosie, dear, you do remember that we're not meant to get too attached to these children? It's almost October already, and the doctor was saying that most of them will be placed before Christmas."

"Before Christmas..." Rosie repeated in dismay. She had thought the children wouldn't be moving on until the new year, which seemed so much farther away than Christmas, even if she knew it really wasn't.

"Yes, everything will be closed down by the beginning of January," Jean confirmed. The money will have run out by then and, in any case, the children need to get on with their lives, don't they? The older ones will have to find trades." Her face took on a pinched look. "And the little ones will have to get used to their new families, of course," she added, trying to sound matter-of-fact, but not quite managing it.

"How is Isaak?" Rosie asked. "Is he recovered from his sickness?"

"Oh yes, he's as right as rain, the little fellow," Jean replied with a smile full of affection. "And so lovely and jolly again, too. I don't know why he came over so sad that time—it just about made my heart break, to see him crying so. Dr. Friedmann said that falling sick like that could have made him remember some experience or other from the camps." She gave an unhappy, little shudder. "He said the children are bound to have a good many issues around food, because they would have been starving, of course, with so little food given to them. And the Nazis apparently played all sorts of diabolical games with them, things I hardly can imagine—teasing and taunting them with food, holding it back, even offering it as a prize for doing something terrible." She bit her lip, looking near tears before she managed to compose herself. "It's so very dreadful to think about, especially with someone as small as that. I can't quite get my head around it, really. How anyone could... especially to a child..." She pressed her lips together, her eyes flashing for a moment before she resumed, "It really is hard to credit, especially when the children seem so happy and well now, but then these things slip out, don't they? And then you realize they're not well at all, not really." She let out a sad, little sigh. "As much as you want them to be."

"But they're *getting* well," Rosie said, thinking of little Daniel who had commanded her to draw, a happy grin on his face. "They really are getting well, Jean. You must hold onto that."

The other woman nodded slowly. "Yes, you're right, and I will try. It is nice to see them looking so rosy and plump!" She smiled in a way that made Rosie think she was thinking particularly of Isaak. "And laughing, too, right down in their tummies. I've found they quite like hide-and-seek, and they can stay hidden for ever so long, I've been rather put out!" She bit her lip again as unhappy realization flashed in her eyes. "Of course, it stands to reason, doesn't it? They must have become very good at hiding indeed."

"Yes, I suppose so," Rosie agreed quietly.

"Goodness, but sometimes it feels like there is nothing that evil hasn't touched." Jean sighed again and then rose from her stool. "But never mind all that for now. You need your sleep. I'll tell your Frieda that you're on the mend, don't you worry. I know she'll be pleased."

Jean took away the tea things and helped Rosie to lie down again; already she felt very sleepy, her eyes drifting shut before Jean had even closed the door behind her.

The last thing Rosie thought about before sleep finally

claimed her was how Jean had said *your Frieda*. She liked the sound of that.

When Rosie woke again, it was still bright out, but she knew some time must have passed because she felt a little lighter in herself, her body less leaden and sluggish, although her head still felt fuzzy. She scooted up in bed, grateful she was able to manage it on her own without the room spinning or feeling as weak as a kitten. Someone—Jean, most likely—had left a jug of water on the bedside table, and Rosie managed to pour herself a glass and drink thirstily before she rested her head back against the pillows with a sigh.

It had now been three days, maybe even more, since the evening of the trip to the theater, when she'd fallen ill. It felt like an absolute age, and she was eager to see not just Frieda, but also Jean again and the little ones, too, and even, she realized, with a flush of surprised pleasure, Leon. They barely knew each other, but he'd seemed so kind when she'd spoken to him about Frieda, and she hoped they might become friends. Although what must he think of her, to have collapsed on him as she must have? Rosie squirmed inwardly with embarrassment at the thought. What a way to have carried on! She would apologize when she saw him again, although maybe when she did, he'd be back to being his reserved self. Who could say?

She glanced out the window at the sunlight streaming down and decided she felt well enough to get up. She needed a wash quite desperately, after three feverish days in bed, and so, slowly, aching as if she was an old woman, Rosie rose from her bed.

It took some time, but she managed, with great effort, to give herself a wash and then dress and even do her hair, before Jean came into her room, horrified to see her up and about.

"Good heavens, what do you think you're doing?" she

demanded. "You were very nearly at death's door, my girl, and now you're prancing about as if you're Cinderella, about to go to a ball!"

"I'm not," Rosie protested, laughing a little, for she'd never heard Jean sound so fierce.

"Well, you can get right back in that bed," Jean told her, "because you have a visitor, although I suppose all things considered, it's just as well you're not in your nightdress."

"What... why...?" Rosie began, only to stop as Jean chivvied her back into bed, helping her to take off her shoes and pulling the covers over her as if she were still an invalid, which, she realized she sort of was, for the simple act of washing and dressing had exhausted her more than she'd realized.

A few moments later, Jean ushered in her visitor—and Rosie could not keep from gaping in surprise to see it wasn't Frieda, as she'd been hoping and even expecting, but Leon. Leon Rosenblat, here in her bedroom, to see her!

Rosie blushed furiously, unable to stop, even though she told herself there was nothing terribly scandalous about a man seeing her lying on her bed, fully clothed, even if she was under the bedcovers.

He smiled wryly, as if he guessed the nature of her thoughts, or perhaps just saw the truth of it in her scarlet face. "I'm glad to see you are feeling a bit better," he told her.

"I am, thank you," she replied, folding her hands on top of the blanket and willing her flush to fade. "I think I must have caught a chill when I went into the lake, after all."

"So it would seem. It can happen quite easily, I find." He paused, his dark eyebrows drawn together, his gaze turning distant, and then he gave himself a little shake and managed a small smile. "I was worried for you, as was Frieda, when we heard you had a fever."

"I'm sorry to have caused distress," Rosie replied, hating how stilted she sounded, how absurdly formal. She wasn't even sure why she did; she'd so much rather she didn't, and yet, for some silly reason, she couldn't manage it. "Frieda didn't catch cold, did she?"

"No, not at all." His smiled deepened, his eyes crinkling at the corners. "I think she would have rather that than you being so poorly. She was so very worried about you."

"Jean told me as much, and I was very sorry to hear it." Rosie pleated the bedcover with her fingers. She *did* hate to think of Frieda worried on her account, although she was glad she cared enough to worry at all. "I do hope she'll visit me soon," she told Leon, hearing the throb of fervency in her voice. "I'd like to see her, if just to put her mind at rest."

"Yes, I'm sure she will, soon." He took a step closer into the room, seeming hesitant all of a sudden. "You are... very kind, to be so concerned for her."

"I care about her," Rosie replied, simply, compelled to honesty. "I'm not even sure why, but from the moment I saw her sitting all alone, that first night..." She swallowed and looked away. "I don't know, maybe it sounds silly, but I felt... almost as if I *knew* her." Maybe because Frieda had reminded her of herself, Rosie admitted to herself.

Leon was quiet for a moment and Rosie wished she hadn't said so much. It had sounded rather ridiculous when she'd said it aloud. And in two months, maybe less, she would never see Frieda again. Something, perhaps, she needed to remind herself of more often.

"You said," Leon remarked after a moment, his gaze moving slightly to the left of her, "that you knew how Frieda felt... wanting not to feel, that is, when she went in the lake. What did you mean by that?" He turned to look at her then, and Rosie quelled under the sudden intensity of his gaze. He looked like he wanted to know the answer, and he would wait until she gave it.

And yet the question was so personal, so intimate, that

Rosie struggled to know how to reply. How honest should she be? Leon had been kind to her, yes, and she was realizing more and more that she *liked* him, but the truth still was, she didn't know him very well at all. In any case, she hadn't told anyone here about the sorrows in her past—not even Marie or Jean. She had no idea what Leon would think of what had happened to her, what she'd done, and she realized she wasn't ready to find out.

"Just that I've felt... sad sometimes," she hedged. "The war has brought that out in everyone, I think, one way or another. It's nothing like what Frieda has experienced, of course," she added quickly.

"It is not a competition," Leon replied quietly.

"No," Rosie agreed, "but... it feels like I oughtn't complain, considering..." She trailed off, unsure how to finish her sentence.

"Considering how much these children have suffered?" Leon filled in, and she made herself look at him; his eyes were drooping again, his expression both thoughtful and sad. Although she suspected he wasn't much over thirty, in that moment he looked old, aged by suffering, the lines from his nose to mouth deeply scored. She wondered what he had endured, whom he had lost? Parents, brothers, sisters? Children? A *wife?* It felt far too invasive to ask, and yet she felt she had to say something; to skate over the moment was surely wrong.

"And the adults, as well," she said at last. "You... you were in the camps, weren't you, Leon?"

His mouth tightened and he looked away, his body tensing before he did his best to relax again. "Yes," he answered briefly. It seemed as if he didn't want to talk about the past, either, and Rosie knew she could hardly blame him.

A silence descended upon the room that did not feel entirely comfortable, and she wished they hadn't spoken of such things at all. Much better, and certainly much easier, to only look forward, to what the future held.

"I am glad you are feeling better," Leon told her finally, and Rosie realized he was going to go, and, more significantly, that she was disappointed to see him leave.

"Thank you," she said helplessly, unable to think of a way to keep him there and not sure why she wanted to so much, anyway. "And... thank you for visiting me."

He gave a little formal nod and then withdrew, closing the door softly behind him.

A sigh escaped Rosie in a gust of sound. Before she could untangle the unsettling welter of her own feelings, Jean swept into the room, moving around quickly, folding clothes and twitching her blankets.

"Well! Mr. Rosenblat has seemed very interested in your welfare," she remarked, not, Rosie thought, sounding altogether approving.

"He was just being polite," Rosie replied quickly.

Jean glanced at her, an eyebrow arched. "Was he? Was that why he came several times a day to check on you, just as Frieda did?"

She stared at Jean in surprise; that was certainly new information. "He didn't!"

"I assure you did," she returned smartly. "Always asking after you, seeming concerned indeed. *Very* concerned."

Rosie, having no idea what to say, said nothing.

Jean hesitated, a folded blanket in her hands, and then she said slowly, "It's not my business to interfere, but it doesn't seem quite... proper, does it?"

Rosie stiffened in affront. "Mr. Rosenblat is simply concerned for my welfare, since I collapsed in front of him. What could possibly be improper about that?"

"Maybe proper isn't the right word," Jean returned hurriedly. "I'm not accusing you of anything untoward of course, but..." She hesitated, refolding the blanket carefully, even though it hadn't needed it. "It's a bit like with the children, isn't it? We oughtn't to get too attached... to anyone here."

"I assure you, I am not attached in any way to Mr. Rosenblat," Rosie said, and now she knew she sounded positively frosty. She did her best to moderate her tone. "Jean, the truth is, I barely know the man. In fact, before the trip to the theater, I rather thought he disliked me."

"Well, I can assure you, he doesn't dislike you now," Jean replied, with the glimmer of a smile. "Not the way he was asking after you, at any rate."

Rosie shook her head, everything in her resisting such a notion, even as a tiny little tendril of pleasure unfurled inside her. "I really think you must be imagining things, Jean," she insisted, with an attempt at a laugh. "In any case, I'm not interested in anyone like that, least of all Mr. Rosenblat." *Are you sure about that?* a voice inside her whispered, and she silenced it at once. "The truth is, I... I lost someone during the war." She swallowed hard; it was painful just to speak of it. "So I'm not ready—not ready in the least—to think about... about loving someone again, and I doubt very much that Mr. Rosenblat is, either, considering what he must have been through."

"I suppose that's just as well," Jean returned on a sigh, "although I'm sorry for your loss, of course. Seems like everyone has lost someone, but that doesn't make it any easier to bear, does it? As for you and Mr. Rosenblat..." She frowned and put the blanket down. "After Windermere, he's going to go on to live his own life, isn't he, with... well, with his own people? Just like the children will have to."

Rosie knew her friend meant well, and maybe she was even right, but all the same, she found herself saying, "Leon is an adult, not a child, and he will live his own life as he sees fit— with his *own people* or without them."

"Of course, of course," Jean said quickly. "All I meant is—

he's Jewish. Nothing wrong with that, of course, nothing at all, but he's going to want to marry a Jewish woman, isn't he?"

Rosie shook her head, deciding this had gone on long enough. "I have no idea about any of that." She felt, suddenly, quite tired, and a bit dispirited. "But it seems a bit silly to wonder about who the man is going to marry when I barely know him." She tried to smile to soften any implied rebuke in her words.

"Yes, I suppose." Jean sounded unconvinced, and Rosie turned her head away from her and closed her eyes.

"I'm sorry, but I think all this activity has quite tired me out. I'll rest again, if you don't mind."

"Of course," Jean exclaimed. "Maybe I shouldn't have allowed visitors yet. I'd be so cross with myself if you had a relapse."

Rosie opened her eyes and smiled at the older woman, feeling bad for making her fret. "No, I'm glad you did. And thank you, Jean, for taking care of me so well. You've been so very kind."

"Well, I've become fond of you, I suppose," Jean returned, ducking her head. "And you've seemed so worn out and well... sad, really. I'm not surprised to hear you lost someone. You can tell sometimes, can't you, when a body's known grief? I think you can, at any rate."

Broken calls to broken.

"Yes," Rosie replied quietly, looking down at her lap. "I suppose you can."

As Jean left the room, she opened her eyes and stared out the window; dusk was starting to fall, the trees on the far side of the yard lost in shadow. She felt rather unsettled, restless, and she knew it was because of what Jean had said about Leon. It had been ridiculous for her to talk about romance and even marriage when it came to Leon Rosenblat. She barely knew the man, and yet...

And yet... what?

She liked him, she knew, or at least thought she could, if given the chance. She found herself seeking him out, if just the sight of him, from across the room. Was that simply because of natural curiosity, or because she wanted to make a good impression, or because... *because...*

Rosie shook her head, annoyed with herself and her spiraling thoughts. She closed her eyes and determined not to think about Leon at all.

CHAPTER ELEVEN

"*Rosie!*"

Rosie almost didn't recognize the joyful voice as she set down the tray of toast she'd been bringing into the dining hall, and looked up to see Frieda barreling toward her, only to skid to a stop a few feet away and duck her head, suddenly shy.

It was the day after Leon had visited Rosie in her room, and that morning she had insisted to Jean that she was well enough to resume at least some of her normal duties. She'd showed up at the kitchen before breakfast, determined to help, even as the cooks had clucked about her, saying she still looked peaky. She hadn't had a chance to see Frieda until this moment, and now she was hanging back, looking uncertain, and Rosie decided she wasn't having it. Not anymore.

"Come here, you," she ordered with a ready smile, and she pulled Frieda into a quick and firm hug. Frieda looked astonished, but, as Rosie put her arms around her and pulled her toward her, she suddenly started to cling to her, pressing her cheek against her shoulder, her arms wrapped tightly around her waist. Rosie's heart felt as if it were expanding and melting and squeezing all at once as she hugged her back. "I heard you were worried about me," she murmured gently as she stroked Frieda's hair. "But, as you can see, I'm as right as rain. Nothing a few days' rest wouldn't cure. I'm not planning to take another dip in the lake, mind!" She'd kept her voice purposefully light, and was surprised when she felt a shudder go through Frieda, and realized she was crying silently, her hot cheek still pressed to Rosie's shoulder, her tears dampening her blouse. "Oh Frieda, Frieda, darling." Rosie hugged her more tightly. "I promise you, I'm all right now."

"I... I thought I'd killed you." Frieda's voice was a suffocated whisper, filled with both deep fear and regret. Rosie ached with sadness for her.

The dining hall, she decided, was not the place to have this conversation. "Come with me," she said, and she tucked her arm through Frieda's and led her away from the children filing into the room for breakfast, shooting Frieda curious glances, and upstairs to the empty art room. Sunshine poured in from the windows, and the puddles on the yard outside glinted in its light, although the sky was still the color of stone, the morning fog misting the tops of the fells. Rosie brought Frieda to one of the tables, and sitting down, patted the seat next to her.

Frieda's head was lowered, her blotchy face streaked with tears, but she sat down obediently, folding her hands in her lap. As she did so, Rosie saw the reddened welt on the inside of her arm again, and it looked worse than ever, swollen and sore.

"Frieda," she told her gently, "nothing that happened is your fault. My illness—even if I'd *died* from being in the lake!— that wouldn't have been your fault."

Frieda looked up at her, her face so full of misery that Rosie had to draw a breath. The poor girl looked as if she had been torturing herself with guilt and blame. "But you wouldn't have gone in the lake if I hadn't," she whispered.

"It was my choice to go in the lake, Frieda," Rosie stated firmly. "And, in any case, I'm fine. *Fine.*" She leaned forward, putting her hands on Frieda's shoulders, her face close to hers, so she could see Rosie's certainty for herself. "I had a bit of a cold, that's all, and who knows, I might have been catching it anyway. You know how there have been all sorts of colds and flus going around here, with so many people about."

Gently, she reached out to wipe the tear trickling down Frieda's cheek; thankfully, Frieda let her, blinking rapidly to keep another from falling as she gazed at Rosie with so much sorrow in her dark eyes.

"What is this really about, Frieda?" Rosie asked gently. "What has tormented you so? Sometimes I feel you make yourself miserable on purpose, to... to punish yourself, for some reason. But what? What is tormenting you so?" She hadn't realized she'd thought that completely through until she said it out loud, but now Rosie knew how much she believed it. Frieda had been so deliberately unhappy since she'd arrived in Windermere, more so than any of the other children, almost as if she *wanted* to be, or she felt she should be. Why? Would Rosie finally learn the truth now?

Frieda was silent for a long moment. Then, in the barest breath of sound, she whispered, "I killed them."

A frisson of shock went through Rosie, because she sounded so *certain*, but her own voice was steady and warm as she asked, "Who, Frieda?"

"My... my mother and my sister." A tear slipped down her cheek and this time Rosie wasn't able to catch it. She stared at Frieda in confusion, longing to comfort her, but sensing that her feeling of guilt, her utter conviction of it, was too deep for her to simply shrug it aside with a few words.

"Why do you think that?" she asked.

"Because it's true." Frieda sniffed, another tear slipping down her cheek unchecked, and then another; so intent was she on confessing her guilt, that she seemed heedless of the fact she was crying, little shudders going through her as her words came out in fits and bursts. "It was... my fault. All my fault. Everything."

What a terrible burden for a child to bear, Rosie thought, her heart aching with both love and grief for this young girl who had clearly borne so much.

She rested a hand on Frieda's shoulder, a gesture of solidarity and comfort, longing to imbue her with a sense of both. "Will you tell me what happened?" she asked gently. "If you can?"

Frieda didn't reply for a long moment, and then, finally, after a few gulps to compose herself, she began in jerky starts and stops, her gaze firmly on the floor, "It was why we had to go to the camp. Because of me. Mama was trying to get away—to Sweden. We were going to take a train to Gdansk, and then a ship. It was all arranged." She looked up at Rosie with a desperate sort of urgency. "It could have worked. We could have been safe. I know we could have." She gulped back her tears, wiping her face.

"What happened?" Rosie asked quietly, her hand still on Frieda's shoulder.

"Mama went to the window to get the train tickets. She had papers for all of us. She'd paid for them. I don't know how, because we didn't have much money. But she'd done it." Frieda sniffed. "She told me to wait in the station with Marijana. My sister." Frieda's voice wavered. "She was little—only six." For a second, she looked as if she might break down, her lips trembling before she pressed them together. "I was told to keep her quiet. I... I tried."

With a lump forming in her throat, Rosie found she could picture the scene so clearly—two little girls buttoned up in woollen coats, waiting with a couple of battered suitcases at their feet, full of uncertainty and confusion, not truly understanding what was going on. The rush of people in the station, the buzzing sense of fear like static in the air, their mother hurrying away for just a few minutes, intent on procuring their passage to freedom, little Marijana becoming impatient, frightened...

"Oh Frieda," she said sorrowfully, full of grief for the girl. She didn't know the whole story, not yet, but she was afraid she could guess what must have happened.

"Marijana missed Mama," Frieda explained in a quiet, now lifeless voice. "She began to fuss. I told her to stop, because she was making noise. She wouldn't, and when I spoke sharply to her, she began to cry. And then... the soldiers saw us, and they asked for our papers."

"Oh, Frieda," Rosie said again, softly.

"Mama had them," Frieda continued, the words now coming in a tumbling rush, as if she needed to get them all out. "I told him we were waiting for her, and I hoped he'd go away, but then Marijana said we were going to go on a big boat... I told her to be quiet... Mama came back..." She shook her head. "I don't remember it all, but there was shouting, and questions, and the soldier hit mama in the face. I remember that." She was silent for a moment, composing herself, one last shudder going through her before she went very still and then stated quietly, "The soldiers took us to a train. A different train."

"To Auschwitz," Rosie finished softly, an ache of grief in her voice. *Oh Frieda.*

"It was terrible," she resumed after a moment, her voice soft and sad. "Marijana cried for so long, until she stopped, and then it seemed worse because she looked so... so empty. As if there wasn't anything in her head anymore at all. Mama didn't talk to me. I think... I think she was angry with me, for what happened. She blamed me."

"Frieda, she wouldn't have," Rosie exclaimed, although she could not know any such thing, not for certain. But still, she knew about the bond between mothers and their children. She knew about a mother's love for her daughter. "She wouldn't have been," she said again, firmly.

"It was my fault," Frieda replied staunchly, lifting her chin. "I know it was. All of it."

The import of her words, the deliberateness of her tone, made Rosie ask cautiously, "*All* of it?"

Frieda nodded, a confirmation that there was even more to this terrible story. "When we got to the camp, Mama was taken from us. I think she knew she was going to... to die. They pretended it wasn't like that, but we all knew it was. The way they separated us..." She gave a little gulp. "She'd had a cough all winter, and it had got worse. When we got off the train, she looked very sick and weak. They wouldn't want her, for work." Another gulp. "As she was leaving, she told me to take care of Marijana. She asked me to promise, and I did." Frieda's voice caught, broke, and she leaned forward, to gaze imploringly at Rosie, as if asking for understanding, for absolution. "I *did*."

"I know you did," Rosie whispered. "Oh Frieda, I know." Except she didn't really know, not the full extent of it all. She couldn't possibly, because how could anyone imagine or understand what this dear child had gone through, what she'd endured, how terribly she'd suffered? Rosie felt as if her heart was splintering into pieces just to think of it, and yet Frieda, at all of what—? Eight, nine years old?—had *lived* it. And blamed herself for it, which made it even worse.

"When they took Mama away," Frieda continued, her voice wavering before it firmed and she met Rosie's gaze with a heartbreaking steadiness, the determination to tell the whole story blazing there in her eyes, "Marijana started to shout out for her. I couldn't let her shout—I knew I couldn't! They'd take her too, I *knew* it." A sob escaped her, an unruly, desperate sound. "I told her to keep quiet and she wouldn't—*again* she wouldn't— and I thought this time I will make her quiet. I *will*. And so I... I pinched her." Frieda's gaze was wild as she continued on, the words tumbling over themselves, "I wanted her to be quiet, *bitte, bitte*, please just be *quiet...*" Another sob escaped her, and then another, and then Frieda doubled over, her arms around her waist as her shoulders shook and Rosie took her into her arms, stroking her hair, murmuring endearments, longing to make it better, and knowing she couldn't, except through this. The pain had to come out. Like lancing a wound, letting out the poison. Every tear Frieda shed was part of the healing, Rosie told herself, but her heart broke all over again to hear the shattered sobs coming out of the girl, as if they were coming from deep within her, torn from her heart, her soul, emptying her out.

Still Rosie held her, overwhelmed with both sorrow and love for this girl who had been so brave, and blamed herself for so much. And yet there was still more for Frieda to tell.

After a few minutes, she eased back from Rosie, wiping her eyes. "Marijana began to cry when I pinched her," she explained dully, her gaze fixed unseeingly in front of her. "And one of the guards noticed. He pulled her out and slapped her across the face. She cried more. And then..." She stopped, and Rosie stared at her, appalled, fearing what was coming next and yet resisting it, because surely, *surely* not...

"*Frieda...*"

"And then he shot her," Frieda finished, and a shudder went through her. "He shot her in the head with his gun, like she was..." She gulped. "Like she was a horse that had to be killed. Or a fly you'd smack. Like she was *nothing.*"

"Oh, *Frieda.*" Rosie had no idea what to say.

"All my fault," Frieda finished as looked up at her, dry-eyed now. "It was all my fault."

"No..." Rosie took Frieda firmly by her shoulders; the girl's head lolled back as she stared up at her with lifeless eyes. "*No*, Frieda. It wasn't your fault. It wasn't anyone's fault but the guard who had the gun, this whole evil system that allowed such things, that encouraged and even delighted in them..." A choked cry escaped her as the realization of all Frieda had had to endure crashed over her again, and she forced it back. "Please, please, don't blame yourself," she told her, her voice throbbing with conviction. "Your mama, your papa, Marijana... they would all want you to live and to be happy. I *know* they would. You mustn't blame yourself for their deaths. You mustn't, Frieda. You were only trying to help them."

"But if I hadn't—"

"You can't think that way," Rosie cut her off, keeping her voice both firm and gentle. "You simply can't. Why, if anyone thinks about the 'ifs', they'd go mad. I know I would."

Frieda shook her head slowly. "If I hadn't pinched her..."

"No ifs, Frieda. You are not to blame. You *must* believe that." A sudden thought occurred to her, and gently Rosie picked up Frieda's arm; she did not resist at all. The mark was there, in her inner elbow, red and livid. "Frieda," Rosie said quietly, "have you... have you been pinching *yourself*? Because you pinched Marijana?"

Frieda did not reply, but the answer was there on her face. She'd been punishing herself, Rosie realized, for the deaths of her family. *All this time...*

As she looked at the tender, marked skin, she realized the wound was deeper than she'd thought. There would almost certainly be a scar. *Oh Frieda.*

"Your family would not want you to punish yourself like this," Rosie whispered. "I know they wouldn't. Oh Frieda... Frieda, darling." She hugged her again, and Frieda clung to her, and neither of them spoke, because there were no words. There was just this, Rosie realized. Letting the grief out. Letting the guilt go. And holding her all the while.

Eventually, they broke apart, and Rosie smiled at Frieda and brushed her cheek with her fingers. She felt limp with emotion, but also strangely hopeful, as well as thankful.

Thankful that Frieda had told her all this, that she had trusted her enough to, and hopeful for the future, for Frieda's future.

For surely today was the first step toward whatever lay ahead of the young girl, and Rosie would do her utmost to make sure that whatever was ahead was good.

Even, she acknowledged painfully, if she had to say goodbye to Frieda in just two months.

CHAPTER TWELVE

The next few weeks felt like a golden time to Rosie; even the weather changed, the dank, drizzly days of September giving way to a crystalline October, the air pure, the sky bright, the fells tipped with frost. Rosie was glad her health had completely recovered, but even more so that her friendship with Frieda had both deepened and strengthened. Her heartbreaking confession in the art room had turned a page in their relationship, begun a new welcome chapter, and it was noticeable most of all in Frieda herself.

Gone were the defiant looks, the disdainful expression, the haughty tone. Frieda did still remain cautious and guarded, and she continued to be reluctant to interact with the other girls, but Rosie knew small steps were still steps, and better than none at all. As Marie would say, there were no quick fixes, no magic buttons to press, or pills to swallow. Healing took time. It continued to be painful, but it could also be good.

And Frieda was, by Rosie's measure, flourishing. She smiled so much more, and sometimes even laughed, and had seen the doctor about the self-inflicted wound on the inside of her elbow. He'd put ointment on it and bandaged it and Rosie hoped

fervently that Frieda would no longer feel the need to pinch—
and punish—herself for what had happened to her mother and
sister.

Although Rosie was as busy as ever, helping around the
estate, she made sure to spend time with Frieda every day,
whether it was dabbling in the art room, walking by the lake or
simply chatting over a cup of tea. She learned much more about
Frieda's life—that her father had wanted to emigrate to America
—thus the English lessons—but hadn't been able to get a visa.
That her mother played piano beautifully but Frieda had never
learned. That she'd liked to write, before the war, before the
camps, but wasn't sure how to begin again, wasn't sure the
words were even inside her anymore. The only person she
didn't talk about was Marijana, and Rosie understood that.
Some things were still too painful. Perhaps they always
would be.

She was incredibly thankful that Frieda had shared her
story with her, but meanwhile Rosie felt as if her own was still
locked tightly inside, and she wasn't even sorry. Conversely,
Frieda's sharing had made Rosie less willing to share her own;
her personal losses seemed almost paltry in comparison with the
younger girl's, and to compare them was somehow offensive.
And, she acknowledged, she wasn't ready to talk about them
anyway, and she wanted to focus on Frieda.

Better to simply enjoy being with her, watching her unfurl
like a flower, while Rosie continued to push her own sorrows
down, down, down. If she focused on Frieda, and didn't think
about herself, Rosie hoped she might just be able to forget them,
or at least act as if she had, and maybe that could go on forever,
or for long enough.

In any case, there was plenty to keep herself occupied: trips
were organized for the children to Carlisle, to Kendal, and even
once to Blackpool. There were walks up in the fells and around
the lake, and a dozen of the children put on an amateur

theatrical one evening, cheeky Ari in the lead role, with Rosie helping with the costumes and props. There were always children in need of a plaster, or a cup of tea, or even a quick hug, and they were always coming and going from the art room, where Rosie continued to assist Marie, often accompanied by Frieda, who sometimes drew, and sometimes merely watched.

"Your Frieda seems quite happy," Marie remarked one afternoon as Rosie helped her tidy up. "I do not think I had seen her smile until recently."

"I don't think I had either," Rosie replied with a little laugh. "It is good to see, isn't it?"

"Yes, I am glad she is adjusting. This will be a time away from reality for these children," Marie remarked reflectively as she gazed out at the lawn, now awash in pools of sunshine, some boys kicking a football, girls holding hands in a circle playing some sort of game. "These precious months, free from worries and cares. In January, they will have to think about their futures."

"Yes, I know." With every day that passed, every leaf that fell, the future—and the children's departure—loomed closer. Rosie tried not to think about it, wanting simply to enjoy this borrowed time, but it was getting harder and harder not to wonder what would happen—and to brace herself to say goodbye to Frieda. "It will be hard when they leave," she admitted quietly.

"And what about your future?" Marie asked, her eyebrows raised. "Will you return to Canada when this is over?"

Rosie shrugged as she stacked the crayons in a tub. "I haven't really let myself think about it too much."

"Perhaps you should?"

"Yes, I know." Another sigh escaped her, this one seeming to come from the depths of her being. She'd started a letter to her mother several times before she'd finally written a short, almost impersonal note, focusing on what she was doing, rather than anything she was feeling. It had almost felt like a betrayal, to write in so neutral a way to her dear mother, and she'd been reluctant to post such a letter, but finally she had, simply because she knew her parents would want to hear from her. But Rosie suspected her mother would be hurt, or maybe just worried, by her letter's brevity.

"You don't have to return to Canada, you know. I myself will be returning to London to continue my work there, with Anna Freud. You could help me there, if you'd like."

"I don't know how much use I'd be," Rosie protested. "I don't know the first thing about psychotherapy, or anything like that." It was kind of Marie to offer, but if Rosie felt out of her depth here, among the volunteers, how much more so would she feel in a psychologist's office, with professionals?

"You managed to reach a child no one else could reach," Marie replied with a small shrug. "You are useful, Rosie, whether you think you are or not. But..." She paused to give Rosie an uncomfortably knowing look, the kind that made her feel as if Marie could see every thought flitting through her head—or, more alarmingly, the ones buried down deep. "Do you know," she remarked in an offhand way, "what many, if not most, children draw, once they have moved on from their trauma?"

"Trees, flowers?" Rosie guessed. She had seen quite a few drawings of those in recent weeks.

Marie gave a little shake of her head. "Homes," she said succinctly. "Right now, Windermere is their home, and so they draw that. When I worked with the war orphans in London, they almost always drew homes—square houses, only a couple of lines, and yet with so much yearning. Homes feed and fill the soul. They give us a place of rest, and also a sense of hope, of meaning."

"Yes, I suppose," Rosie replied after a moment, for it seemed as if Marie was waiting for a reply.

"I think at some point everyone has to return home, whether that is physically, or simply emotionally. Metaphorically, even. They must go back to the beginning, before they can go forward and find another home, a new meaning." She gave Rosie that faint, knowing smile, her full lips curving just a little. "And you, Rosie, I think, have been running. Running away—from home. One day you will be out of breath, out of road, and you will stop. Then what will you do?"

Rosie held the other woman's gaze with effort; she felt as if Marie had just reached inside her with a great big hand and jumbled her thoughts and feelings all around, and it was not a comfortable feeling at all. She opened her mouth to say that she wasn't running; if anything, she was standing still. But she already knew what Marie would say, with that little smile of hers. *You can run from things while staying in the same place.* As for going home... what, really, had kept her from returning to her old life, and the people she knew who loved her? It wasn't them, or even Kingston, she was afraid of returning to, she realized. It was *herself.*

She was the one who had changed. She, like Frieda had, felt guilty and ashamed for all that had happened, all she'd done. She wasn't ready to face those feelings, or the overwhelming grief that threatened to rise up in her like a tide if she let it—and so she didn't. She didn't think about it at all, but one day she would have to, especially if Marie kept pushing and pressing.

"I don't know," she admitted at last. "I don't know what will happen then."

"This is a good place to think about it," Marie advised gently. "While you have the time and space, the freedom to do so."

"Yes, I suppose," Rosie replied after a pause, knowing she sounded unconvinced. She *felt* unconvinced and also... afraid. She wasn't ready to think about all that, and yet, with every word that Marie spoke, she felt something rising within her, no matter how she'd tried to push it down. It was surging up and up, and she gave a gulping sort of swallow as she turned away from Marie, trying to compose herself. She didn't *want* to feel all these emotions. She'd done her best not to for months now. Why couldn't she keep on as she was?

She took a deep breath, meaning to change the subject, say something innocuous, but then she found she simply couldn't. It was beyond her, now that Marie had made her feel so raw, so exposed, with her gentle prodding.

"I think... I think I might go for a walk," Rosie said instead, a bit unsteadily.

"A good idea." Marie sounded as if she knew exactly why Rosie was suggesting such a thing. "It is a beautiful day today, after all."

It was beautiful, with a purity to the air that Rosie had felt nowhere else, not even back in Ontario. She quickly shrugged into her coat and headed down the lake road, toward Troutbeck, walking with her arms folded, her hands cupping her elbows, and her head down. She was blind to all the beauty, walking faster and faster, as if she was trying to outrun something. Maybe she was.

After a few minutes, she veered off onto a footpath that ran close to the shore, away from any potentially prying eyes, or nosy neighbors.

She walked with long, fast strides, the movement enough to keep her mind occupied, especially as the path was uneven in places, and strewn with loose stones. She'd walk and walk and walk...

And at some point, the road would run out, just as Marie said. *And what then?*

The sky was a bright blue above her, the sun starting to lower, sending its golden rays across the ruffled surface of the lake. Rosie's eyes smarted from the chilly breeze—at least that was why she told herself she had to wipe them more than once.

She'd built a wall in her mind, brick by laborious brick, but memories were slipping through the cracks, like shadows and ghosts, their vaporous tendrils winding around her heart, *hurting* her.

Thomas, presenting her with a 'bouquet' of a dozen eggs, because they'd been so precious in wartime. The way he'd clung to her, at their last goodbye. The smell of his Pinaud aftershave, the easy carelessness of his laugh as he threw his head back...

And other memories, these ones darker, harder. The round swell of her stomach, the joyous kick of her child inside her. The accompanying fear, along with the ferocity of feeling—she would keep this child, no matter what. She would love him or her, with everything she had.

Then the bloody blur of her time in the hospital, when she'd gasped and wept and clutched at her belly as her body relentlessly emptied itself of her child. The pale wisp of hair, the round cheek, was all she'd ever seen of her daughter before a stern-looking nurse, without a shred of sympathy, had whisked her away.

A cry escaped her, a sudden, jagged sound she hadn't meant to make, and Rosie clapped a hand over her mouth. Then she fell to her knees, heedless of the damp, muddy ground, the hardness of the earth, as another sound escaped her, a sob that splintered on the still air.

No, she wasn't going to cry. She *wasn't*. She hadn't wept once since it all happened, hadn't let herself because she feared if she started, she'd never stop. She'd be nothing but memory and pain, and she couldn't do that, she absolutely couldn't, which was why she'd stayed so blessedly numb, forced herself to be...

And yet, for once, finally, her control failed her. The sobs slipped out and she bent over double, her arms wrapped around her waist, as if she had to physically hold herself together, as her body shuddered with the force of her remembered grief.

Thomas, teaching her to jitterbug. Giving her her first kiss in the long grass of the meadow at Turnham Green, both of them bathed in summer's sunlight. Slipping a wedding band on her finger so they could go to a hotel together. She'd been so nervous, and yet so happy. Being held in his arms, his lips pressed to her hair, as sunlight streamed through the crack in the blackout curtains... Learning she was pregnant, filled with fear and wonder as she pressed her hands to her barely-there bump.

So many memories. So many regrets. So much loss.

How did the children bear it? she wondered as the sobs finally subsided, leaving her wrung out and empty, like a husk, a shell. She was lying prostrate on the ground, her cheek pressed into the dirt, her eyes closed, her body utterly spent. How did they go on at all, never mind laugh and joke, play football and paint, learn and love, after they'd lost so much? It felt impossible to her. She would never love anyone again. She wouldn't be able to make herself.

And yet if these children could heal, shouldn't she be able to, as well? What made her grief so special, or so deep, that it kept her from trying again, from learning to live, to *really* live, once more, just as they all were?

At some point, Rosie wondered wearily, did grief become tiresome, even selfish? If dear Frieda could go on after what she'd endured, then certainly she could, as well. Couldn't she?

"Rosie."

Her name was spoken softly, almost tenderly, and Rosie tensed as she heard it. She was lying face down on the ground, her skirt rucked up past her knees, everything muddy... She couldn't bear for anyone to see her like this, and for a second, she simply closed her eyes, half-hoping whoever was speaking would go away if she just refused to see them.

"Rosie," he said again, and she knew who it was. Leon. How had he found her out here, by the lake? She'd deliberately chosen a little-trod path! She'd *wanted* to be alone. Why had he come across her, why had he spoken to her, when he knew, he must have known, what a private moment this was?

Somehow, Rosie managed to get to her knees. Her hair had come undone from its neat roll and her cheeks were smeared with mud. Her stockings were damp and torn and she knew she must look a fright. She felt too tired to be embarrassed, although she knew she surely would be, later.

She hadn't really spoken with Leon properly since he'd visited her after she'd been ill, and he hadn't tried to speak with her, either, as far as she could tell. After a brief foray into friendship, they'd retreated into their usual wary reserve. So why was he here now?

"What do you want?" she asked, knowing she sounded ungracious. She tried to wipe the mud from her face but succeeded only in smearing it further.

Leon took a handkerchief out of his trouser pocket and then went to the lake, crouching down so he could dab it in the water. He turned to her, his expression as serious as ever. "Will you permit me?" he asked, and Rosie wasn't even sure what he meant as she nodded dumbly, too weary to resist.

Gently, tenderly, Leon began to wipe at her face. He treated her as if she were injured, as if she were broken, and she realized in that moment that she was. Rosie had been sure that she'd cried all the tears she had in her, spent them in noisy sobs, but now she found there were more, because as Leon dabbed at her face, she felt them slide silently down her cheeks, and he wiped those away too. It felt like the most intimate thing anyone had ever done to her, more tender than an embrace, or even a kiss. Once again, Rosie felt too exhausted, too emotionally spent, to be embarrassed.

After several minutes, Leon stepped back, the muddy, sodden handkerchief held in one hand. "There," he said, smiling faintly. "Better."

"Is it?" Rosie put her hand to a cheek. "I must look like a madwoman."

"No."

"I feel like a madwoman." She dropped her hand and looked away. "How did you find me?"

"I followed you," Leon confessed, without any seeming embarrassment or apology that he'd done so.

Rosie turned back to look at him in surprise. "You did! Why?"

"I was... concerned. You were walking into the wood, toward the lake, like..." He stopped, and after a few seconds' pause, Rosie finished his sentence quietly.

"Like Frieda did?"

He nodded. "You looked upset. I did not want you to be alone, in such a state. But perhaps I shouldn't have...?"

Rosie shrugged, wrapping her arms around herself. "I don't know," she admitted. "I feel as if I don't know anything anymore."

"Sometimes it helps," Leon ventured, "to talk."

"I haven't really talked to anyone," Rosie replied. "About... about this. I haven't been able to." She glanced at him uncertainly. "And it feels wrong to talk to anyone who has been in the camps. It's so much worse—"

"Remember when I said it was not a competition?" Leon's voice held the faintest trace of humor.

"Not a competition," Rosie agreed, "but still." She paused and then said abruptly, "Frieda told me her little sister was shot right in front of her eyes. Shot and killed." A shudder escaped her. "Nothing like that has ever happened to me. Nothing even close."

"But *something*," Leon replied as he settled himself on a fallen log, "happened to you."

Rosie stared at him for a moment, and he seemed so patient, so kind, his dark eyes drooping, the corners of his mouth lifting up into a small, encouraging smile. He was so different from the man he'd first seemed to her, the man she'd assumed him to be. Had that reserve been a form of armor, the way her numbness was, to keep from feeling, from hurting? She still had no idea what he'd endured, who he might have lost, and yet here he was, willing to listen to her... if only she was able to tell him.

"Rosie?" Leon prompted gently, and she took a deep breath.

She would tell him, she decided. She had to tell someone, because today's episode had made her realize that her numbness hadn't been any such thing at all. Beneath it had been so much feeling, so much seething despair and grief. She would never let go of it if she couldn't share it. Like the children with their drawing, or Dr. Friedmann offering his talking therapies, the pain had to get out. It might kill her otherwise, suffocate her slowly, or leave her to drown.

"All right," she said quietly as she settled herself on a rock opposite him. "I'll tell you." She realized her fists were clenched and she forced herself to relax them. "I'll tell you everything."

CHAPTER THIRTEEN

Leon waited, eyebrows slightly raised, that faint, encouraging smile curling at the corner of his mouth, everything about him seeming gentle and attentive. Still Rosie struggled to know how to begin. What to say, to confess, because already she knew he would think differently of her once it was said. Of course he would. She took another breath to steady herself.

"It's a common or garden story, I'm afraid," she warned him, right at the start. Best he knew that upfront. From somewhere, she summoned a false, brittle-sounding laugh that made her wince to hear it, although Leon's expression did not change. "And rather sordid, as well. You will think less of me for it. I know so." She cringed inwardly, knowing she was trying to push him away. Part of her, she realized, was desperate to talk about what had happened... and another part wanted to back away as fast and far as she could. If Leon left, if he told her she didn't need to speak of it, after all, she wouldn't say another word. She would, she decided, never, ever speak of it again, to anyone.

"Tell me," Leon replied, "and let's see."

It was not the response Rosie had been expecting, and yet she admired him for his honesty. He wasn't going to give her any false assurances that he wouldn't think less of her, because, of course, he couldn't know. And she respected that honesty, that fairness. But did she really want to tell him everything? Could she bare her heartbreak, her shame, after all this time, and in front of someone she didn't know all that well?

The alternative, she knew, was simply to push it back down, and she feared she couldn't do that anymore. The pain, the poison, had to come out, otherwise it really might damage her forever.

"I met someone when I was serving in London," she told him after a moment, choosing her words with care, her tone flat and strangely unemotional, almost as if she were simply telling a story, talking about someone else. It was easier that way. "His name was Thomas. He was charming and funny and kind, and he looked like a movie star. He swept me off my feet—do you know that expression?" She turned to look at Leon, who shook his head.

"I do not, but I think I am able to guess."

"Yes, I suppose you would. I was very naïve, really, with so little life experience. Romance had completely passed me by, and I didn't even mind, not really. I'd always been quiet..." She trailed off, thinking of her cousin Violet, who had always encouraged her to creep out of her shell, and she *had*, oh, she had... with Thomas. Always with Thomas. "Anyway," she resumed, "Thomas brought me out of myself. He made me laugh, and, amazingly, I made him laugh too, which felt almost like a miracle. I'd always been serious, you see. I have a cousin— she was my best friend, although we barely talk now. Maybe that's my fault. But she was also encouraging me to... to live life more, I suppose. Come out of my shell." She let out a soft huff of laughter as she looked at him again. "Do you know that expression?"

"Again, I can guess," he said quietly, that faint smile crinkling his eyes.

Rosie looked down at her hands, clenched back into fists in her lap. She'd barely begun, and yet already she felt more raw and exposed than ever before. Even just talking about Violet made her ache. She missed her cousin, and she missed who she had been with her.

"Well." Her voice sounded a little clogged. "I don't suppose our romance was much different from anyone else's." She looked up suddenly, surprising Leon, she thought, with the ferocity of her expression. His eyes widened slightly, but he waited for her to speak again, as patient as ever. "Have you ever been in love, Leon?"

He paused and then said carefully, "Yes. Once."

"Did you lose her... during the war?"

"Before." His tone was brief but not repressive. Now it was Rosie who was waiting, and after a moment Leon continued, "Her father forbade the marriage. My family was not grand enough. Or, I suppose, *I* was not grand enough." He gave a little shrug and a small smile. "She was the daughter of a wealthy banker, and my father was only a tailor."

"And you?" Rosie asked. "What were you doing before the war?"

"I was studying medicine at the University of Warsaw. I thought my prospects would be respectable enough, considering, but her father did not think so. Our romance ended in 1938, a year before the war came to Poland, and then, of course, I could not be a doctor at all." He gave a little shrug, as if it were all negligible, but Rosie ached for him. To have lost so much, even before the true atrocities of the war—both love and the hope of a future. "But what about you, Rosie?" Leon asked gently. "And this man? Thomas? What happened?"

Rosie took a deep breath. "We were going to get married," she said quietly. "At least, I thought we were. Thomas had said he would ask me to marry him, properly..." She trailed off because while he'd made that promise, he hadn't kept it. There had been time enough before he'd gone to Normandy with the 101st Airborne to ask her properly, "*down on one knee, with a ring*," as he'd told her. "But he didn't," she resumed, "and so we never married. He went to France in the invasion, and I was volunteering with the Canadian Women's Army Corps in Leicestershire." Doing work as a listener that she was still not allowed to talk about.

She fell silent, and after a few moments Leon asked quietly, "Did he die in France?"

"In the Netherlands, during the Battle of Ardennes." She paused, not wanting to say any more, yet knowing she needed to tell the whole story. "I was expecting a child at the time. He didn't know about the baby. At least, I don't think he did. I wrote him, but he never wrote back, and I can't be sure he ever received the letter." She couldn't look at Leon, didn't want to see the condemnation on his face. Unmarried and pregnant! She knew it was a matter of shame for any respectable woman. He would judge her, and she wouldn't blame him for it. "I lost the baby," she said, her voice barely a whisper, her gaze firmly on her lap. Tears crowded her eyes, and she blinked them back. She didn't want to cry yet again. "It was a little girl. I wasn't even able to hold her. I only saw a little bit of her hair. Blond, like Thomas." A tear dripped from her cheek to her hand, and she swiped it away. "I was dismissed from the Corps, of course, in disgrace. That was back in March. And for the next few months I didn't do much at all. I had a room at a boarding house with a kindly landlady who didn't ask too many questions. That time is all a bit of a blur now, to be honest. The days passed, but I can't even remember what I did." She'd walked the bombed-out city, and she'd stared into space. Other than that, Rosie's mind was a terrible blank.

"Then I met Marie Paneth at a children's center in London," she continued, "and she invited me to come here and help. But before I came..." Did she have to tell this, too? In some ways, it felt the most shaming part of all. And yet, after admitting to everything else, how could she leave out this last, devastating act of treachery, especially as it had shaped the way she'd thought about everything that had gone before? "I wrote to Thomas' parents, after he'd died," she explained quietly. "I think I wanted to feel some sort of connection to him, through them. I knew they would grieve him, as I was grieving him, as no one else I knew was. And so I wrote, and they wrote back." Another breath, this one hitched.

Leon waited, completely still and alert, although Rosie couldn't bear to look at his face.

"They told me..." She paused, her throat tight, and found she had to start again. "They told me he was already engaged to a woman in the States, that he had been for a long time... since before I met him, even. And they also wrote that they never wanted to hear from me again, and they doubted whether Thomas had ever loved me, or even known me." She let out a sound that was meant to be a laugh, but wasn't. "He certainly hadn't mentioned me to his parents at all," she finished, "even though he'd told me he had. And when I received that letter..." She paused, the memories roiling through her in a maelstrom of emotion—the shock, the devastation, and then the comforting, blanketing numbness. She'd put the letter in her pocket and done her utmost never to think of it again. "It felt like another grief," she told Leon. "On top of the first of losing Thomas, and the second, of losing our daughter. I didn't think I could bear any more loss, and so I never let myself think about any of it, even though it was always there. Waiting for me, in a way." She looked away from him, afraid to see the expression on his face. "Today is the first time I've let myself cry about any of it."

"It is good to cry," Leon said after a moment. Rosie couldn't tell anything from his tone—whether he felt sorry for her, or whether he judged and condemned her for her behavior, or maybe something in between.

"Is it?" she asked wearily. She wasn't sure she felt much better for her tears; she felt tired and spent and nothing had actually changed... except Leon must think less of her now, which actually made things worse. Why had she told him anything at all? Why had she opened herself to yet more sorrow?

"There is a saying I know," he said slowly. "In Yiddish, it is *'geveyn mahtt likhtiger das harts.'*"

Rosie let out a wobbly, uncertain laugh. "I'm afraid I don't know what that means."

Leon cast his gaze to the sky as he attempted to translate. "It means, I think, 'weeping makes the heart grow—lighter,' I suppose."

"Weeping makes the heart grow lighter," Rosie repeated slowly. She gazed out at the still waters of the lake, the surface without so much as a ripple, and let the words trickle slowly through her. *Was* her heart lighter? Right now, she felt too tired to be sure, and yet... she'd let go of *something*, in the telling. Something she'd needed to release. She felt as if, with every tear she'd shed, there would be one less to have to weep and wipe away in the future. Did grief work that way? She hoped it did. "Thank you," she said at last as she finally turned to look at him. His expression was grave but not condemning. Still, she felt compelled to ask, "Do you think worse of me for it?" She realized, as she asked the question, just how much she cared about his answer.

"Worse of you?" he repeated, sounding almost surprised by such a notion. "Rosie, why would I ever think worse of you for something like that?"

"Because... well, because..." She didn't want to have to explain or say it all again. "Because of what I did."

To her surprise, Leon let out a huff of tired laughter. "Rosie," he said, "I have seen and done too much to care a—" He frowned, struggling for the word. "A... a fruit for that."

An answering laugh bubbled up inside her. "I think you mean a fig."

"Ah, yes, a fig! I knew I didn't have the right word." He smiled, his eyes creasing at the corners, everything about him so gentle and kind and accepting that Rosie felt a rush of emotion for him, a grateful affection, and maybe even something deeper and more abiding, something she would let herself think about later. It had felt good to laugh, she realized, like stretching a sore muscle.

As their laughter subsided, she looked at him seriously. "Tell me your story, Leon," she asked, her voice quiet. "That is, if you want to. I know how painful it can be..."

"Yes, it is painful." He gave a little nod, frowning in thought. "And, sadly, it is a story that any of the children or other adults here could tell, or one very like it." He shifted on his perch on the log, his hands clasped between his knees, and then began. "We were all in the ghetto at Warsaw, at the start. The Nazis put all the Jews of the city there in 1940, and from other cities, as well. There were so many of us in there... Hundreds of thousands, at least. A dozen people or more sharing a room, no food, no doctors, nothing, and the Nazis would come in and steal our things, shoot anyone they liked, whatever they wanted, they did it, just like that." He snapped his fingers before he shook his head, smiling faintly. "I look back at it now and I almost want to laugh, because at the time we thought that it was so very bad. But it was just the beginning."

"It sounds awful to me," Rosie replied quietly. Too awful even to envision, she thought, at least properly.

"It was," Leon agreed, his tone turning sober again. "My sister died in the ghetto, of typhus. There was an epidemic right at the start. My mother was—what is the word?" He paused, thinking. "Fanatical," he finally said, "about us all using a comb, to get the lice. We all had them, of course, because of the conditions, and that is how typhus is passed. '*Comb, comb!*' she'd say, and shake it at us. It was her prized possession, I think, a silver comb from her bridal set. One of the only things she had left from our life before. But my sister got the disease anyway. She was so weak, from lack of food. She was only fifteen."

"Oh, Leon." Rosie shook her head slowly, knowing there were no words.

"It was a mercy, in the end. She would have suffered and died in the camps, far worse than back in the ghetto. The Nazis... they might have done terrible things to her." His face darkened and he looked down at his lap. "I do not think I could have borne to see that."

He was silent for a moment, still looking down, and Rosie longed to comfort him.

"I'm so sorry," she whispered, because what else could she say? Just as with Frieda, any sentiment she could offer felt so lamentably paltry and inadequate.

"Well." He looked up, trying to smile. "It was a mercy. There is that. We were deported in 1942. By that time, people had begun to guess—the Nazis had been telling us we would be resettled in the east. Some people started to hope, that it would be better there. We would be given houses, jobs. *'Ukraine isn't so bad!'* they said to each other, but you could see in their eyes... that they didn't really believe it. But you have to try to hope, in a way, no matter how bad it gets. If you cannot find hope, what point is there to life? But the more people went, the more we knew. There were whispers, rumors, of trains, of camps, of smokestacks stretching to the sky. And yet..." He shook his head slowly. "It still felt so unbelievable. No matter what the Nazis did to us, we kept saying to ourselves, *All right, yes, but they wouldn't do* that! We told ourselves it had to get better, when, of course, everything we had experienced showed that it never would. It would only get worse."

He stopped for a moment, lost in thought, his gaze distant. Then he cleared his throat and resumed. "We were taken to

Dachau." He spoke matter-of-factly, but his eyes still held a distant, dazed look, and Rosie knew he must be remembering the camp, the dreadfulness of arriving at such a hellish place. "My mother was taken right away to the crematorium. We knew. They pretended otherwise, but everyone knew. She did not fight it. She blew us kisses, I remember. She was even smiling. She'd been so tired... when Jerusza died—my sister—she lost her hope. She tried to hold onto it, but sometimes that is not possible."

He was silent again, and Rosie had the sudden, desperate urge to tell him to stop, not to remember. It was clearly so painful, and yet there was an acceptance in his voice, a weary sort of peace that amazed her. How could he speak of such atrocities in such a way, when she had just wept and wept over her own small-seeming sorrows?

"My father and two brothers and I, we were sent to work, digging gravel pits. It was hard labor, and they did not give us enough food. If you slowed down, you would be beaten, perhaps even shot. Roll call every morning at four o'clock, while it was still dark... making us stand there for hours, even in the pouring rain or the snow, with nothing at all to eat... we'd hold each other up, because if you fell down, you would be shot. Sometimes, the guards would call us out, for sport. Make us fight each other, or one of their terrible dogs. Great beasts, they were, trained to kill. Their jaws..." He shuddered, shaking his head. "Even in all this, we thought, *It will end. One day, it will end. We just need to survive.* We did not let them separate us. They wanted us to hate each other, but we refused, even when they did things, terrible things—made us beat one another, or worse. We accepted it. We understood. We forgave each other."

He paused again, his throat working, and Rosie tensed, because she knew what he said next must be difficult, even more difficult than all that had come before.

"Then, one day, they picked my father. He was working in

the gravel pit, and yes, he was a little slow. He was an old man and he'd been starving for so long. The guard smashed his hands with his shovel. Those hands had sewed the smallest, most perfect stitches... my father was a tailor, but he was also an artist. Every finger broken." He drew a breath and let it out slowly. "Well, there was nothing to do after that. He couldn't work. We knew he would be killed. We said our goodbyes that night, in our barracks. We sang the Kaddish over him, while he wept and kissed us. He was taken the next day."

"How could they...?" Rosie began, uselessly, because, of course, they had, and worse, so much worse.

"I do not know the answer to that question." Leon took another breath before continuing, "One of my brothers died of typhus after we'd been there maybe a year and a half. There was an outbreak in the camp, and many died. My other brother made it to the end. The Nazis had become frightened by then, because they were so clearly losing the war, and that made them even more dangerous. They sent many prisoners on marches, many miles away, and killed others. Every day we lived in fear, knowing that freedom might be so close, but also that it might be taken from us. We had to survive. We *had* to."

He fell silent, shaking his head slightly, and then resumed. "My older brother took part in a revolt, in the village of Dachau. He'd had enough, we all had. There were only six prisoners, along with some local *Volkssturm*. Even they were desperate, frightened. They took the town hall, but the SS killed them all within minutes. The Americans arrived to liberate the camp the very next day. If only he'd waited... by that time I was the only one of my family left alive."

"Oh, Leon." Rosie shook her head. "How did you survive it?" she asked in a whisper. "Not the physical part, I mean. Emotionally. How did you make yourself go on? How do you still?"

Leon was silent for a long moment, his gaze turning pensive.

"It was hard. It still is. Every day can be a... struggle. But I realized, when I was in the camp, that I had to make peace with it. With all of it. Or the Nazis would have destroyed me, along with my family."

"Yes, I can understand that," Rosie said slowly. To make peace with the past. Perhaps that was the only way to face the future. To mourn, to grieve... and then to let go.

"I think," Leon said after a moment, smiling a little, "that we have talked enough of sad things. I have been sad for a long time. I do not wish to be sad any longer."

"I don't, either," Rosie admitted, surprising herself, for she realized just how much she meant it. "I'm *tired* of being sad." And maybe, just maybe, *not* being sad could be a choice. Like Leon, she could choose to make peace. Choose hope, rather than regret. The memories of Thomas and her baby daughter did not need to torment and haunt her. She could let them go, look forward. Finally. For the first time, it felt, if only a little, possible. "Thank you, Leon," she said. "For listening to me, and for letting me listen to you. You have helped me, truly you have."

"I am glad. I have not liked seeing you so sad."

He stood up, and then reached out a hand to help her up. Rosie took it, noticing the feel of his hand in hers; although his fingers were delicate, long and slender, they were also strong. As he pulled her up, she stumbled a little, and took a step toward him, his shoulder brushing her arm, his hand tightening on hers.

For a second, something flared deep within in Rosie, a sweet and poignant yearning she'd never expected to feel again. She saw the golden glints in Leon's eyes, the way they widened with awareness, his hand still holding hers, fingers wrapped around her own. Her breath hitched audibly and then she pulled her hand from his and took a step back.

"Thank you," she said unsteadily, and then she turned and began walking back to the estate.

CHAPTER FOURTEEN

October slipped into November like a pearl off a string, the long, lovely days becoming all the more fleeting and precious. The nights were drawing in, the air sharp with cold, and the children had started to sense that this time away from reality, as Marie had said, would have to come to an end—and soon.

Some of them, Rosie knew, were looking forward to moving on—finding jobs or going to school, settling down in a new life, one that felt more real than the holiday atmosphere of Windermere. The younger children had begun to ask about their futures; the Central British Fund would be arranging their adoptions, although first they intended to move them to another home, so they could stay together.

"They've become like a little family of their own," Jean explained. "And they believe they should stay together for a while longer. One of the board members of the Central British Fund, Sir Benjamin Drage, is donating part of his estate down in Surrey for them. Weir Courtney, it's called."

"Oh, Jean!" Rosie had looked at her friend with affectionate excitement. "Will you accompany them?"

The smile Jean gave her was tremulous. "I have not yet

been asked, but I hope so. They'll need a familiar face, won't they? Alice Goldberger will be matron."

Although she was hopeful for her friend's plans, Rosie didn't like to think about her own, or talk about the future with Frieda; they had both, by silent, mutual agreement, decided to act as if their time in Windermere would never come to an end —and yet, with every passing day, that became more difficult to do.

Then, in early November, Leon suggested a trip. Since their conversation by the lake, when they'd both shared their stories, they'd become friends, good friends; Rosie often found herself seeking him out, and Leon did, likewise. She'd managed— mostly—to convince herself that that strange, electric moment when he'd held her hand hadn't happened, or at least it hadn't happened the way she'd thought it had. She'd been emotional, vulnerable, and so had he. That's all it had been, she told herself, because anything else felt too overwhelming—and frightening—to think about, even as the possibility remained on the fringes of her mind. Yet how could she possibly risk her heart again, after Thomas?

And yet, a little voice whispered, *you are trying to let go. To look toward the future...*

But not, Rosie told herself, like that.

"A trip?" she repeated when he suggested it one morning, as she helped to clear away the breakfast dishes. "I feel we've been everywhere there is to go around here. Windermere, Bowness, Kendal..."

"I want," Leon said with a small smile, "to go to the seaside. Do you know I have never been?"

"Never?" Rosie asked in surprise.

He shook his head solemnly, although his eyes glinted gold and there was a hint of a smile about his mouth. "No. Never. And neither has Frieda. She told me so, the other day."

Rosie knew Leon and Frieda had been spending some time

together; it had happened naturally, with her as the link, and she was glad. "Hasn't she been?" she asked, realizing that she and Frieda had never talked about such a thing. "You want to go to the seaside," she mused, smiling, "In November, in Westmorland? It will be freezing, you know. Utterly."

He shrugged, smiling now, too. "But we will still see the sea."

"Yes, I suppose we will." She paused for a moment, imagining it—the three of them at the seaside together. Almost like a family—No, she could not let herself think like that, even as she knew she already had. In any case, she could surely enjoy a day out, especially if Frieda wished to go, as well. How many more opportunities would they have to do something together? "All right, then," she told Leon, with a smile. "Let's go to the seaside."

They went to Grange-over-Sands, since it was closest, and possessed a lovely, long promenade along the seafront, along with a lido, although that was certainly not in use in November. They took the train from Windermere, just the three of them; it wasn't uncommon for the children to go off in little groups, but it felt both cosy and intimate, just their three, almost, as Rosie had thought when Leon had suggested it, like she kept wanting to think, like a family.

She had been planning to pack a picnic, but Leon had told her he would treat them all to a cream tea at the Grange Hotel, which sounded very elegant. The day was fine, but cold, the sun bright, yet barely seeming warm; Rosie suspected the seaside would indeed be freezing, although she found she didn't really much care. It felt like a holiday, to take the train south and then traipse along the glorious seafront to the promenade, the sea stretching out in front of them endlessly, glittering all the way to the horizon.

"I have never seen so far," Leon exclaimed, as he stared out at the expanse of water. "I feel as if I know how explorers might have felt, looking out at distant lands."

Rosie laughed and agreed that she knew what he meant. "When I did my training, during the war, I was on an island out there," she told him. "To the northwest, on the Irish Sea. The sea was all around us then, you could see it from every window. Sometimes it felt as if I was floating in the water."

"Yes." He nodded, his gaze still on the sea. "Yes, I can understand that."

"Please, can we go down to the beach?" Frieda begged, seeming as excited as a small child.

Laughing, Rosie took her hand and led her down the steps from the promenade and onto the sand.

It was truly freezing right there on the water, with a punishing wind that came straight off the sea and chilled Rosie right through. She pulled her hat down over her ears as they ventured onto the long, flat stretch of damp sand, the tide far out, their shoulders bowed beneath the wind's relentless onslaught.

If she'd thought the weather might put Frieda off, however, she was glad to see it didn't; the young girl ran and played on the beach, turning in dizzy circles before falling on the damp sand, arms and legs outstretched, smiling up at the sky.

"I've never seen her so happy," Rosie told Leon, and he smiled at her.

"I have never seen *you* so happy," he said, and Rosie let out a little laugh of protest, until she realized it was true. She *was* happy... happier than she could remember being, in a long time.

"You're right," she told him. "I *am* happy." She smiled at him, feeling a rush of affection for him, his kindness and thoughtfulness. "Thank you for thinking of this, Leon."

As Frieda ran off down the beach to explore, Leon reached for her hand. Once again, Rosie felt that electric jolt, just as strong as before, when they'd been by the lake. His fingers were strong and dry wrapped around hers.

"I would like to be able to make you happy, Rosie," he said quietly.

Rosie stilled, knowing she could not pretend to mistake his meaning. She was not even surprised; over the last few weeks, they had been, inexorably, heading toward this moment, with every smiling glance, every quiet conversation, every moment where they simply stood together, content even in silence. Yet what to say? What, even, to feel?

She felt as if she were a jumble of emotions: yearning and fear, apprehension and hope. She did not know which one of those held sway and so she stood there silently, her mind and heart both racing and yet also strangely still, as Leon gently clasped her hand and his thoughtful gaze scanned her face, before he nodded slowly.

"It is too soon for you," he stated. "I can see that."

"Leon..." Rosie shook her head helplessly. "I... I don't know whether it is or not," she told him honestly. "I..." *Care about you.* She knew it was true, she felt it through her whole being, yet she found she could not make herself say the words; it seemed physically impossible, as if a stone were lodged in her throat, blocking speech. Maybe Leon had been right, and it was too soon. *And yet...*

"Never mind," he said, smiling, although his eyes, drooping, looked sad. "Let us leave it for another day. There is a cream tea waiting for us."

Rosie nodded, grateful to let the discussion drop, yet when Leon slid his hand from hers, she found she missed its comfort and strength. Still, she wasn't brave enough to reach for it again.

Her mind remained in a ferment as they collected Frieda and walked back down the beach and across the promenade, to the grand hotel set in its own gracious lawns, overlooking More-cambe Bay.

The dining room was every bit as elegant as Rosie could have ever hoped, rivalling even the swanky hotels she'd visited during that long-ago trip to Los Angeles. There were crystal chandeliers, and tablecloths of heavy linen, and plates of porcelain, cutlery of heavy silver. Despite the continued strain of rationing, they were able to have two scones each, bursting with currants, a dab of clotted cream and plenty of jam, and cups of tea with milk and even sugar, besides. Rosie couldn't remember when she'd felt so pampered.

Leon made sure to keep their conversation light, making Frieda laugh as he murmured humorous speculations about the other guests, or messed about with his napkin, pretending it was his tie. Rosie had never seen him act so silly, and it made her smile, for there was a joy in his lightheartedness, along with a freedom she had never seen before, and even though she tried not to, she found she could imagine a future, hazy and yet real, where it was the three of them, not just for a day, but for always.

And yet how, when they would all go their separate ways in mere weeks? Surely that was just a futile dream...

After their tea, Frieda insisted on returning to the beach one more time before they took the train back to Windermere, although it was late afternoon by then, and the shadows were lengthening.

The tide had begun its relentless, determined creep toward the shore, and Frieda raced toward the waves that were now frilled with white. "I dare you to dip your toes in!" she called back over her shoulder, to Rosie and Leon.

"*Brr*, no thank you!" Rosie replied, laughing, and then turned to check Leon's response, only to still when she saw the strange, almost transfixed look on his face. "Leon...?"

"Yes, all right," he called to Frieda, but Rosie didn't think his voice sounded as light or easy as it had been just moments ago.

She rested one hand on his arm, looking at him in concern. "Leon?"

He smiled at her and patted her hand. "It will be very cold, I think."

"You don't have to..." Rosie began, unsure why she was saying it. Of course Leon didn't have to.

"I cannot resist a challenge."

He strode toward the water and Frieda, and Rosie thought there was something resigned, almost fatalistic, about the set of his shoulders, along with a steely sort of determination. She watched, apprehensive, although she couldn't say why.

Frieda was gleefully kicking off her shoes and socks while Leon sat down on the damp sand and carefully unlaced his shoes, rolling down his socks and placing them inside. It reminded Rosie, bizarrely, of a man preparing for his execution.

"Come on then, Frieda," he said cheerfully. "In we go!"

Frieda's bloodcurdling scream as she waded into the water made Rosie tense before she saw the girl was laughing. But as for Leon...?

He wasn't laughing, Rosie saw quickly, or even smiling. His hands were clenched, his face a rictus grimace of someone in pain.

"Leon!" Rosie called to him, uselessly, yet longing to reach him.

"Oh Rosie, you must come in, it's so cold!" Frieda shouted joyfully. "I can't feel my feet at *all*!"

"Too cold for me!" Rosie called back, her gaze still fixed on Leon. He'd managed to relax a little, but he still looked as if he was enduring not just the cold water, but something more emotional and elemental. Something inside of him. *But what...?*

After another minute or two, both he and Frieda had had enough, and they turned back to the shore, drying off their feet before pulling on their socks and shoes. As Frieda ran down the beach again, Rosie went to Leon.

"I was concerned for you," she said in a low voice, and he gave her a small smile, but Rosie sensed it took effort.

"That was more difficult than I expected, it is true."

"Why? It wasn't just the cold, was it?" She already knew that instinctively, from his odd reaction.

"No." He was silent for a moment, straightening his trousers, his tie, before he turned to look at her. "There is something I have not told you, about Dachau." He paused, his gaze distant, before he looked back at Rosie. "The Nazis—they used prisoners in experiments, truly dreadful experiments. They cut them open, they gave them poison, they even amputated their limbs and attempted to attach to them others, as if we were... monsters. It was... a horror beyond all others, what they did."

Rosie's breath caught in her chest. "I didn't know any of that," she whispered, appalled.

"They chose me for an experiment with freezing water," he continued, his gaze becoming distant once more. "It was to test how to save German pilots who had been shot down in the North Sea, or so I was told. There were a few hundred of us who were forced to do it. They'd put us naked into the icy water, leave us there for hours to see if we died. Then, if we were still alive, they'd take us out again and find various ways to warm us up. One poor fellow had boiling water thrown over him, and then died from the burns. Hardly a success." The smile he gave her was positively grim. "I had the experiment done to me twice. In a way, it was helpful, because it made me realize that the Nazis would do anything. *Anything*." His voice choked briefly before he resumed. "We'd been telling ourselves that it wouldn't get worse, but then I saw that it could, and it would. Of course it would. They were *evil*, Rosie." He turned to face her, the look in his eyes urging, even begging, her to understand. "More evil than I could have ever imagined. How does a man become that evil? How does he allow himself? I do not know. Somehow, he does—for these men, they were children, once. They were infants. Innocent. How did they come to this?" He shook his head slowly. "I do not know. I do not know."

Rosie stared at him, utterly aghast, having no idea what to say.

After a few moments, his gaze on Frieda racing happily down the beach, Leon continued, "They tried to make me do the experiment a third time, and I resisted. I'd been so—what is the word? Like a servant."

"Meek?" she suggested in a whisper, and Leon frowned.

"I do not know that word, but whatever they had wanted, I had done it. I'd thought that was how I would survive. But this? Again? No. And so I fought. It is how I got this limp." He smiled faintly, gesturing to his leg. "They beat me near to death. They let me go, thank God, but my leg was broken, among other things. That would have been enough to have me shot, of course, if I did not work." He shook his head. "But I would not let it be so. I went to work the next day—with a broken leg."

Rosie let out a gasp and Leon smiled.

"How, you think? I do not know. Truly, I do not know. Only that I was determined not to die, and that was the only way I could manage it." He released a long, low breath in a gust. "The bone set improperly, of course, which is why I now limp. But it healed, and I survived. They did not try to put me in the water again. And better yet—they gave me hope. Yes. They did." He nodded, registering her silent surprise. "Because I did not let them defeat me. I was stronger than they thought, I was stronger than *they* were. That knowledge was like a gift to me. It helped me to go on." He let out a small, sad sigh before he nodded and resumed, "That is when I came to know the boys, the ones here at Windermere. My father was dead by then, my brother, too. My older brother—he was so angry. He let it consume him, like a poison, but I wanted to hope. I wanted to give that hope to those boys." He turned to her with a faint smile. "Those *chil-*

dren. Which is why, perhaps, I spoke so sharply to you, on that first day."

"Oh, Leon." Rosie shook her head, blinking back tears. "I was being foolish, I know I was..."

"No, *I* was. I knew we were safe, there was no evil here, but there was part of me that still felt afraid."

"That's understandable."

He gave a small shrug. "Maybe."

"Is that... is that why you reacted the way you did, when Frieda went into the lake, that day at the theater?"

He turned to her, looking bemused. "How did I react?"

"I don't know. For a moment, you seemed... afraid, I suppose. I thought it was just because of Frieda, but it felt strange at the time."

"Perhaps, then, yes. And also why I was so concerned for you. I, of all people, know what it is like to catch a chill." He let out a laugh then, surprising her, and making her both smile and want to weep. This man was so incredibly strong. So wonderfully brave. *So very dear.* And he wanted to make her happy. "Going in the water today was a test," Leon told her. "I do not know if I succeeded or not, but at least I went in. I felt the freezing water, and I did not let the memories consume me or make me bitter."

"I'm so proud of you," Rosie said, and, impulsively, she reached for his hand.

Leon threaded his fingers through hers as he looked at her seriously. "I am glad, but you must know I want you to be more than proud of me."

"Leon..." *I am,* she wanted to say, cry, *I am, I know I am.* Yet, once again, she found she couldn't; it was as if her throat had stopped up completely.

"It is all right," Leon told her quietly. "I am patient—maybe too patient! Let us go find Frieda."

And still holding her hand, he tugged her round to walk down the beach, to the girl cavorting on the sand, her face tilted toward the sky.

CHAPTER FIFTEEN

In November, the Red Cross came with news of some of the children's families. While there was no news from Frieda's family, one boy found his aunt was alive and ready to welcome him; another, to everyone's amazement, found out his own brother was alive and had been fighting in the RAF during the war. The news was joyous yet also sad, for those were the only two who found anyone at all. For everyone else, it was a story only of unmarked graves.

"It does not come as a surprise," Dr. Friedmann told the volunteers, "to hear of their deaths. Of course it does not. And yet things that do not surprise us still have the power to shock. It is strange, yet it is so."

Rosie knew exactly what he meant. Hadn't she felt that when she'd learned Thomas had died? Or when she'd fallen pregnant, and then later lost her daughter? Each time, some part of her had been waiting for the worst, and yet, when it came, just as she'd thought it would, it felt like a shocking blow. But she longed for a different ending for these children, and even for herself. A different ending of their own choosing... and hers.

Ever since that day on the beach, Rosie had thought about

Leon, wondering if she could have a future with him. Was she ready to love again? Could she be, in time? And what about what Jean had said to her? Leon was Jewish; surely he would want a Jewish wife? And yet, he'd said he wanted to make *her* happy. She didn't think she had misunderstood him. She didn't care he was Jewish; perhaps he didn't, either.

And then there was also Frieda. As the days passed, Rosie realized more and more how she did not wish to envision a future without her. Her mind spun scenarios of staying in England, finding a way to visit Frieda on occasion, maybe even regularly. And then one day Frieda herself mentioned it.

"I don't want to be adopted," she told Rosie bluntly. It was late afternoon, the light liquid and golden, and they were walking around the lake with a few of the younger children, who had skipped ahead. They would be leaving for their new home in Bulldog Banks the following week.

"You don't want to be adopted?" she said to Frieda as they walked, her gaze on the children running in the distance. "Don't you want a home, Frieda?"

"They'll be strangers." Frieda stuck her lower lip out, looking as sulky as when she'd first come to Calgarth. "That is not a home."

"But in time..." Rosie protested, half-heartedly, because she knew she didn't want Frieda to be adopted, either. "In time," she persisted firmly, putting her own feelings aside, "they will come to love you, and you them. And that *is* a home."

Frieda looked stubbornly unconvinced. "I don't want a home," she insisted, her tone turning truculent, and Rosie tried for a playful smile.

"Do you want to stay at Calgarth forever?" she teased, only for Frieda to give her a sudden, burning look.

"Yes," the girl burst out. "Yes. With you."

"Oh, Frieda." Rosie reached for her, and Frieda came into her arms, burrowing her face into Rosie's shoulder. The other children had sat down on the ground by the side of the road and were playing in the piles of damp leaves. Their clothes, Rosie knew, would be terribly muddy, and Jean would be cross, but they seemed to be having so much fun. She hugged Frieda tighter. "I wish that could be, but you know it can't," she murmured, as she stroked her hair.

"But..." Frieda hesitated, and Rosie eased back so she could look in her face.

"But?"

Frieda nibbled her lip, looking uncertain.

Rosie had a feeling she knew what she was going to say, and yet she needed to hear her say it. "But, Frieda?" she prompted gently.

"Couldn't *you* adopt me?" Frieda whispered. "If you wanted to?"

"Oh Frieda, I would want to," Rosie assured her, an ache of longing in her voice. "I *would*."

Frieda's eyes widened, her hands clasped in front of her, her expression turning painfully hopeful. Rosie couldn't bear to disappoint her. "Then why don't you?" she asked eagerly. "You could, Rosie, I'm sure you could!"

"Frieda, darling..." Rosie gazed at her with both deep affection and a sense of despair. "They wouldn't let me." She hated to see Frieda's expression fall so dramatically, collapsing in on itself as she looked down at the ground, blinking hard and scuffing one shoe against the road. "I'm a young woman on my own," Rosie explained, keeping her voice gentle, "and I'm not even from this country. And, of course, I'm not Jewish."

"I don't care about any of that," Frieda insisted. "I *don't*. Papa wasn't Jewish, and my mother wasn't... she didn't care that much about it, I don't think. I don't care. *Rosie...*"

Rosie couldn't bear for her to beg. "Frieda, if I could—"

"Have you asked?"

Rosie fell silent, because, of course, she hadn't. She hadn't even considered asking, because, after all of Dr. Friedmann's warnings about not getting too attached, and the way Jean had presumed she would not be able to adopt, she had similarly assumed it was impossible.

"No," she admitted slowly. "I haven't. I suppose I just assumed it wouldn't be allowed." She hesitated, her mind whirling with new thoughts, impossible ideas. And yet maybe, just maybe, actually possible…

Could she adopt Frieda? What would that even look like? She could take her back to Kingston, but how would she provide for them both? She didn't have a job; she'd only completed one year of university. She had just turned twenty-four years old.

And yet… her parents would accept Frieda, Rosie knew. They would, of course they would. They would love her as she did. She could live at home until she could find a job, a way to provide for them both. Frieda could go to school; maybe Rosie could even go back to university.

For the first time, the prospect of going home didn't fill her with a nameless sort of dread. It gave her a sense of hope, even excitement, that rose within her even as she told herself to be cautious.

"I will ask," she promised Frieda. "I'll speak to Dr. Friedmann about it."

Frieda beamed with joy, her eyes brightening as a smile split her face, and Rosie felt she had to warn her.

"But don't be too hopeful, Frieda, please, because I really don't know if it would work. If I would be allowed. The Central British Fund has been organizing the adoptions, and they have been quite clear they wish for Jewish families to adopt the younger children eventually."

"But shouldn't I be able to decide my own future?" Frieda demanded, and Rosie smiled at her strident tone, her determination.

"Yes, of course you should." She wasn't a small child, like the others. Frieda should have a say in her destiny, but whether she—or Rosie herself—would be listened to at all, she had no idea. "Come on, let's get the others," she said, nodding toward the children who were still playing among the piles of damp leaves. "I think it's time for tea."

A few days later, Rosie worked up the courage to talk to Dr. Friedmann about the idea. Although she knew he himself could neither refuse nor give permission, he could certainly advise, and she'd come to respect the gentle doctor's wisdom. She wanted to know what he thought before she approached the Central British Fund; in truth, she wasn't sure she'd know how to approach the Fund without some help and advice.

"Ah, Miss Lyman." He stood up from behind his desk, the right half of his mouth lifting in a smile that seemed warm and genuine. "A pleasure, as always. It has been a delight to see Frieda blossom under your care."

"I'm sure it's not just because of me," Rosie replied with a small smile, "but it is Frieda I'd like to speak to you about."

"Of course." The doctor sat down and gestured for Rosie to sit, as well. "How may I help?"

"Well..." Her heart was thudding, her mouth dry, her hands clammy. She had no idea if what she was about to suggest was utterly outrageous or really rather sensible. Possible, at least... hopefully. "I was wondering... that is..." She swallowed and started again. "I wanted to inquire about the possibility of adopting Frieda."

A second's beat felt endless and electric as Dr. Friedmann stared at her, his eyes widening before he composed his expression into something more thoughtful. "You want to adopt her, you mean?" he asked, and Rosie heard the surprise in his voice, underneath the solicitous tone.

She nodded. "Yes. And Frieda... Frieda wishes for me to adopt her, as well."

"You spoke with her about this?"

Rosie did not miss the very slight note of censure in his voice. "Only because she spoke to me of it first," she said quickly. "I wouldn't have dreamed of doing so otherwise, I assure you."

"I see." Dr. Friedmann was silent for a moment, his fingers steepled together, his forehead furrowed in thought. "Of course, there are obstacles," he said at last. "That, I'm sure you already realize. You are a young woman, you do not reside in this country, and, most importantly, perhaps, you are not Jewish."

"Yes, I know." Rosie bit her lip. "I told Frieda as much already. Has... has a family been found for her yet? That is... she will be adopted by someone, won't she? She won't have to go into a hostel like the older children?"

"Frieda's future has not yet been determined. It might be that a hostel is the most appropriate place for her. It is not as unfriendly a place as it sounds," Dr. Friedmann assured her with a small smile. "The children will live together, with a matron supervising them, while they go to work or school. In a way, it is like a family, a large family, and it might be the kind of an arrangement they are comfortable with, after everything they have experienced. Many of them would prefer to stay together."

"That may be," Rosie allowed, "but the truth is that Frieda has not made many real friendships here. I don't know that she would actually like such an arrangement."

"Possibly," the doctor agreed after a brief pause, "but, in any case, we are still hoping to find her aunt, her father's sister. Since she is a Gentile, her chance of survival is understandably much greater. If she can be found, the hope, of course, is that Frieda would live with her."

"Yes, of course." The words came automatically, but Rosie didn't feel them. Frieda hadn't even written the aunt's name down, she thought despondently. The only reason the Red Cross was looking for her at all was thanks to Rosie's intervention, something she half-wondered whether she should regret. "But if the aunt isn't found?" she asked after a moment. "Would it be possible then?"

Dr. Friedmann considered the matter, his gaze lifting up to the ceiling. "I do not know the answer to that question. The Central British Fund has a high priority to place children with Jewish families, understandably. However, they would, of course, wish to take Frieda's views into consideration. And then there are the other matters, of your age and marital status. If you were married, with a husband who was employed, I must confess that would be a different matter entirely." He paused, his smile gentle yet seeming disconcertingly knowing. "Perhaps even a Jewish husband?" he suggested kindly.

Rosie flushed, knowing he had to be thinking of Leon. Their friendship had not gone without notice at Calgarth, especially after their trip to the seaside with Frieda. Rosie didn't mind the speculation or lighthearted gossip she suspected was flying around the estate; her friendship with Leon was something she both cherished and was proud of... even as she wondered if she could ever possibly be ready for more.

And if it meant she could adopt Frieda...

But, no. She could not let herself marry Leon simply to get Frieda. The thought was unconscionable. *And yet...*

"I have no intention to marry at this moment," she told Dr. Friedmann carefully, her voice slightly stiff with embarrassment.

"Ah, well." He gave a little shrug. "There is no harm, I am sure, in speaking with the Central British Fund personally. You could travel to London to meet with them. It is always helpful to have a representative from the program here to update them on our progress."

"I could?" Rosie asked, surprise audible in her voice. She

had not thought it could be as easy as that. Of course, she cautioned herself, speaking to them directly might yield no satisfactory results... and yet she felt hopeful, simply because of the doctor's suggestion, more than she expected to. At the very least, it was a chance, and while she was in London, she could visit Violet, as well. She felt badly that she had fallen out with her cousin, even though it had not been in an overly dramatic fashion. Violet hadn't been as sympathetic as Rosie would have expected, or at least hoped, and she'd been too raw and wounded to not let it matter. Still, she knew now that she'd like to see Violet before her cousin returned to Ontario, although perhaps she already had. The last time her mother had written, she'd mentioned that Violet was waiting for Andrew Smith, now her fiancé, before she returned to Canada, but that had been some weeks ago.

Still, surely it was worth a try? Especially if going to London could help her—and Frieda.

The arrangements to travel to London were made with surprising ease—and haste. Rosie knew she had not a moment to lose, for the Central British Fund could very well be making other plans for Frieda already; the time in Windermere for all the children was coming to an end in just six weeks, and dozens had left already.

Rosie told Frieda of her plans, cautioning her against becoming too hopeful, which, judging from Frieda's excited reaction, was futile, yet still, Rosie thought, necessary.

"It's just a discussion, Frieda," she told her. "They will have concerns. It might not be possible—"

"I know," Frieda replied, grabbing her hands. "But still."

Rosie laughed, unable to keep from catching a little of her infectious excitement. It was fun to let herself dream, even to plan. "Would you like to live in Canada?" she asked. "It wouldn't be too far away?"

"Too far away?" Frieda replied, with her usual direct look. "Far away from what?"

It was a reminder that despite her happiness now, she had lost absolutely everything—and everyone. Rosie didn't want to disappoint her yet again.

Leon's reaction was, understandably, more measured. "I would hope the Central British Fund would listen to what Frieda herself wants," he told her, "considering her age. She is not a small child, after all. But it is not always possible."

"I know, and I wonder if I'm a bit mad, to take on the rearing of a twelve-year-old girl, when I am only twenty-three myself." She gave Leon an abashed smile. "Perhaps it will be too much for me."

"Perhaps it will be the making of you." The smile he gave her was tinged with sorrow, and Rosie felt a sudden, urgent need to explain to him how she felt, even if she didn't entirely know herself.

"Leon... what you said, that day at the beach..."

Instantly, he became alert, watchful. "Yes?"

"I... I care for you," Rosie blurted. "I do. I'm just not... I'm not..."

The light in his eyes dimmed, but he still smiled. "I understand, Rosie."

"I..." She blushed, fighting with herself, her own feelings, the deep-seated fear of revealing them, even *feeling* them. "I don't want to lose you," she finally whispered. "And I'm afraid I might."

"You won't," Leon replied simply. "I'll always be here."

"But in six weeks we'll all be somewhere else," she pointed out rather miserably, for as she made herself imagine a future without Leon, she realized she didn't like the look of it at all.

"Yes, that is true," Leon allowed, "but I will make sure you know where to find me."

"Where will you go, after this ends?" She had not asked before, because they had made a silent, unspoken pact not to talk about the future in that way, to live in the very precious present.

"I am planning to go to Sheffield," he answered, "with some of the boys from Dachau. They will have a hostel there. I will stay with them, at least for a while, and see them settled."

"And after that?" Rosie asked tremulously.

Leon smiled faintly and shrugged. "After? I cannot yet say. I would like to continue to train as a doctor. Whether that is truly possible in this country, I do not know."

Rosie nodded slowly. So much of the future was a morass of uncertainty that had yet to take any kind of form—for Leon, for Frieda, for herself. And yet she trusted Leon's promise, and it reassured her. She would, she thought, believing it, being comforted by it, always know where to find him.

CHAPTER SIXTEEN

The hustle and bustle of London felt overwhelming after the calm beauty of the Calgarth Estate; although Rosie had gone on a few day trips over the last few months, to Windermere and Kendal and Bowness, she had not been in a proper city since July, and London's noise and crowds, the grime and dirt, all threatened to send her scuttling back to the train.

She'd heard from Violet before she'd taken the journey; with the barracks in Mayfair now given back to their owner, her cousin was staying at a boarding house in Battersea, and working for CMHQ as they continued with the massive effort of demobilization of the Canadian forces. Violet was hoping to return to Canada by Christmas—accompanied by her fiancé Andrew.

Rosie couldn't help but feel a little quiver of trepidation as she headed toward the tearoom around the corner from Trafalgar Square, where CMHQ was located, and where she had arranged to meet Violet. She had not seen her cousin since June, and they had not parted on particularly good terms, or written to each other since.

Her relationship with Violet had always been somewhat

tumultuous, Rosie reflected; her cousin was chatty and sociable, a veritable force of nature, and when they were younger, Rosie had always been content enough to remain in her shadow. But the war, and their service in it, had changed that particular dynamic; several years ago, Rosie had been selected for officer training while Violet had not, much to her ire, a decision that had led them to not be on speaking terms for over a year. And then, when Rosie had told her about Thomas and her baby daughter, Violet had been sympathetic but decidedly brisk; she clearly hadn't wanted to dwell on such tedious sadness and she had told Rosie that everything that had happened had been for the best, a sentiment Rosie had found difficult to stomach at the time, and still did.

But now... what would Violet be like? How would they relate to one another, after so much time had passed and so much had happened? Rosie knew she wasn't angry with her cousin, not any more, but she wasn't entirely sure what she did feel toward her.

"Rosie!" Violet rose from the table in the window where she'd been sipping a cup of tea, nearly upsetting her cup and even the whole table as she waved madly at Rosie, who had only just come in the door.

"Hello, Violet." Rosie was heartened to see her cousin was still her cheerful, indefatigable self. The last vestiges of the hurt and resentment she'd felt back in June melted away, and she thought suddenly of Leon, telling her how weeping made the heart lighter. Yes, perhaps it did. It certainly felt lighter now, and she was able to greet her cousin with genuine warmth and gladness.

Violet wrapped her in a tight embrace, giving her shoulders a good squeeze before she let go. "It's so good to see you," she said, and then, tellingly, sniffed, dashing at her eyes. "Look at me, a regular waterworks! I'm so glad you wrote, Rosie. I was afraid... well, I was afraid I'd put my foot in my big fat mouth the last time we met. I know I shouldn't have said what I did, about it—you know—all being for the best." She bit her lip, crimson with lipstick, her hazel eyes wide and luminous as she gazed at her in appeal. "I'm so sorry, Rosie. I know I handled that terribly."

"Oh, Violet." Rosie shook her head as she shed her coat, hanging it over the back of her chair before she sat down. "It doesn't matter, really, it doesn't. Perhaps it was for the best, after all."

"Don't say that," Violet implored. "Please don't. I know you can't mean it."

"Well." Rosie poured herself a cup of tea from the pot in the center of the table. "It's in the past now, anyway." Even if it still hurt. At least it didn't hurt as much. She really was moving on, Rosie thought, in small, careful steps, if not leaps and bounds, and for that she was both glad and grateful.

"Tell me how you've been," Violet said. "All this time. Up by the lakes! I've heard it's wonderfully beautiful up there, with the mountains and things, but the weather can be terribly gloomy."

"It can," Rosie agreed with a laugh. "It rains an awful lot. But it is truly one of the most beautiful places in the world, at least one of the most beautiful places I've ever been. And I've so enjoyed getting to know all the children there." She paused and then added with careful deliberation, "And one young girl in particular, in fact. Frieda." Saying her name out loud gave Rosie a warm glow. *Frieda, my daughter.* Would she ever be able to say that and mean it? Have it be true?

"Frieda." Violet wrinkled her nose, her forehead furrowed. "Do you mean one of the Jewish children?"

"Yes. Those are the only children there, Violet." Rosie strove to moderate her slightly stern tone. She'd been at Calgarth for five months, but for Violet, it was all new and strange, and she understood that. "She's a little girl from Katowice, in Poland. I've actually come to London today to meet with the Central British Fund for German Jewry about adopting her."

"Adopting...!" Violet's jaw dropped rather comically before she snapped it shut, her eyes wide and round as she stared at Rosie. "You mean you want to adopt a... a baby?"

"A child, actually, a girl. Frieda is all of twelve now," Rosie explained, a touch of pride to her voice.

"*Twelve!*" Violet practically yelped. "Goodness, Rosie, you don't do things by halves, do you? What on earth would you do with a twelve-year-old Polish girl?"

"Love her," Rosie replied simply. "Care for her and love her, as I already do."

"*Well.*" Violet shook her head slowly as she sat back in her seat. "That's one for the books, I guess! Will they let you do it, though? You're not married, are you?" Her eyebrows arched high. "That hasn't changed since I last saw you?" She let out a laugh, only to subside when she saw Rosie's thoughtful look. "Rosie...!"

"No, I'm not married," Rosie assured her with a smile. "But there is a man in my life... a man I care for." As she said the words, she realized just how much she meant them. "But I don't think I'm ready yet, to think that way." She paused to take a sip of her tea, steeling herself. "But I might be," she added a bit recklessly, "one day." Maybe even one day soon.

"A man! Goodness." Violet looked dazed. "Is he another volunteer?"

"Yes, he came with the children from Poland."

Violet's forehead crinkled. "You mean... he's Jewish?"

"Yes," Rosie replied. "He's a survivor, as well. He was in the camps, just as the children were."

"Goodness." Violet still looked dazed, but also, Rosie thought, slightly scandalized by the notion.

"You wouldn't mind if I married a Jewish man, would you,

Violet?" Rosie asked, her voice deceptively mild. She wondered if other people would mind, people back in Kingston, where there weren't many Jewish people at all. Would her parents care? Her brother?

Violet's eyes widened. "*Mind*? No, no, of course not. But... well, it *is* a bit strange, isn't it? I mean..."

"What do you mean?" Although she strove to keep her voice neutral, Rosie heard the slight edge to it, and knew Violet did, too.

"Just that it would be... different..." she began, only to suddenly throw her hands up in the air. "Oh, Rosie, I don't much mind what you do!" she exclaimed. "I reckon I've given you enough lectures over the last few years, telling you how to be. Yes, it is a bit strange, to think of you marrying a Jewish man, adopting a Jewish daughter! People back home might talk a little, but *I* wouldn't. And I'll stop looking shocked, I promise. If you love him and he loves you, then I suppose that's all there is to say about it."

"I don't know if we love each other yet," Rosie replied. "Like I said, it's too soon." She gave her cousin a quick, grateful smile. "But thank you."

The conversation moved on then, to talk of Violet and what she'd been doing at CMHQ—"the most dreadfully boring work imaginable, lists and lists and lists! The army makes more of 'em than they need." She also told Rosie about Andrew, and how he'd told her he'd be demobbed before Christmas.

"If we could make it home for the holidays, that would be wonderful. Mum and Dad are so excited to meet him, but we might have to wait till January. There's still plenty of work for me to do at CMHQ, so I don't suppose it will matter too much."

"You sound happy, Violet," Rosie told her quietly, and her cousin smiled.

"I am. I never thought I'd settle down like an old housewife, and yet here I am, about to do just that." She gave a little laugh.

"I don't mind, though. If I don't see another typewriter for the rest of my life, that would suit me down to the ground." Her laughing expression turned serious. "And you seem happy, too, Rosie, if I do say so, and... more than that." She paused, her forehead crinkling in thought. "When Thomas was in the picture, you were happy, of course, but it was a bubbly, fizzy sort of excitement, and that doesn't always last, does it, as lovely as it is? But now you seem more settled. Peaceful, even."

Rosie smiled at Violet's apt description of that "fizzy feeling" she'd had around Thomas; it was certainly true. "I am happy," she said, a thrum of sincerity in her voice. "I really am."

As they were parting, with hugs and kisses on the cheek, Violet suddenly slapped her forehead. "I almost forgot! A letter came to you at CMHQ a few weeks ago. Major Davis is still there, the old tyrant, and she gave it to me to pass onto you, since she knew we were cousins. It's from somewhere in Worcestershire... did you know anyone posted there?"

"No, I don't think so." Rosie took the letter and examined the postmark, somewhat mystified, but not particularly curious. The handwriting looked a bit spidery and she didn't think she recognized it, but CWACs had moved all around during the war, and it could have been from any of the women she'd met and served with over the last three years. "Thank you," she told Violet. "I don't suppose I'll see you before you go, but maybe we'll meet back in Kingston."

"You will come back to Ontario, won't you, Rosie?" Violet asked anxiously. "You're not going to stay in England forever with this girl, if you adopt her?"

Rosie thought of Frieda, of Leon, of Lake Ontario, shimmering blue-green in the summer sunlight, Amherst Island perched in it like a jewel.

"I'm going to come back," she told Violet, and for the first time she knew she meant it.

. . .

The office for the Central British Fund was located in Woburn House, on Tavistock Square, a grand, brick edifice that hummed with activity. As Rosie stepped inside, telephones rang, typewriters clacked, and secretaries and office clerks bustled around, looking busy and important.

"There is so much work to do," Elaine Blond, the woman in charge of relocating the Windermere children, told Rosie as she led her to a cramped and cluttered office on the second floor. She sat behind a wooden desk and gestured for Rosie to take the only other seat in the small room. "We must strike while the iron is hot—while the British and American governments are still concerned about what has happened to the Jews." Her pretty mouth twisted. "In a few more months, no one will care anymore at all."

"Surely that can't be true," Rosie exclaimed, "considering what has happened to them?"

"One would think, but..." Elaine sighed and shrugged as she spread her hands wide. "The CBF was founded in 1933, when Hitler first came to power, and we have always struggled to find sympathy. Our main problem has been convincing governments that Jewish refugees are not, in fact, a threat to them."

Rosie knew Elaine had been involved in the *Kindertransports* before the war, when ten thousand children had traveled to England, separate from their parents. It had been stopped in 1940, due to the conflict. Most of their parents had died back in Germany during the war.

"But that is neither here nor there," Elaine continued with a brisk smile. "How are things up at Windermere?"

"They are very well, thank you," Rosie replied with an answering smile. "The children have truly flourished there. It has been a delight to see."

"I am glad to hear it."

"Many of them have gone already now, but of course you know that." Rosie twisted the strap of her handbag resting in her lap between her hands, feeling tongue-tied and more nervous than ever now that the moment to explain herself had finally come. "Some are even planning to travel all the way to Palestine, I believe." Dr. Friedmann had mentioned it recently; some of the older teenagers were Zionists, longing to return to what they saw as their homeland.

"Yes, that has been a particular focus for some refugees." Elaine nodded and smiled in agreement, although Rosie sensed a slight impatience from her, a bristling need to get to the bottom of why Rosie had requested this appointment. She was clearly a woman with a great deal of work to do.

"There is one girl at Calgarth," Rosie told her in a rush, "who has not yet been placed anywhere, as far as I know. Her name is Frieda Weber. She is twelve years old, and she has asked if I will adopt her."

Just as Dr. Friedmann's had, Elaine Blond's eyes widened slightly, her nostrils flaring, her lips pursed in thought or perhaps even disapproval.

Rosie continued doggedly, trying to keep from sounding as desperate as she felt, "We have become close, and I... I would like to adopt her, if I could. I am from Canada, in Ontario, and I would take her there to live with me."

"Assuming a visa could be arranged," Elaine remarked, her tone giving nothing away.

Rosie had not even thought of visas. "Y-yes," she agreed stiltedly. "Assuming."

"You are not Jewish." This was stated as fact.

Rosie shook her head, her hands now clenched tightly in her lap. "No."

"And you are quite young," Elaine continued.

Elaine was, Rosie thought, making all the objections that she'd feared. "I am twenty-three."

"Hardly old enough to care for such a child," Elaine returned succinctly. Rosie's heart sank even more. "I appreciate your interest and concern, of course," she continued, "and I am quite sure that the experience at Windermere has created a good deal of affection on both sides when it comes to you and this girl. But the time there was never meant to be a permanent solution, Miss Lyman. These children have lives to lead elsewhere."

"But does Frieda?" Rosie burst out. "If I don't adopt her, where will she go?"

"As it happens, I received a letter only yesterday about this very girl," Elaine Blond replied. "I am sure you will be pleased to hear her aunt has finally been found."

Rosie stared at her dumbly. This, she realized, she had not expected, even though she knew she should have. "Her aunt..." she repeated numbly. "And she is willing to take her in? Where does she live?"

"She is in Dresden, where Frieda's father was born, I believe. We have not yet corresponded about whether she will take Frieda."

"But does Frieda even want to go back there?" Rosie pressed. "She told me she's never even *met* her aunt."

Elaine's mouth became pinched. "I do not know the particulars."

"But if this aunt isn't Jewish either," Rosie continued desperately, feeling the hope of caring for Frieda slip away from her. She hadn't fully realized until that moment just how much she wanted it to happen. "And Frieda has never met her... surely I am as like family as she is, if not more—"

"As I said," Elaine cut across her, "the experience at Windermere clearly created a close bond of affection between the two of you. That does not mean it will last. You are a young woman, Miss Lyman, with your whole future ahead of you. I imagine you will return to Canada and take up your life there, and you will forget Frieda after a time."

"I will *not*," Rosie declared with fierce dignity. "I would never do such a thing. I know my own heart, Miss Blond, of that I assure you."

The other woman looked unmoved, albeit a little weary. "Even so."

"So you will not consider it?" Rosie asked, and she heard the ragged thrum of tears in her voice that she choked back. "Not at all?"

"Not at this time," Elaine replied, in the manner of someone making a concession. "If the aunt proves as unamenable as you seem to suggest, perhaps... perhaps it can be considered. *Perhaps.*" Her voice was quelling. "But there are ramifications to consider, Miss Lyman, that you seem blithely unaware of. A visa is not an easy thing to obtain, for one."

"I'll obtain it," Rosie replied fiercely. "If that is all it takes—"

"I assure you, that is not all it takes. But it is a beginning." Elaine sighed. "It would be far better for you to return to Canada on your own," she told Rosie wearily. "You are young, emotional, and I do not think you realize what you would be taking on." She paused and then continued carefully, "These children, they have experienced unimaginable horrors—"

"I am well aware of that," Rosie inserted quietly.

"They are damaged," Elaine continued flatly. "Unbearably damaged, perhaps irrevocably so, I am very sorry to say. It might not seem so now, when they have been laughing and playing by the lake, but it is true, nonetheless. There is deep, deep trauma within them that will take many years to process and accept. Do you really think you are capable of dealing with all of that, Miss Lyman?"

Rosie swallowed hard and then lifted her chin, meeting the other woman's probing stare directly. "I believe I am, Miss Blond, because I am damaged, as well. Not like Frieda, it is true, but with my own sad scars. Marie Paneth—the art therapist up at Calgarth, as I'm sure you know—told me some time ago that broken calls to broken. I didn't really believe her at the time, perhaps because I was too broken myself." Rosie smiled faintly, appreciating the irony. "But I understand it now, because I've lived it. I've helped to heal Frieda—and she has helped to heal me. And I know we are not perfectly healed, nor perhaps will we ever be, or anyone else for that matter, but we *need* each other, Miss Blond. We love each other. That much I do know, absolutely." She stopped, knowing she had no more to say, gazing at the other woman in challenge, with pride, because she meant what she said, utterly, and she would stand by it.

"Well." Elaine looked, for the first time, truly sympathetic. She gave a slow nod and a small smile. "We'll see what we can do."

It was, Rosie knew, the most she could hope for, and, in truth, she did feel hopeful as she left Woburn House. She felt shaky too, for having said so much, and for being so bold. What if Frieda's aunt *did* want her? And what if Frieda decided she wanted to go and live in Dresden with her, after all? Rosie wanted her to be happy, of course she did, but she knew she'd feel a huge sense of loss, of grief.

Well, that was a worry for another day, she decided. For now, she would be content with what she had—something that was not quite a promise, but close enough.

Rosie had arranged to spend the night at a modest hotel near Piccadilly before heading back to Windermere in the morning, and it wasn't until she was in her room, having had a meager dinner of Spam fritters and cold boiled potatoes in the hotel's dining room with a few other, rather dour guests, that she remembered the letter in her bag that Violet had given her, and she took it out with little more than a flicker of curiosity.

Her old friend Susan, with whom she'd served at Beaumanor Hall, had stayed on at CMHQ before heading back to Canada in October; another friend from her London days, Beth, had applied to work in the Pacific but the war there had ended before they'd even sailed. Had she stayed in England after that?

Rosie slit the envelope and then unfolded the letter, scanning the first few lines before it felt as if her heart had frozen in her chest, her breath in her lungs, her whole body going rigid with shock.

Rosie, dearest Rosie, if you're reading this, you probably believe I am dead...

It was, she realized with a wave of utter incredulity, from Thomas.

CHAPTER SEVENTEEN

The convalescent hospital in Worcestershire smelled of carbolic and infection, cabbage and damp wool. The men there had all been wounded in the last months of the war, and they were still recovering, as of yet too ill to return to the States. There were men with grievous head injuries, and men in wheelchairs, and those who had had limbs amputated, the cloth now neatly pinned across empty sleeves or trouser legs. There were men playing cards in the dayroom, and others who lay in their beds and simply stared at the ceiling. It was a part of war that Rosie had never seen before, the aftermath of it, and she was both horrified and filled with pity.

Thomas was in the ward at the end of a long, tiled corridor, seated in a chair by the window, facing a garden that was bare and brown in winter. There were only a few other patients in the room, asleep or as good as, barely stirring as Rosie stood in the doorway for a moment, studying the man she'd loved and composing herself, for the sight of him there brought a sudden flood of emotion.

She'd received his letter last night, and spent hours simply staring into space, trying to make sense of it all. Thomas... alive. *Thomas... alive!* How could it be? How was she meant to feel? Because she didn't, she knew, feel the way she once would have expected—elated, thankful, filled with wonder.

The next morning, gritty-eyed but determined, she decided she needed to see him. His letter had been so brief, merely stating he was alive, convalescing in an American military hospital in Worcestershire, and that he wanted to see her. She knew no more than that, and she knew she needed to.

It had been a simple matter to take a train, and then a bus, on her way back to Windermere, and so here she was... with no idea what to say. What to think? How to feel?

She took a step into the room. "Thomas," she called softly.

He turned, and his face lit up like a firework when he saw her. "*Rosie!*"

For a second, she didn't know how to react; she knew she did not feel the same sense of joy he clearly did, and, just as before, she could not entirely understand why she did not, despite all that had happened—his parents' rejection, his potential lies. Six months ago, surely, she would have been excited, thankful. She *knew* she would have. She would have run to him, weeping with joy, her arms stretched out, incredulous and so very hopeful. But now, beneath the understandable sense of relief that he hadn't been killed, she only felt confused, and tired, and sad.

It was clearly not the reaction Thomas was expecting, for he dropped the arms he'd stretched out to her. "Rosie?"

"Hello, Thomas." She walked into the room, and then, because this was, after all, *Thomas*, she leaned down to put her arms around him and kiss his cheek. He didn't smell the same, she thought, of his Pinaud cologne and hair pomade. He smelled stale, and also of medicine, but that, of course, wasn't his fault. Still, it felt strange.

His arms came around her briefly, clumsily, before he dropped them.

She eased back, smiling at him, although part of her still felt like crying. He was terribly thin and haggard-looking, and his hair had gone white at his temples and sides. There was a scar from his forehead to his chin, a pink line running right in front of his ear.

"A little surprised at how I look, huh?" Thomas said, trying to smile, but there was a slightly bitter edge to his voice that made Rosie feel guilty.

"I am a little surprised," she admitted quietly. "But mostly because I thought you were dead, Thomas. I... I can't believe you're alive!" She smiled, even though her lips felt as if they weren't working properly, and eagerly he leaned forward in his chair.

"You received my letter?"

"Yes, Violet gave it to me only yesterday. I haven't been in London, you see, and so I didn't get it at CMHQ." She hesitated, the silence between them feeling both expectant and a little tense, and then she asked quietly, "Did you receive mine?"

Thomas's brows drew together. "Yours? When?"

"Before the battle of Ardennes." She drew a quick, steadying breath. "September, it would have been, of last year."

He gave a restless sort of shrug, his fingers twitching at the blanket that covered his knees. "I don't know. I can't remember what letters I received. A lot has happened since then, Rosie."

"You would have remembered this letter." She turned to look out the window. So, he didn't know that she had been pregnant with their child. Was there any point telling him now? And yet, how could she not? "Will you tell me what happened, Thomas?" she asked quietly. "After the battle? How did you survive?"

He hesitated and then began in a flat voice, gesturing to his scar, "I was shot in the head. They left me for dead, and I was as good as, there in the snow. But then the Huns picked me up... took me to one of their prisoner-of-war camps, a 'Guest of the Reich.'" He smiled mirthlessly. "Stalag Luft, it was called, in Barth, on the Baltic Sea, north of Berlin. 'Beautiful Barth on the Baltic,' we called it, although there wasn't anything beautiful about it, not at all. There were about seven thousand of us there, along with a bunch of Brits. For the first few weeks, I was in the hospital, practically in a coma. Even after that I couldn't remember my own name for months. It came back to me slowly, over time... and *you*, Rosie. You came back to me most of all." He looked at her then, with a bright, burning longing in his eyes.

Rosie found she could hardly speak past the lump in her throat. "Oh, Thomas. That sounds dreadful. I'm so very sorry."

"The guards abandoned the camp right before the end of the war, just left in the night," he continued. "We woke up and they weren't there. It was so quiet, eerie, really. Then the Americans liberated us, before the Soviets took over. It was dicey for a while, let me tell you, but eventually they got us out. They finally shipped me over here about a month ago, and that's when I wrote to you." He paused to look at her again, his expression turning bleak. "I know I'm not the same as I was the last time you saw me. The head injury, it's healed up, but I'll be honest, it still affects me. Memory, mostly, but sometimes other things. They had to teach me how to tie my shoes." He let out a laugh, the sound edged with despair before he rallied, squaring his shoulders, lifting his chin. "But I'm getting better every day, Rosie. I really am. And I... I still love you." His voice cracked. "Do you still love me?"

"Oh, Thomas," Rosie said again. She stared at him helplessly, not sure she had any other words. *Did* she still love him? She had no idea how she felt anymore. So much had happened, so many things she'd endured and then gotten over, and now she felt as if she were back at the beginning, reeling once more.

"Yes, I do," she finally said, because it was true, at least in part. "I was devastated when I thought you had died, Thomas. Utterly devastated."

He shook his head sorrowfully "I wish there was some way I could have let you know I was alive."

"So do I." Although, she wondered, how much difference would it have made? Her daughter would still have died. And what about Thomas's parents? Would she ever have been accepted into his life, no matter what he said now?

More importantly, Rosie thought, she most likely wouldn't have gone to Windermere in search of herself... and she wouldn't have met Frieda, or Leon. A sound escaped her, something between a ragged laugh and a sigh. The situation felt impossible, everything happening at the wrong time—too soon, too late, too much, too little. "How long will you be here for?" she asked, and he brightened, eager and hopeful once more.

"They say I might be ready to ship home after Christmas. That's not very long, is it?"

"No, not long at all." By Christmas, Frieda would have a placement... with her aunt or elsewhere, or with Rosie. "That's good news, Thomas."

"For sure it is, Rosie, but the truth is, I don't want to go home without you." He gave her a direct look, both determined and desperate. "Do you really still love me, Rosie?"

"Thomas..." She hesitated, and then made herself ask quietly, "What about your fiancée back home?"

For a second, the look on his face was completely blank, and Rosie felt a strange, uneasy sort of hope. Had she got it all wrong? Had his parents been lying, for some reason? Then a shadow of guilt crept into his eyes and his mouth puckered like a prune before he looked away.

"How did you hear about that?" he asked, his face averted.

Rosie's heart sank, even though she didn't actually feel disappointment. She felt sad, and a bit confused, and very, very tired. "I wrote to your parents," she explained in a low voice. "After I'd heard you had died. I... I wanted to feel close to you, I suppose."

"You wrote to my parents?" He sounded surprised and not at all pleased. "Rosie—"

"They wrote back," she cut him off, her voice sharpening, "a not very nice letter saying they never wanted to hear from me again, and that there was a lovely young woman back in Greenwich, Connecticut, who you'd asked to marry, and who was now devastated by grief."

He turned back to her, his expression turning desperate again as he reached out one hand. "It wasn't like that, Rosie, I swear."

"How was it, then? Maybe you could tell me, because you never did before." She'd tried to sound gentle, but her voice came out even sharper. The hurt was still there, she realized, at least a little bit, maybe even more than that.

Thomas sighed heavily. "We had an understanding, it's true. Maureen and I were high-school sweethearts. Everyone thought we'd get married."

"Did *you* think that?"

He shrugged restlessly. "Yeah, I guess I did."

"Did you ask her to marry you?" Rosie asked pointedly. "Down on one knee, with a ring?" she added, and now she was the one who sounded bitter.

Thomas hung his head. "All right, yeah, I did, right before I shipped out," he confessed before adding in a rush, "I thought I might die, Rosie! And everyone expected it. Life felt... precious."

"Yes, I think I remember hearing that before." He'd said the same to her, before he'd slipped a ring on her finger—not an engagement ring, but one for the wedding they'd never had, a cheap thing of brass, simply so they could go into a hotel and spend the night together... and all the while, another woman had been wearing his ring, a real one.

She looked away, a sour taste roiling in her stomach, rising in her mouth.

"*Rosie.*" Thomas lurched forward, grabbing her hand. "It wasn't like that, I promise."

The feel of his hand in hers, thinner though it was, was familiar. Beloved, even, but in the way a photograph was, something you looked at and then put away. *Could* she love him again, properly? Did she even want to?

She glanced down at their clasped hands, remembering how they'd walked arm in arm down Piccadilly, laughing and chatting. Lying in the meadow at Turnham Green, dancing at Rainbow Corner, the whole world stretched before them, shimmering with possibility and delight.

Was it all gone? Had it ever been real? Thomas seemed to want her to believe it was, despite Maureen, who had been waiting for him in Connecticut all this time.

"What was it like, then, Thomas?" she asked quietly. "Did you ever tell your parents about me? Because in the letter, they seemed to not know I existed. And what about Maureen? Did you ever break it off with her? Did you write to her to tell her you'd fallen in love with a CWAC in London, when she told you she didn't know how to flirt?" Her voice broke then as the memories flooded back, and she tugged her hand from his, shaking her head and wiping her eyes.

"Ah, Rosie. Rosie, darling." Thomas sounded near tears himself. "I can tell you think I was a cad, and I know it looks like it too, but it really wasn't like that, I promise. I loved you. I love you still..."

"You must have written your parents since you returned," Rosie said, still wiping her eyes. "Did you tell them about me then?"

He hesitated, and she let out a despairing laugh.

"No? Not even then, Thomas?"

"Rosie, I haven't, it's true, but only because I hadn't found you yet." He spoke in a rush, the words tumbling over one another. "That's really the only reason why! I didn't know if you'd still care for me, and the truth is, I *still* don't. I love you. I want to build my life with you. If you want me to write my parents and Maureen right now, and tell them all about you, then I will. Just give me a pen and some paper."

He looked at her defiantly, one hand outstretched, but all Rosie could think was that he must have never written to Maureen before about her. He'd never even told his fiancée it was over... if indeed it had been. Had Thomas ever meant what he'd said about wanting to marry her? Was Maureen still wearing his engagement ring? Did she think they would marry, even now? Rosie had no idea what to believe. And she still hadn't told him about their daughter.

"Rosie, please."

"I need to think," she told him. "This has been so sudden... I was just getting over you!" The words burst out of her in an accusation. "I was finally moving on, Thomas, past my grief. For months, I was like a... like a ghost, just walking around blankly, numb and even dead inside. But..." Her voice hitched and she drew a breath. "I was finally getting over you."

Thomas's mouth twisted. "I'm sorry it's so *inconvenient* for you that I'm alive."

"You know I don't mean that!" she protested in exasperation. "But it's a shock, Thomas. It's a very big shock."

"I know and I'm sorry, Rosie. Please believe that I am." Once again, he was back to being eager, a penitent in love. "I'm sorry. I know I'm handling this all wrong, and I don't want to! It's just that I've been dreaming of this day for so long. It's what got me through everything—the hospital, the prison, here— knowing one day I'd hold you in my arms again."

What on earth could she say to that? A few months ago, she

would have dreamed of it, too. Oh, how she would have! But did she—could she—still?

"I need to think," she said again. "My life has changed since we last saw each other. It's changed rather a lot."

Thomas's eyes narrowed as his shoulders slumped. "Is there someone else?"

"Not like that," Rosie said, mostly truthfully. "But I've been up in Windermere, Thomas, with children..."

"What?" Now he looked completely nonplussed.

Wearily, Rosie explained about the children, the Calgarth Estate, although she didn't mention either Frieda or Leon. She wasn't sure why—whether it was to protect Thomas, Leon or Frieda, or perhaps herself.

"But you say that's ending soon?" Thomas said when she'd finished, without, Rosie thought, asking so much as a single question about her time there, or showing any interest in it at all.

"Yes, in the new year."

"Which is when I'll be able to return home." He reached for her hand again, and Rosie let him take it. "Rosie, darling, this is perfect. We can travel home together. You can meet my parents—"

"I don't think they want to meet me," she interjected rather tartly.

"They'll come round, once they know you, and they realize how much I love you," Thomas replied, with far more certainty than Rosie felt. "I'll take a job in Dad's law firm in the city. We'll buy that little house. Remember, Rosie?" He squeezed her hand. "Remember the house and the dog and a couple of kids? Our dream."

Your dream, Rosie thought, but didn't say, because she knew it wasn't really fair. It had been her dream too, for a little while. When she'd been pregnant with his child...

Resolutely, she tugged her hand from his. "Thomas, that

letter I sent you in September, before Ardennes? Do you know what it said?" She heard the hurt in her voice, and she knew Thomas did, as well.

He gazed at her in confusion. "Rosie, what...?"

"I was pregnant, Thomas," she blurted brokenly. "Pregnant with your child." She drew a shuddering breath. "I lost the baby, a little girl. She died in the womb, they didn't know why."

His mouth opened, then closed as his eyes widened and he reached for her hand again, holding it tightly. "Oh, Rosie. Rosie, darling. A little girl... our little girl..."

Tears pooled in her eyes and resolutely she blinked them back. "I didn't even get to hold her. I wish I had. But I was dismissed from the Corps. I really lost my way for a while. Coming to Windermere changed all that. But... I'll always miss her." She squeezed his hand. "I thought you should know."

Thomas shook his head slowly, his expression distant and dazed. "A little girl," he whispered, before looking up at her with all the old hope and eagerness. "Rosie, we can have another little girl! And a boy! Lots of each. We can still have the dream—"

"Don't, Thomas." Telling him about their baby had felt like lancing a wound. It had hurt, but in a strange way, it had also provided relief. It left her feeling drained, but as undecided as ever. She'd loved him so very much. Why couldn't she remember how to love him again, especially as he seemed to love her?

But what about Frieda?

What about Leon?

"Oh, Thomas. I... I don't know," she said helplessly. "This is all so much to take in. You have to give me a little time." Maybe then she would have some clarity, some certainty, because right now she felt as if she were spinning, in so many ways.

"Of course." Thomas let go of her hand. "Of course. Like I

said, I'm not being shipped home till Christmas. There's time, Rosie. We have plenty of time."

"Yes." Rosie nodded, feeling hollow inside. "Yes, there's plenty of time."

He smiled at her then, and the curve of his lips was like a ghost of the cocky grin he used to give her, that charming smile that had slipped onto his face so easily. He'd been so carelessly confident then, so used to having anything and everything. She hadn't minded it, because he'd chosen her, and that had felt like a miracle.

But now? Now she was a different woman, and he was a different man. Could they fall in love all over again, pick up the remnants of what they had once shared?

"May I visit you again?" she asked. "I can take the train from Windermere."

Thomas's face lit up, and Rosie found herself giving a small smile. Once, she would have thrilled to have pleased him so easily. She felt a flicker of that old joy again, an ember she could, perhaps, kindle into flame.

"Yes, visit me," he said. "Or I'll visit you. They've said they'll let me out of here soon. Where did you say you were? The Calgarth something?"

"The Calgarth Estate. But I don't want you to have to come all that way." And, she realized, she wasn't entirely sure she wanted Thomas showing up in Windermere, having to explain his presence, not, at least, until she'd had time to think. "I'll come back here, in a week or two," she promised. "And I'll write."

"All right, then." He nodded slowly, giving her a rallying sort of smile. "You promise?"

"Yes, of course, Thomas." She smiled and touched his hand lightly. "I promise."

She walked away feeling strangely guilty for leaving Thomas on his own, sitting in his chair, staring out the window.

Outside, dusk was already drawing in, and the air was bitterly cold. Her feelings too jumbled to make sense of them, Rosie buttoned up her coat, tucked her head low, and started toward the station and the life that awaited her back in Windermere.

CHAPTER EIGHTEEN

The train journey from Worcester to Windermere was a blur; Rosie sat and stared out the window into the oncoming night, her mind whirling, yet also blank. *Thomas... alive.* Thomas, still in love with her and wanting to marry her. The realizations kept tumbling through her mind, and yet every time, they jolted her, a surprise, a shock. How could this be? And what on earth was she going to do?

She should have at least told Thomas about Frieda, she thought, and her intention to adopt her. How would he feel about taking a twelve-year-old girl into their lives? She couldn't be sure, and that made her wonder how well she'd ever known him, before she told herself that wasn't fair—adopting a twelve-year-old girl was hardly something he'd expect her to do.

And yet, and yet... Her mind seethed with questions and worries, as well as a sudden, deep longing to turn back time, back, back to when she'd loved Thomas with a love that had felt pure and true, and things had seemed so simple. He would marry her, they would have their little house, the picket fence, the dog, the children... *oh, the children.*

Rosie leaned her head against the train's grimy windowpane

and closed her eyes. She felt as if she couldn't think about it anymore, but neither could she stop thinking about it. Thomas, oh Thomas...

"Miss, are you all right?"

She opened her eyes to see the kindly-looking conductor smiling down at her.

"We're almost at Windermere."

"Thank you," she murmured. "And yes, I'm fine."

She gathered her belongings as the train pulled into the darkened station. She'd taken a later train than she'd expected, thanks to her stop in Worcester, and she'd have to walk back to the estate if there wasn't a bus—a distance of three miles. The prospect, on a cold and dark winter's night, was dispiriting.

She'd barely alighted from the train when she heard a familiar voice. "Rosie!"

She turned, her heart lifting to see Leon standing on the platform.

"What... how...?" She shook her head, smiling, as she came toward him. "I thought I'd have to walk."

"I knew the bus had stopped running."

"But how did you know I'd be on this train?"

He gave a smiling little shrug. "It's the last one today."

"Oh, Leon!" Suddenly, she felt near tears and without even thinking about what she was doing, she threw her arms around him.

Surprised, Leon stiffened for a mere second before he wrapped his arms around her, drawing her to him, and Rosie pressed her cheek against the scratchy wool of his coat.

"What's all this about?" Leon asked with a little laugh as he eased back. He touched her hair gently. "Not that I mind, of course."

Rosie let out a shaky laugh, embarrassed she'd hugged him, yet not having it in her to regret such an impulsive action. "I'm sorry. It's been a rather trying day."

"Don't be sorry." Leon's concerned gaze scanned her face. "What happened with the Central British Fund?"

"Oh..." In all the tumult of finding out about Thomas, Rosie had practically forgotten yesterday's meeting with Elaine Blond. "It went about as well as I expected, I suppose."

"Why don't you tell me about it in the car?"

He took her case and led her to the car, and once they were headed back toward Troutbeck and the Calgarth Estate beyond, Rosie told him the essence of the meeting.

"So not yes, but also not no," Leon surmised once she'd finished. "Well, there is reason to hope."

"Yes." Rosie gazed out the window at the woods sliding by in the dark. She felt Leon's thoughtful glance resting on her, but she did not turn to look at him.

"Today was trying?" he prompted after a moment. "Was that because of the trains?" His tone suggested he thought it wasn't.

"No, not the trains," Rosie admitted, but did not say any more. She wasn't ready to tell Leon about Thomas until she'd sorted out her own feelings a bit more. "I can't talk about it just yet," she said as she turned to him with an apologetic smile. "But I will soon, I promise."

Leon frowned, his lips pursed, his forehead puckered, and Rosie wondered whether she was being fair to him by not telling him when he could so clearly sense something was wrong. He might be envisioning all sorts of things—but could he have ever envisioned this? She certainly hadn't been able to.

They didn't speak for the rest of the short journey back to Calgarth, but at least, Rosie thought, the silence did not feel tense. She was glad to be in Leon's company, to rest in it in a way she realized she never had with Thomas, not even in their happiest days.

As Leon pulled up to the main hall, Frieda came running out; she'd clearly been watching and waiting for them.

"*Rosie!*" She barreled into Rosie as soon as she got out of the car, and she pulled her, laughing, into a hug. "Did they say yes?" Frieda demanded. "Did they? Did they?"

"Not yes and not no," Rosie told her, parroting what Leon had said, "but that's about what I thought they'd say. Come inside and I'll tell you more." She would have to tell Frieda about her aunt being located, she realized. She'd pushed the whole existence of the woman to the back of her mind, but now it rose to the front. What if Frieda was pleased? What if the aunt decided she wanted to care for her niece? Rosie knew she would be happy for Frieda, to have finally found some family, but it would be hard, so hard, to lose her now.

At the end of one of the tables in the empty dining hall, she, Leon, and Frieda sat with cups of tea while Rosie told them the gist of what Elaine Blond had said. It felt natural to have Leon sit with them; since their day at the seaside together, they had been spending more and more time together as a three. Almost like a family.

"My *aunt?*" Frieda repeated in disbelief when Rosie told her, gently, what the Red Cross had discovered.

"She is living in Dresden, apparently."

"Dresden!" Frieda looked horrified. "But I don't want to live in Dresden!"

"But your aunt—"

"My aunt will not want me," she burst out fiercely. "I know she won't. Papa's family wouldn't speak with him after he married my mother, because she was Jewish. That is why I've never met her. I won't live with her!" Frieda banged the table with her fist, her face wild. "I *won't!*"

"Frieda, no one will make you live with her," Rosie assured her, resting her hand over the girl's, hoping it was a promise she could keep. "Especially if what you say is true."

"It is!"

Rosie glanced at Leon, who looked troubled, his lips thoughtfully pursed. "We need to wait to find out more," she said. "Perhaps your aunt will write."

"But I don't *want* to live with her!" Frieda exclaimed, and then she scrambled up from the table and ran out of the room.

A sigh escaped Rosie in a gust of sound. "I think I probably could have managed that better," she remarked wryly.

"She's frightened," Leon replied. "And that makes her..."

He paused, his forehead crinkling as he thought of the word, and Rosie filled in, "Lash out? Yes, I know. But I don't know what else to tell her. I don't want to make promises I can't keep, and that's what I might have just done."

Leon rested his hand over Rosie's, just as she had over Frieda's a minute earlier. The feel of his warm fingers on hers was comforting and strong—yet they also gave her a little jolt of electricity, of awareness and even attraction. It was not, she knew, unwelcome. "This can keep for another day," he told her. "Can't it? The Red Cross will not be arriving this evening and you have had, as you said, a trying day, and not just because of the trains." He smiled faintly, seeming to be waiting for her to reply, and Rosie knew he wanted her to tell him what had tried her, just as she knew she couldn't. Not yet, not yet...

"You're right," she said, with an attempt at a smile. "I think a good night's sleep for Frieda, as well as for me, might make everything look better in the morning."

And then, she hoped, she would know what to do—how to feel—about Thomas.

The next week passed in a blur of activity. Frieda remained a bit sulky, but also clingy, which saddened Rosie even as she understood it. After years of the worst kind of suffering, Frieda had finally found both happiness and stability—and now they were being threatened by a faceless organization, an unknown aunt. No wonder she was frightened, and yes, lashing out.

Meanwhile, the other children were leaving Windermere in dribs and drabs; the younger children, accompanied by Alice Goldberger, Jean, and a few other staff members, left for Weir Courtney on the first day of Hanukkah. The smallest children, those few under four, had already been placed elsewhere back in October.

Rosie hugged her friend tightly as she said goodbye; she knew Jean was thrilled to be able to stay with the young children, especially Isaak.

"Who knows what will happen," she told Rosie. "Alice is recommending that the children remain at Weir Courtney for some time, so they can remain settled."

"And you will stay with them?"

"As long as they need care," Jean replied. "My mother's gone to live with her friend. There's nothing keeping me in Scotland anymore."

"God bless," Rosie said, hugging her again. "I'm so happy for you, Jean."

Other children had already gone to hostels around the country, some even planning to emigrate to British Palestine. A few had gone to distant relatives in the States. By new year, they would all have to be gone... and so would Rosie.

As each day slipped by, she knew she had to think more practically about her own future. She'd had a letter from her mother, telling her that Jamie was home, and that she hoped Rosie might return home soon, as well. She'd written of the annual Santa Claus parade in Kingston, and skating in Market Square, and Rosie had felt a sudden wave of longing rise inside her. She wanted to be *home*. She just still wasn't sure how to get there.

There had been a letter from Violet, as well; she would be home for Christmas, with Andrew Smith in tow.

And a letter from Thomas, desperately effusive, the handwriting strangely spidery, unlike his former, firm stroke.

Dearest Rosie,

Please forgive me for the way I acted when I saw you. I know I must have seemed like an old grump, but the truth is, I'm desperate for you—and desperate to be the man I once was. Maybe I'll never be that man again, but I want to be... with you.

Please come visit me and we can talk again and remember how we used to be. Remember Turnham Green, Rosie, where I kissed you for the first time? Remember Rainbow Corner, where we danced the night away? Marry me, Rosie, and I'll take you back to Greenwich, to that little white house, and all the dreams we'll make there. It's waiting for us, Rosie, I swear it is.

Rosie had hardly been able to bear reading it. It hadn't filled her with any sort of desire, she'd realized, to visit Thomas, or talk to him again, much less marry him and return to Connecticut, and her own deep reticence surprised her. Was she so fickle in her affections, that a few months could change her heart? Or even worse, had her heart changed because *Thomas* had, and as he'd said, he was no longer the man he'd once been?

The possibility was shaming. Could she really abandon Thomas, the man she'd once loved, the father of her child, when he was so in need of her love and care? And if she did, what then? She decided she needed to visit him and talk with him again, properly. She needed to gauge her own feelings—and tell him about Frieda. Although there had been no word from the Red Cross about her aunt, Rosie was hopeful that she still might be able to adopt her... and if Thomas was going to be in her future, he needed to be agreeable.

But first, she realized, she needed to tell Leon about Thomas. It had been over a week since she'd returned from London—and Worcestershire—and she saw the confusion in the crinkle of Leon's forehead, the shadow in his eyes. He wouldn't press her, but he knew she was keeping something back, and Rosie needed to be honest with him. Unfortunately, she wasn't entirely sure how to be honest, when she didn't truly know how she felt.

The moment came when she was in the art room, tidying up the few paints and brushes that had been left out; not many children came to the room anymore, although the walls were plastered with their pictures.

"There you are," Leon stepped into the room as Rosie turned, her hands full of jars of cloudy water that had been used to clean the brushes.

"Were you looking for me?" she asked.

"I wondered where you were." Leon shoved his hands into his pockets. "It's been so quiet here, hasn't it, with many of the children gone."

"Yes. It feels a bit sad, to be honest." Rosie tried for a laugh and didn't quite manage it.

"Have you thought any more about the future?" Leon asked quietly. "With Frieda, I mean," he clarified quickly.

"I am waiting to hear from the Red Cross," Rosie replied with a sigh. "If her aunt doesn't wish to take her—"

"But even if she does?" he pressed. "Frieda does not want to go."

Rosie frowned. "I imagine the Central British Fund will want her to stay with family."

"I think," Leon replied, "that they would rather she stay with someone who is Jewish."

She gave him a small, wry smile. "But, as you know, *I* am not Jewish."

"No, but..." Leon lifted his head to look at her, his jaw set, his eyes dark and determined. "I am."

Rosie's heart lurched even as she went completely still. For a second, she could not speak; her mind was spinning too much. "What..." She moistened her dry lips with the tip of her tongue. "What are you saying, Leon?"

"What do you think I am saying?" he answered evenly.

Rosie glanced down and saw her hands were trembling. She put the jars down and hid them in her skirt. "I... I don't know," she said, knowing it was a coward's answer. She did know, or at least she suspected, but she was afraid to say it out loud.

"Rosie, I told you I wanted to make you happy." Leon took a step toward her. "I care about you, and I care about Frieda. What if—"

"Leon, Thomas is alive," Rosie blurted out in a rush. As soon as she said it, she wished she hadn't. It was the worst possible moment, and yet she'd felt as if she couldn't keep it from him a moment longer, not with what he'd been about to say.

"Thomas," he repeated, his tone neutral, flat. He took a step back.

"Yes, Thomas. The man... the man I told you about."

"I remember who Thomas is." His gaze, revealing nothing, scanned her face. "You learned this in London?"

"Yes," she confessed miserably. "There was a letter waiting for me there, from him. He's been at a convalescent home in Worcestershire. He'd been shot in the head at the Battle of Ardennes, but survived, and the Germans picked him up. He ended up as a prisoner-of-war in Germany, but he didn't remember anything for a long time. I suppose it has happened to quite a few soldiers. Everything was in such a state as the war came to an end."

She stopped, waiting for him to say something, but Leon remained silent, his expression alarmingly inscrutable.

"Leon..." she began, but then stopped again, because she did not know what she'd meant to say.

"Did you see him?" he asked after a moment, his voice toneless. "That is why you took the later train, isn't it?"

"Yes, I stopped in Worcester."

Leon nodded slowly.

"He... he still wants to marry me," Rosie admitted in a whisper.

"Does he?" He raised his eyebrows. "And what of the woman back in America? The woman he was going to marry?"

Rosie shrugged, feeling worse by the second. She hated seeing Leon looking so cold, so *condemning*. It reminded her of when she'd first met him, and how uncertain and wrong-footed he'd made her feel. "He said he was planning to tell her the wedding was off." But he hadn't yet, and part of her wondered if he had ever intended to, before he'd been taken by the Germans.

"I see," Leon said quietly.

"Do you? Because I don't." Rosie let out a wobbly laugh that sounded too close to tears. "Leon, I don't know what to do. Thomas is still recovering, and he seems so unhappy. He wants to take me back to his family in Connecticut, but—"

Leon shrugged, no more than a twitch of his shoulders. "Then I suppose you should go."

"You... do?" She stared at him in surprise. "You think I should go with him?" *Marry him*, she wanted to say, but didn't. She hadn't expected, hadn't *wanted*, Leon to be so coolly matter-of-fact about it all.

"You loved him, yes?" he replied. "Only months ago. That hasn't changed?"

"I..." It felt wrong to admit that maybe it had. Rosie just shook her head, more miserable than ever.

"And he still loves you. There are no obstacles, are there?"

He spread his hands, making it sound so simple, so obvious. "None at all."

Rosie knew she shouldn't be hurt by his seeming sensibility, and yet she was, dreadfully so. How could he say such things, when moments ago it had seemed as if he'd wanted her to marry *him*?

"I haven't told him about Frieda," she said instead, determined not to show how wounded she felt by his cool words.

"And will you?" Leon returned, a note of challenge in his voice. "If her aunt decides to take her, I suppose there won't be any need."

"*Leon*." She couldn't bear for him to suggest such a thing, to *think* such a thing. "I wouldn't—"

A sudden sound from the doorway had Rosie stopping abruptly, and she turned to see the end of a plait flying out as Frieda bolted from the door. Rosie's stomach curdled with dread. How much had she heard? What had she believed?

"Frieda!" she called, and then she turned back to Leon, angry now. "That wasn't fair! I haven't changed my commitment to Frieda at all. I'm not about to abandon her, no matter what happens."

"No," Leon agreed quietly. "You are not abandoning *her*." And then he turned and walked swiftly from the room.

Rosie let out a cry of frustration. That conversation had not gone at all well, and she supposed it was her own fault. She shouldn't have told Leon about Thomas like that. She'd wanted to be honest, but she could have certainly picked a better moment... any other moment! And yet she hadn't expected him to be so cool about it all. If he really loved her as she'd been thinking he did, surely he wouldn't have been willing to let her go so easily? Had she wanted him to fight for her?

Well, he certainly hadn't.

Rosie finished tidying up the art room, needing a few moments to compose herself before she went looking for Frieda.

She needed to think about Frieda, she knew, and not Leon. But when she finally went in search of her, she couldn't find Frieda anywhere. Anxiety swirled in her stomach as she searched through the dining hall, the dormitories, the classrooms. She walked down the path around the lake, until the darkness forced her to turn back. She knew Frieda could be anywhere, curled up in some corner, not wanting to be found, but what if she'd done something foolish... again?

By evening, when Frieda had not come to dinner or evening roll call, it was clear to Rosie that something had to be done. Frieda, she suspected, had run away.

CHAPTER NINETEEN

"Where do you think she has gone?"

Rosie could hardly bear to see the gentle concern on Dr. Friedmann's face, hear it in his voice, for she felt as if she didn't deserve it. *She'd* driven Frieda away, even if it had been without meaning to. She and Leon, arguing about the future. About themselves.

"I don't know," she replied miserably. "She's... she's gone to sit by the lake before, when she's been upset, but it's so dark and cold out. I hate to think she might be out there now."

Dr. Friedmann steepled his fingers beneath his chin. "Are there any other places she might go?"

Rosie shook her head. "None that I can think of."

"She has gone to the lake before," Leon stated in a low voice. Over the last few hours, he had helped her to search for Frieda around the estate, although they hadn't spoken of Thomas again. They hadn't spoken at all, until Leon had suggested they speak to Friedmann.

"Yes," Dr. Friedmann replied now. "So Miss Lyman said—"

"What I mean is," Leon continued in that same low voice, "she has gone *in* the lake."

"What?" The doctor's gentle expression dropped, his eyebrows snapping together as he looked between the two of them. "What do you mean?" he demanded. "When did this happen?"

"In Bowness, months ago, when we went to the cinema," Rosie answered in a near-whisper, taking up the wretched story. "She left the theater and went to the lake—I found her there, about waist deep in the water. She said she wasn't... she wasn't trying to harm herself... But then she lost her footing, and so I went in and rescued her."

"And no one thought to tell me what had happened?" Dr. Friedmann asked. His voice was quiet, but somehow that made it worse.

Rosie swallowed. "I was going to tell you, but I caught cold and fell ill from being in the lake... and when I'd recovered, Frieda seemed so much better. She *has* been better. She wouldn't..." She glanced apprehensively at Leon. "She wouldn't do that again, would she?"

He shrugged his ignorance, not looking at her.

Guilt rushed through Rosie like a corrosive acid. This was all her fault. She should have told Dr. Friedmann about Frieda's escapade in the lake; she shouldn't have told Leon about Thomas the way she had. So many regrets. If something had happened to Frieda, she would never, ever forgive herself.

"I'm sorry," she whispered. "I didn't think Frieda was truly in any danger."

Dr. Friedmann raked his hands through his hair, looking more annoyed than Rosie had ever seen him before, but also resigned. "I do not believe that was your decision to make," he told her quietly, and Rosie blinked, absorbing the stinging rebuke, feeling even guiltier. No, it hadn't been, and she hadn't even realized she'd made it until this moment. "But as it is, we have no choice now but to send out a search party to walk around the lake. God willing, we will find Frieda safe and sound."

"This is my fault as much as yours," Leon told her in a low voice when Dr. Friedmann had gone to alert the others. Rosie was doing her best to hold back tears of both guilt and a deep, wild fear. "If not more so. I shouldn't have said what I did. I know you wouldn't abandon Frieda, Rosie."

"But does she know that?" Rosie asked despairingly. She felt too overwrought to talk to Leon about anything other than Frieda. She *had* to be found. She simply had to. "Do you think she actually would go into the lake?" she asked him, her voice scared and small.

"I don't know. I hope not. I pray not." He was silent for a moment. "But I don't know."

"*I* know," Rosie returned, forceful now. "Frieda wouldn't do something like that, not now. She has so much to live for, to hope for. She would talk to me first about... anything. She *wouldn't* just run away."

Leon regarded her soberly. "Let us hope so."

Half a dozen volunteers walked round the lake with flashlights, the bright beams sweeping the water as they called out Frieda's name. The only answer was the lonely whistle of the wind through the leafless trees. With every step she took, her head lowered against the icy, unforgiving wind, Rosie didn't know whether to feel hopeful that Frieda hadn't been found by the lake—or worse, *in* it—or despairing, that she hadn't been found at all.

It was nearing ten o'clock at night when they finally returned to the main hall, dejected, no farther ahead than when they'd started. There had been no sign of Frieda at all.

"Perhaps she left the estate?" Rosie asked Leon wretchedly.

"She could have taken a bus or a train, even. She could be *anywhere*."

"But where would she go?" Leon returned, his tone determinedly reasonable. "Where would she *want* to go?"

As they approached the hall, Marie came running out, her face alight. "She's been found!" she cried, and Rosie sagged with relief, so Leon put his arm around her to keep her upright, and she leaned into him, grateful for his support.

"Where?" she called back. "*Where?*"

"A policeman rang from Grange-over-Sands, of all places," Marie returned. "She was on the promenade there, all by herself, and as it was getting dark, someone became worried and rang the police. They picked her up."

Grange-over-Sands. Instinctively, Rosie turned to look at Leon, who gave her a small, sad smile of acknowledgement. Grange-over-Sands, where the three of them had been so happy, for a day. Where they'd been like a family.

"May I see her?" she asked Marie. "Have they brought her back?"

"No, the policeman rang just now," Marie said. "Someone will have to go to fetch her."

"I'll go," Rosie said immediately, and Leon spoke immediately after.

"I'll drive."

They drove in silence down the lane toward Troutbeck, before turning off for the road south to Grange-over-Sands, the single-lane track swathed in darkness, with tall hedgerows on either side hemming them in.

"It is good she has been found," Leon said at last. "And that she is safe."

"Yes." Rosie spoke mechanically, her unseeing gaze on the dark road ahead of them.

She was relieved that Frieda had been found, of course she was, but she still felt horribly guilty. What if Frieda *hadn't* been found? What if she'd done something dreadful to herself? If that had happened, Rosie knew she would never have been able to forgive herself, but, right then, worse than that was the fear that she wasn't fit to be Frieda's guardian, to be as good as her mother. How could she be, when something like this had happened, on her watch, *because* of it, even? If this story got back to the Central British Fund, to Elaine Blond...

"Rosie," Leon stated quietly. Meaningfully. "I shouldn't have said what I did. I didn't mean it."

"It doesn't matter," Rosie replied dully. "As long as Frieda is safe."

"It *does* matter," Leon insisted. "Not just for Frieda, but for you." He paused and then said, speaking in a heartfelt voice and yet with difficulty, "For *us.*"

A shiver went through Rosie, rippled along her skin. *For us.* Was there even an *us* for her and Leon? Could there be, one day, with everything else going on? She felt so confused and so unhappy, because she'd never wanted things to happen the way they had.

"I shouldn't have told you about Thomas like that," she whispered after a moment. "I didn't mean to... that is, I wasn't..." She wasn't even sure what she was trying to say.

"It's all right," Leon replied quietly. "I know you loved Thomas. And now that he's back in your life—"

"But he isn't back," Rosie blurted. "Not like that." She took a steadying breath. "Let's find Frieda," she said. "And talk to her. And then we can talk about... about us." If there could be an us, after all. A fragile yearning inside her made Rosie realize that she wanted there to be, very much... if only it was possible.

· · ·

The police station was a humble-looking building of gray stone directly facing the street. Frieda was inside, kicking her legs against the rungs of a wooden chair, her head lowered so Rosie could not see her face.

"Frieda!" she cried, rushing toward her, Leon following behind. Frieda looked up, her defiant expression crumpling as Rosie knelt in front of her and took her into her arms without hesitation. "Oh, Frieda! Frieda, darling. I'm so glad you're safe."

"I'm sorry," Frieda whispered.

"*I'm* sorry, so sorry," Rosie exclaimed as she hugged her. "I don't know what you heard, or what you thought of it, but none of it matters, Frieda, except that you're all right."

"She didn't want to be moved from the prom, that's for certain," the sergeant said, his tone one of kindly benevolence. "I thought she'd stay there all night, but it does get awfully cold, with the wind coming in from the sea."

"I'm sure it does," Rosie replied, still clasping Frieda close to her. "Thank you, officer."

"Poor little blighters," the sergeant remarked softly as they turned to go. Rosie knew he was thinking what so many of the locals thought about the Windermere children, and while she appreciated it, she wanted to tell the man that these children didn't need his pity. They deserved his respect.

"Come along," she said gently to Frieda, as Leon helped her up from where she'd been kneeling on the floor. "Let's get you home."

They didn't speak during the drive back to Calgarth; the darkness made silence easier somehow, and now that the palaver had passed, Rosie realized how strained she'd felt, and how exhausted she was. Yet there was still so much to be said, for losing Frieda for a single afternoon had made her realize, more than ever, that she didn't want to lose her ever again. She would fight for Frieda—fight Elaine Blond, the Central British Fund, the whole world if she had to. Frieda belonged with her—

and she needed to know it, believe in it and rest in the sure and certain knowledge that Rosie would never, ever abandon her. It was, Rosie thought, a promise she would move heaven and earth itself to keep.

Back at Calgarth, everyone had gone to bed, leaving the main hall dark and quiet. Rosie offered a subdued Frieda a cup of warm milk before bed, to which she duly agreed. Rosie moved briskly around the kitchen, heating up milk and bringing it out to the dining hall for her and Leon as well as Frieda.

"I thought everyone could do with some warming up," she said with a smile and set the cups down.

Frieda murmured her thanks as she took her cup.

They sat and sipped in silence, Rosie longing to reassure Frieda about the future, yet uncertain how to begin.

Then, setting her cup down with a thud, Frieda burst out, "Are you going to leave me? And Leon? For this... this *Thomas*?" She said his name with something like a sneer.

"Frieda." Rosie put her own cup down as she reached over to lay her hand on Frieda's. "I am not going to leave you," she assured her steadily. "I was never going to leave you."

"But you said—"

"*I* said something I shouldn't have," Leon interjected quietly. "Frieda, Rosie might not care for me as I wish her to, but she certainly cares for you. And I trust what she says—she'll never leave you. Not if she can help it, at any rate."

Frieda looked between Leon and Rosie. "But you said you weren't sure..."

"I *am* sure," Rosie declared firmly. "I am more than sure. I love you, Frieda." Her voice choked with emotion as she said the words—the truth—out loud. "I love you so much. And if I can take care of you, and think of you as a daughter... well, then I will feel like the most fortunate and privileged person on earth."

Frieda stared at her for a few seconds, her expression fierce, as if she were testing the truth of Rosie's words, whether she could trust them. Rosie waited, knowing the love for this young girl was shining in her eyes, blazing right through her. She just hoped Frieda could see it.

"But what if," Frieda finally said quietly, "they don't agree? Because you're not Jewish?"

"We'll just have to do our best to *make* them agree," Rosie replied with conviction. At that moment, she felt as if anything were possible, simply by the sheer voice of her own will. "If you want to be with me and I want to be with you—"

"*I* know," Frieda exclaimed, her face lighting up. She glanced at Leon, and then back at Rosie, her expression a mingling of defiance, excitement, and hope. "You could marry Leon!"

"Frieda," Rosie protested quickly, blushing in embarrassment. She couldn't bear to look at Leon, considering everything they both had and hadn't talked about that day.

"You could!" Frieda insisted, her voice rising, her eyes snapping with excitement. "You could! And then they couldn't say anything against it because you're not Jewish. Because Leon *is* Jewish!" She looked between the two of them, as if expecting them to leap to agreement, as excited as she was.

"Frieda," Rosie protested. "Sweetheart, it's not that simple..."

"Isn't it?" The words, so quietly spoken, jolted Rosie right through, because they weren't spoken by Frieda, but by Leon.

She turned to him, jolted again by the look in his eyes—as intent as ever, but with a tenderness that just about undid her.

"At least," he amended quietly, "it could be. Couldn't it?"

"I..." Her head was spinning, her heart too. Everything felt jumbled up and in disarray, except... all of a sudden, it wasn't. It wasn't jumbled or confused at all. Rosie stood there, looking dumbly at Leon, and she realized it was actually very clear indeed. She loved him. She was almost certain he loved her. And they both loved Frieda.

But it's only been a few months. And you've loved and lost before. You're not ready, it's too soon, it's too scary, don't be so reckless, so foolish, not again...

"See!" Frieda crowed. "*See!*"

"Well?" Leon prompted, the barest hint of laughter gentling his voice, while Rosie stared at them both helplessly, overcome, still struggling with uncertainty, or really, with fear. Fear for herself, her own heart.

Could it really be that easy? Could she let it? What about Thomas? What about *her*? Was she ready for love, for life, to risk her heart again? Was Leon?

"Rosie," Frieda implored, sounding both impatient and eager. "Say yes!"

"Say yes to what?" Rosie asked, trying to laugh, even though she felt embarrassed, hopeful and scared all at once. Too many emotions to process, to deal with, and most of all, for Leon to see.

"Frieda, perhaps you should let Rosie and I talk about this in private," Leon said, keeping his tone kind. "It's late, and you need to be in bed."

Frieda looked as if she wanted to argue, but then she slid off the bench, now acting as meek as Rosie could please. "All right," she said, her tone positively angelic, and then she practically skipped from the room to her dormitory.

Rosie let out a huff of laughter as she gathered up their cups and brought them to the kitchen. "She's as transparent as a windowpane," she told Leon as she returned, shaking her head. She still couldn't quite make herself look at him.

"I wish I could say the same for others," Leon replied dryly. He stood up, his hands in his trouser pockets as he continued in a low voice, "I still don't know what you think, Rosie. What it is that you feel."

"Leon..." Rosie finally turned to look at him, and the kindness in his eyes made affection and something much deeper sweep through her in a welcome rush. This man. This kind, gentle, *good* man.

"It's all right," he said quickly. "I understand. Frieda, she said too many things. And I did, as well, especially in front of Frieda. I put you in a... in a difficult position. I did not mean for that to happen."

Rosie tilted her chin, feeling suddenly, recklessly, wonderfully emboldened. "Didn't you?" she challenged, and Leon hung his head, flushing.

"I admit, I allowed my feelings to—what is the expression? Get the better of me."

Rosie's heart had started to race, and her head felt light, as if she were poised to jump off a cliff, to fly—or fall. "And is that such a bad thing?" she asked.

Leon looked up, his eyes darkening in a way that felt delicious, scary and wonderful all at the same time. He took a step closer to her.

"Is it?" he asked in a low voice, and Rosie heard such an ache of yearning that she knew she could not postpone or prevaricate any longer. Leon had suffered too much in this life to be denied the truth she knew was shining in her heart.

"It is," she confirmed, a tremor in her voice as she met his dark and hungry gaze with her own, both tremulous and bold. "Because my feelings have got the better of me. Frieda was right. It *is* simple. At least... it could be. Because..." Her heart was juddering, her mouth dry. "Because I love you, Leon."

Leon's lips parted but no words came out. Finally, hoarsely, he said, "But Thomas..."

"I have to talk to him," Rosie admitted. "And seeing him again was strange and hard, but it made me realize... I don't love him anymore. I'm... I'm not sure I ever did, not truly." Although perhaps, Rosie acknowledged, that wasn't fair. She'd been dazzled and swept away by the romance of the thing, it was true, but that didn't mean her feelings hadn't been real at the time.

But they weren't her feelings anymore.

"Are you sure?" Leon asked. "Rosie, this is a decision you must make alone—"

"And I *am* making it," she said simply. "I choose you. I love you, Leon, and I want to make a life with you and Frieda, if you'll let me. If you want that, too."

"I do," he said, his voice a thrum of feeling. "I do." He took another step toward her, and then he held out his arms. "May I?" he asked, and wordlessly, overcome, Rosie nodded.

Leon took her into his arms and as she tilted her face up to his, she felt as if the scattered pieces of herself were finally settling into place. And then as his lips gently found hers and her eyes fluttered closed, she reveled at the full and wonderful whole they had formed.

CHAPTER TWENTY

Watery sunlight spilled through the window as Rosie came into the convalescent home's dayroom, where Thomas was sitting in a chair, his unfocused gaze on the view outside. A few other men were seated in the room, reading or playing checkers, or simply staring into space. Rosie stood in the doorway for a moment, unnoticed, watching Thomas, a thousand memories slipping through her mind like quicksilver.

It had been three days since they'd found Frieda in Grange-over-Sands, since she'd told Leon she loved him, and the world felt as if it had been reborn. The hope and happiness that buoyed her soul to new, dazzling heights came to rest now, in quiet sorrow, as she gazed at the defeated-looking form of the man she'd once loved, or at least had thought she loved. Rosie wasn't sure anymore what she'd felt for Thomas; their relationship had been both intense and fleeting, but it hadn't lasted long enough for her to know if it would have endured through the years, the inevitable challenges and sorrows. And now she had to tell him so.

She took a step into the room.

He turned at the sound of her, and a faint smile creased his face and then he nodded slowly, taking in her serious expression, the way she clutched her handbag to her. Rosie suspected he already knew, or at least guessed, what she was going to say, but that didn't make it any easier to say it.

"Hello, Thomas." She tried to smile as he looked away. "It's a lovely day out. Would you like to walk in the gardens? Are you well enough?"

"I am perfectly well. As it happens, I am going to be discharged very soon." He paused, as if he wanted to say something else and then he murmured, "I'll just get my coat."

He rose from his chair with careful dignity, and Rosie waited while he went to fetch it.

A few minutes later, they were outside, walking through the straggly, frost-tipped grass, the flowerbeds forlornly empty, the sky a fragile blue with the sunlight barely warming the earth.

"I know what you've come to say," Thomas said after they'd walked a few minutes without speaking. He sounded resigned more than anything else. "It's right there on your face."

"I'm sorry, Thomas." She laid a hand on his arm. "I wish... I wish we could go back to the way things were."

"Do you?" Thomas asked, his voice rising in challenge. "Really?"

Rosie fell silent, for she realized then that Thomas was right; she didn't wish it, not really. She could never wish away Frieda and Leon from her life. She wasn't even sure she wanted to be that naïve, starry-eyed girl she'd been before, so grateful for Thomas's affection, for any attention he happened to toss her way.

"Maybe not," she admitted as she removed her hand from his arm. "Too much has happened. I've changed, and so have you. Neither of us is the person we were before."

"How have you changed, Rosie?" Thomas asked tiredly. "Because you seem the same to me."

"I've changed," she replied steadily. "Losing—losing our

daughter—"

"But we can have other children," Thomas interjected, sounding almost exasperated as he turned to her. "It isn't just that, is it?"

Rosie stared at him, knowing he would never grieve their child the way she had. Their daughter was just a distant concept to him, one that had gone before he'd even known of it, but to Rosie she'd been a *person*, a person she'd dearly loved. She accepted this difference, and found it didn't hurt as much as it once would have. She was glad she'd told him, even if he would never feel the way she had.

"No, it's not just that," she admitted slowly. "It's many things. We're too different now, Thomas. I'm sorry." She paused before adding gently, "But there is still a woman waiting for you at home, Thomas, a woman who, by all accounts, still loves you, and who knows you far better than I ever did. Our time together was so short, so sweet, but... it wasn't reality, was it? Not truly."

Thomas let out a sigh as he shoved his hands deep into the pockets of his coat. "I suppose it wasn't, if that's how you feel about it," he replied, trying to sound wry and not quite managing it. "Who knows if it was or not. Maybe I made more of it, when I was in prison, than I should have."

"I can understand why you would," she replied, determined to be fair. "But in any case... we did have fun. I don't regret it." Not exactly, anyway. Not completely, but she didn't need to tell him that.

"Yeah, we did have fun." Thomas gave her a small smile. "Remember how we danced at Rainbow Corner?"

"Yes," Rosie replied softly. "I remember."

They walked in silence for a few minutes, the only sound the crunch of gravel under their feet. It felt neither companionable nor tense; it simply was.

"I hope," Rosie said finally, "that we can part as friends."

He glanced at her, a look of resignation in his eyes, but

without any real bitterness. "What will you do, Rosie?" he asked. "Will you return to Ontario?"

"Yes, I think so." She would have to wait to hear back from the Central British Fund about Frieda, but she and Leon had already discussed going to Canada. He'd even suggested, shyly, about resuming his training as a doctor at Queen's University. Of course it wouldn't be easy as all that; there were visas to think of, and formal adoption papers, and more besides, but for the first time since she'd lost her child, Rosie felt as if she could see her future, or at least its first steps. She hoped Thomas could find the same.

He let out a sigh as he gazed out at the wintry gardens. "I suppose I'll go back after Christmas," he said. "And take up my old job at Dad's firm."

"And Maureen?" Rosie asked gently. "She must know you're alive."

"Yes, she's written to me." He paused and then admitted with a seeming reluctance, "I received her letter yesterday."

And in that simple statement, Rosie saw his future laid out, as plainly as hers, if not more so. He wasn't heartbroken, she realized then; if anything, it was his pride that was hurt that she hadn't rushed to his side, overjoyed, mixed perhaps with a longing for what had been, the way he had been when he'd been with her.

But he had Maureen waiting for him at home, who loved him still, and his family and his future, his job, and even perhaps the little white house he'd told her about, the children and dog. All of it was ahead of him.

She'd never truly been a part of any of it, she saw that now quite clearly, and without any real resentment. It had been a dream, a wonderful dream, hazy and hopeful, but no more than that, and she thought she might have realized that at the time, even if she had tried not to let herself. She'd never truly believed in the picture he'd painted, hadn't quite let herself trust its primary colors. And now she understood why. He'd always had Maureen, waiting in the wings, and now he would go home to her.

"I'm happy for you, Thomas," she said quietly. "Truly, I am."

He glanced at her then, his smile sad. "There's someone else, isn't there? For you?"

"Yes," Rosie admitted, because she knew she had to be honest. "Two someone elses, actually. A little girl and a... a man."

He frowned. "A little girl?"

"One of the survivors where I've been helping." He had never asked about what she was doing up in Windermere. He'd never asked anything about her life at all. "I'm hoping to adopt her."

"Adopt her?" His tone was surprised and not entirely without censure. "You mean, a Jew?"

Rosie stiffened. "Yes, she is Jewish, and so is the man I am hoping to marry. What of it?"

He shrugged. "I thought they kept to themselves, that's all."

"Well, thankfully Leon and Frieda have not," Rosie returned sharply before she moderated her tone. "We're hoping to build a life together, as a family, back in Ontario." If she'd needed any validation of her decision, it was in Thomas's surprised and faintly disapproving reaction to this news, his mouth turning down as he gave a slow shake of his head. "Thomas, my intention was to adopt Frieda regardless. If we... if we had decided... well, would you have welcomed Frieda as your own?"

"As my *own*?" He looked even more surprised, and the brief curl of his lip made Rosie clench her hands into fists at her sides. He let out a weary breath as he shook his head. "Rosie, what's the point of asking that? It's not going to happen, anyway."

"No, I suppose it doesn't matter." But she'd already received his answer in that brief but telling reaction, and she was both saddened by it and glad for the confirmation of her own decision. There seemed to be nothing more to say. "I suppose this is farewell, then," she said, turning to face him, and for a second, the new lines on his face, the scar on his cheek, all of it dropped away, and he was young and careless again, and so was she, and life felt easy and beautiful.

Then she blinked and it was gone; Thomas's lips were twisted into something like a smile, although the set of his expression still held a trace of that old obduracy. The war had changed them both, she knew, and it had turned them into different people than they'd been before, although she couldn't regret the changes, at least for her.

As for Thomas... she truly hoped he found happiness with Maureen and the dream he still cherished of the life he could live.

"Goodbye, Thomas," she said, and she embraced him briefly, pressing a kiss to his cold cheek.

He held her to him for a second, no more, his arms coming around her, his hands gripping her shoulders, and then he stepped back with a nod, his gaze flitting away, and Rosie had the feeling that he had already, at least in some sense, moved on.

With one last smile, she headed out of the garden, back to the train station—and home.

Leon and Frieda were both waiting for her at the Windermere station, their faces wreathed in hopeful smiles as Rosie stepped off the platform, although she saw a certain worry shadowing Leon's eyes and she gave him a reassuring smile as she embraced them both. It was finished.

"Rosie, Rosie, you'll never guess!" Frieda exclaimed as they hugged and then started walking back to the car. "A letter came for Dr. Friedmann from the Central British Fund! They said you can adopt me!"

"What?" Rosie faltered in her step as she turned to look at Leon for confirmation. Could it really be that easy?

"Not quite, *moja kocie*," Leon reminded Frieda with a smile. "They have said they are willing to consider the idea, after receiving some communication from Frieda's aunt."

"She didn't want me," Frieda filled in blithely. "And I'm glad!"

"Well, that's the first step, then," Rosie said. She touched Frieda's hair briefly; even though she could see plainly that Frieda was relieved by the development, she still thought there must be some sting in being rejected by a blood relative. But, she thought with a thrill of wonder, it meant that they were one step closer to becoming a proper family.

"Yes, it's good news," Leon agreed. "Especially as the estate will close down in a few weeks. We will have to go somewhere."

Rosie had not thought about that. She knew she could not take Frieda out of the country until she officially adopted her, and that might take months. What would they do? Where would they go?

Leon, seeing the worry in her eyes, gave her a reassuring smile. "A care for another day," he murmured as they climbed into the car. "As for this day, we are together, and that is what matters."

Yes, Rosie decided as she smiled at Frieda first, and then Leon, feeling as if her love and happiness was brimming up out of her, that was all that mattered. There would be cares for other days, many of them, no doubt, as well as joys... but as for today... she would simply savor what was right in front of her— Leon, a man who loved her, Frieda, the daughter she loved, and a future stretching ahead for all of them, shimmering with possibility.

EPILOGUE
SIX MONTHS LATER

"I see it!"

Rosie laughed as the wind whipped her hair and she tilted her face to the sky and bright summer sunlight. "Yes, of course you can, because it's right in front of us," she teased Frieda. "Amherst Island is only two miles from the mainland, after all. You can see it from the shore."

They were taking the ferry from Millhaven to Stella, an afternoon trip because Rosie had promised both Leon and Frieda she would show them the place she had grown up. Next, perhaps, would be New York City, although since they'd arrived in Canada a month ago, they'd stayed mainly in Kingston. But the future held many adventures, she hoped.

It had been a long, challenging six months in many ways; after leaving Windermere, Rosie and Leon had married in a small civil ceremony in Sheffield, before they'd settled in the hostel with Frieda and the boys from Dachau, helping them to acclimatize to their new life while they waited for Frieda's adoption to be approved. Rosie had become their unofficial den mother, Leon like their father, and in many ways it had felt like a large, happy family; Rosie had been sorry to go, even as she was grateful that the boys had settled so well into their new lives. She'd heard from Jean before she'd left; she was still at Bulldogs Bank, helping to care for Isaak and the others; it had been decided that the children should stay there for the foreseeable future, for their own wellbeing. Jean would stay on to care for them, which was exactly what she had been longing to do.

Securing Frieda's adoption and arranging her and Leon's visas hadn't been easy, involving many trips to London and wrangling with petty bureaucrats. There had been times when Rosie had felt as if all she did was wait in various lines or beg indifferent-looking clerks for progress to be made; she'd wondered, more than once, if they would ever be able to get to Ontario. The longer she stayed away, the more she realized she was finally ready to go home. She longed to.

Then, in May, the paperwork had finally come through. They'd booked their passage on a cruise liner turned troop ship, and traveling that way had reminded Rosie of how she'd come over to England as a CWAC, back in 1943, nearly three years earlier. How much had changed! How much *she* had changed.

She'd already written her parents several times with her news—her marriage to Leon, their adoption of Frieda, and just as she'd known they would, her parents had been, if surprised, then still warmly welcoming. They were planning to have a wedding reception for her and Leon later in the summer, and they'd even met them off the ship in Port of Quebec. Rosie had fallen into her mother's arms, laughing and crying all at once, so very glad to be back where she knew she belonged.

Her father and brother had both, with wide smiles, shaken Leon's hand, and there had been a lollipop and teddy bear for Frieda, whose eyes had rounded, first in alarm, and then in hope, at being suddenly welcomed into this strange, new family.

They'd had a steak dinner, and spent the night in a hotel, before heading back to Kingston. Then there had been more challenges; Rosie had had a painful, heartfelt conversation with her mother, weeping in her arms as she'd told her about Thomas and her baby daughter. And her mother had been, as she'd realized she'd always known she would be, comforting and supportive and not disappointed, or even shocked. Rosie had been glad she'd told her, even though it had been hard. Now there were no more secrets, only healing.

It had taken time and patience to enroll Frieda in the local school, insisting she knew enough English, and for Leon to be accepted into the university's medical program. They would continue to live with her parents until they could find a little place of their own; Leon intended to work part-time in order to provide for them, something Rosie knew he felt strongly about. Frieda, too, was looking forward to the three of them having their own home together, after the busy boisterousness of the hostel in Sheffield.

As for Rosie herself, she had decided to return to Queen's; she was no longer the bright-eyed undergrad she'd been five years earlier, but after living through the war, she'd told Leon, she realized how important it was to study history, to remember the past, to learn from it, and maybe one day teach it. Her cousin Violet had decided not to continue her studies; she'd laughingly told Rosie she'd never been as academic, and she was looking forward to married life and children.

"Children, Rosie! Can you imagine it? Do you think I'll be a good mother?"

Rosie had gazed at her cousin, so bright and vivacious and lively, and seen the vulnerability underneath that she had so often struggled to see before.

"Yes, Violet," she'd told her sincerely, "I think you'll be a wonderful mother."

Now, on this lovely summer's day, they were traveling to Amherst Island, just the three of them, for Rosie to show the place she loved most to the people she loved most.

"I should warn you, there's not much here," she said as they scrambled out of the ferry and walked into the tiny village of Stella, no more than a post office shop and a couple of houses of weathered clapboard, the whole place seeming empty, almost abandoned. They'd been the only passengers on the little steam ferry.

"Yes, so you've said," Leon said, putting his arm around her as they walked along, Frieda skipping ahead. "But it's a beautiful place," he continued. "I don't think I've ever seen water such a color."

"Yes, it is lovely, isn't it? I haven't been here for years, and yet it always feels like coming home."

"Shall we stop in the post office shop to say hello?" he suggested.

"I don't know if anyone will remember me," Rosie protested, but they went inside and bought several bottles of root beer from the cooler; Frieda had developed a love of the fizzy drink.

"You must be little Rosie Lyman," the woman behind the counter said with a wide smile, her face creasing into deep wrinkles. "I'd know a Lyman anywhere. They lived on this island for years and years."

"Lucas Lyman is my father," Rosie replied, "and Jed my uncle."

"Lucas and Jed," the woman replied, nodding. "How long ago it all seems! They sold up around the same time the McCaffertys did, right after the first war."

"Yes, my mother Ellen lived with the McCaffertys when she was a small."

"Ellen Copley! Of course I remember her. Came every winter from the States, as a child, on the train. Looked as if she wouldn't say boo to a goose but loved it here, all right. Came back to nurse, as I recall—how long ago was that?"

"About ten years," Rosie replied, smiling. "I lived here too, with my brother Jamie."

"Ah yes, I remember you now." The woman nodded. "Two little mites, you were! How is your family now? Everyone came through the war all right, then?"

"Yes, mostly we did." Rosie glanced instinctively at Frieda and Leon; their families hadn't come through the war, but it didn't seem as if they were thinking about that now, for they were smiling and nodding at the woman. "I've just come to show the island to my husband and daughter," Rosie said, a throb of pride and joy in her voice at being able to use those beloved words, "because I loved it so here."

"There's no place like it in the whole world," the woman replied with certainty. "No place at all."

They paid for their sodas and walked outside into the sunshine, heading down the dirt road.

"Where was your house?" Frieda called. "I want to see where you lived!"

"It's a bit of a walk," Rosie warned. She'd packed a picnic for them to have along the way, and Leon was carrying the basket. With the sun shining down and the gentle breeze blowing through the long grass of the meadows on either side of the dirt road that led away from Stella, Rosie had to agree with the woman at the store; she didn't think she'd ever been in such a lovely place—or felt so happy.

It took them half an hour to walk to the farmhouse where she'd spent so many pleasant years. It was a humble place, just two rooms on the ground floor and two rooms above, made of weathered clapboard, and now that no one had lived in it for some time, half falling down, its porch sagging, the front door half off its hinges. No one had lived there since they'd left; people had been leaving the island in droves, looking for work.

"It's not much, is it?" Rosie said ruefully, for now that she was here she saw that the place was smaller and shabbier than she'd remembered. "But I did love it so. You can see the lake from the backyard."

"Shall we picnic by the lake?" Leon suggested, and they picked their way through the long grass, past the outdoor pump Rosie remembered her mother using, and the barn where her father had worked, all of it dilapidated and half-forgotten, to the shoreline where the waves lapped onto the flat rocks, ruffled in white.

They found a large, flat, sun-warmed rock and spread out their picnic things—the bottles of root beer, and thick ham sandwiches, and her mother's apple pie.

"This truly is a lovely place," Leon mused. "The lake is so big, it almost seems like the sea. And it's so peaceful."

"Yes, I think that's what I like most about it," Rosie replied as she handed Frieda a ham sandwich and a bottle of root beer. "It feels so far away from all the world's cares, although perhaps that's just how I felt at the time, as a child." She'd already told Leon about their desperate flight from New York to the island, during the Depression. How, after the chaotic months after her father had lost everything, coming here to Amherst Island had felt like coming to a haven. To home.

"Does the island have a doctor?" Leon asked, and Rosie shook her head.

"No, they lost their doctor when I was a child. My mother acted as nurse for quite a few years, but when we left, no one took over."

His eyes sparkled as he gave her a teasing grin. "Hmm..."

Rosie felt a laugh bubble up inside her as she realized what he had to be thinking. "Would you really want to live here one day, Leon? And be the island doctor?"

He shrugged, still smiling. "It's as nice a place as any other, if not nicer."

"Yes, but..." She paused as she looked at the grass rippling in the sunshine, the lake dancing with waves.

"I'd like to live here," Frieda announced. "Then I could swim in the lake every day."

"Not in winter," Rosie reminded her. "Sometimes it freezes over."

"Then I could ice skate," Frieda said, and Rosie smiled faintly, remembering their old conversation about skating, now so long ago. New memories, she thought, could be made. They were making them every day. "Although maybe," Frieda finished thoughtfully, "in a bigger house."

Rosie laughed, the sound carried away on the breeze. "Maybe," she agreed and smiled at the two people whom she loved most in the world, who, amazingly, loved her back just as much. Was there any miracle more wondrous than that? To love and be loved. It felt like a secret she had stumbled on and still marveled at, one that she wanted to shout from the rooftops, to let everyone in the world know the wonderful truth of it. To love and be loved! There was nothing—*nothing*—more important or real.

"Why couldn't we live here?" Leon said softly as he threaded his fingers through hers. "When we have both finished our schooling. I will be a doctor, you will be a teacher. One day."

"Why couldn't we?" Rosie repeated slowly, smiling. Why couldn't they, indeed? Right then, the whole world felt filled with possibility, with purpose, with hope.

Her hand still clasped in Leon's, she gazed out at the lake, its surface sparkling in the sunlight, stretching all the way to the sky.

A LETTER FROM KATE

Dear reader,

I want to say a huge thank you for choosing to read *The Last Orphan*. If you found it thought-provoking and powerful, and would like to keep up to date with all my latest releases, just sign up at the following link. Your email address will never be shared and you can unsubscribe at any time. You'll also receive an exclusive short story, absolutely free!

www.bookouture.com/kate-hewitt

It was so much fun to continue Rosie's story, and learning about the children who came to Windermere was both inspiring and heartbreaking. I was thrilled to be able to include it in this installment of the Amherst Island series.

I hope you loved *The Last Orphan* and if you did, I would be very grateful if you could write a review. I'd love to hear what you think, and it makes such a difference helping new readers to discover one of my books for the first time.

I love hearing from my readers—you can get in touch on my Facebook group for readers (facebook.com/groups/KatesReads), through Twitter, Goodreads or my website.

Thanks again for reading!

Kate

KEEP IN TOUCH WITH KATE

www.kate-hewitt.com

 twitter.com/author_kate

ACKNOWLEDGEMENTS

I am always so grateful to the many people who work with me on my story, and help to bring it to light. I am grateful to the whole amazing team at Bookouture who have helped with this process, from editing, copyediting, proofreading, designing, and marketing. In particular, I'd like to thank my editor, Jess Whitlum-Cooper, as well as Sarah Hardy and Kim Nash in publicity, Melanie Price in marketing, Richard King in foreign rights, and Alba Proko and Sinead O'Connor in audio. Most of all, I'd like to thank my readers, who buy and read my books. Without you, there would be no stories to share. I hope you enjoyed Rosie's journey as much as I did. Thank you!

Made in the USA
Middletown, DE
24 July 2023

35690734R10149